WILD SHADOW

ALSO BY MARTHA DUNLOP

THE STARFOLK TRILOGY

The Starfolk Arcana

Starfolk Falling - coming soon

**Subscribe at www.marthadunlop.com
to hear about new releases first.**

WILD SHADOW

MARTHA DUNLOP

TanLea

For my Parents,
thank you for your never-ending support.

1

DYLAN

THE BARN OWL SCREECHED AS IT LANDED ON A TREE BESIDE the removal van. It fluffed its wings and peered into the open door of the small, grey stone cottage. 'Well, I'll be …' Dylan tailed off. He stopped walking and smiled. The owl settled onto the branch, apparently unconcerned by the sway of the perch in the blustery wind and turned its head impossibly far around to look at him.

The man unloading furniture from the lorry in front of the house stopped beneath the branches and looked up into the tree, shielding his eyes from the bright, autumn sunshine. 'Is it normal to see owls in the middle of the day?'

'I don't know.' Dylan shrugged. 'But I've lived here my whole life and I've never seen a single owl before, day or night.'

'It's not normal, as such, but it happens,' a woman's voice said.

The two men spun around. The woman leaning against the doorframe had arrived so silently she seemed to have come from nowhere. Her long hair shone copper in the chilly sunshine, the tresses glossy, curling into ringlets at the ends. She was framed by the spread of dark-green leaves that claimed the stone cottage back into nature. In the summer it would be ablaze with pink roses. Right now, it was hunkering down, a reminder of the bad weather to come.

Dylan caught his breath and shifted so he was sheltered by the hedge that bordered the cottage. She looked ethereal in her wide-leg trousers, clutched in at the ankle. A top with spaghetti straps that spread across her shoulders like a web, stopped just above the red stone that glinted in her belly button surrounded by pale skin and taut, flat muscle. Even her slender arms and shoulders were sculpted and well-defined. He couldn't take his eyes off her. She held all the grace, power and beauty of a predator.

The removal man nodded towards her. 'Sorry, miss. I didn't see you there. Any chance of a cuppa?'

She laughed, and the sound was deeper than Dylan expected. 'If you can find the box with the kettle, I'll make you one.'

'Well there's an incentive to get back to work if ever I heard one.' The removal man chuckled. He looked up at the owl, and then went back to the van for another box.

When Dylan turned back to the woman, she was gone. He took a ragged breath. Why had he been so thrown? What was wrong with him? He walked through the wooden gate and up the paved path to the front door of the cottage. The lawn was over-long and weeds filled the flowerbeds. He knocked. There was no answer. He looked through the front windows into a room that was filled with boxes. They were piled one on top of the other and arranged in rows. Just one box had been opened and an easel was set up in front of the window. Paints, brushes and sponges were spread over every available surface.

Dylan knocked again on the open front door. 'Hello? Is anyone there?'

Nobody answered. Only the sound of a meow broke the silence. He looked around for a cat but didn't see one. He shrugged. 'My name's Dylan, I just popped by to welcome you to Wildley Forest Village,' he tried again. Nothing. Shaking his head, he turned and walked back up the path. 'Do you know her name?' he asked the removal man, who was headed back to the cottage with an armful of boxes.

The man laughed. 'You too, eh? Tabitha, she told me. That's all I know. I wouldn't mind knowing more, but she's a private one, that's for certain. Maybe if I looked like you, she'd welcome me in and spill the beans. As it is …' He chuckled.

Dylan smiled, not sure what to say to that. He nodded to the man and walked away. He knew the owl was still behind him and noticed the silence of the other birds as he made his way down the road for his shift at the café in the centre of Wildley Forest. There was another meow. He stopped. A white, long-haired cat with black tiger stripes watched him from beside the rose bushes, head tilted to one side. He bent down, holding out one hand. The cat walked over and snaked around his ankles, rubbing its body against his legs.

'Aren't you the pretty one,' he said, scratching behind the cat's ears. Straightening up, he looked back at the house. The removal man was headed to the van for another load of boxes. Dylan shook his head. He wasn't sure why he should care where the woman had gone, but he saw her face so strongly in his mind's eye, and he had a weird conviction that she was watching him in return.

TABITHA

TABITHA LEANED AGAINST THE WALL AND PEERED OUT through the window.

She had no idea why she was still watching. He was too perfect. His blond hair was carefully messy, his stubble well-intentioned. His jeans were both faded and immaculate, and his shirt was smartly buttoned under a fitted black jacket. He looked like he belonged in a romantic comedy.

She looked around her new room. To her, it was heaven. To him it would be a mess. There were boxes everywhere, as well as paints, easels, paper, pencils and a huge pile of paintings. Most people her age were out socialising. Tabitha spent her time in her studio, painting the tigers at the zoo or putting on her work face and attending art events. Her reputation as a reclusive artist was her armour. Men like *that* guy just didn't understand her differentness.

She smiled when he walked up to the door, but ignored his knock. Shifting further out of sight, she held her breath while he peered in at the window. Talking to him outside had been a mistake. She wasn't ready to meet the locals.

He knocked again.

'Hello? Is anyone there?' His voice was deep and resonant. She wondered if he sang. She held her breath, not saying anything.

'My name's Dylan. I just wanted to welcome you to Wildley Forest Village.'

Silence. He turned and walked back up the path.

'What am I doing?' she muttered. 'I've completely lost the plot, hiding in my own front room.'

Emily meowed and rubbed up against her legs.

'You can't go out now,' Tabitha said, leaning down to stroke the silky white-and-black fur. 'We've just moved in.'

Emily tilted her head.

'I don't want you to get lost.' Tabitha frowned.

Emily ran over to the door and meowed again.

Tabitha rolled her eyes. 'Okay, but please, prove I can trust you to remember your way home and not run off, or end up underneath a car.'

Tabitha opened the door and stepped back, allowing Emily to slip through the gap. It clicked shut after her and Tabitha sighed, adjusting her position and watching the cat pad up the path. The man was walking slowly towards the village, but Emily caught up with him. He reached down to stroke her. Tabitha wondered whether the cat was purring when she rubbed her ears against his leg as though he was one of her people. Emily had never been unfriendly, but she kept her distance. She trusted Tabitha, protected Tabitha, adored Tabitha. No one else mattered.

Watching Emily love this man, Tabitha felt oddly jealous. She clearly needed to socialise more. She shook her head. 'Enough of this,' she said out loud.

She went back into the main room and surveyed the space. She loved this room. She loved it so much she had given up a much larger house in favour of the tiny stone cottage. This room would be her gallery. It wasn't the ultra-modern, airy space her work was usually displayed in. Instead it had an organic feel that matched the impressionistic wildlife that inhabited her paintings. There would be tigers everywhere. She would have an easel over to one side so she could paint while people browsed, and a kettle in the small room at the back so she could offer her customers a hot drink in the winter.

There was a thump as Emily jumped in through the window and padded over to Tabitha. She purred as Tabitha crouched down. 'What do you think, Emily? Have we found somewhere good to settle?'

Emily padded over to the closest box, jumped inside, turned around a few times and then curled up and went to sleep.

'Well, I guess that's a yes,' Tabitha said with a chuckle.

She ignored the hum in the air that she had learned to recognise as a forerunner to change. Picking up the instructions for the first shelving unit, she frowned at the tiny, imperfect pictures, pretending she couldn't hear the annoying sound. Moving house had been enough. She wasn't ready for more upheaval.

2

DYLAN

'I CAN'T GET USED TO YOU TURNING UP TO REHEARSE IN your work clothes.' GJ adjusted his guitar and rolled his eyes as Dylan shrugged off his smart coat and laid it over the back of a chair. 'You're not seriously going to perform like that, are you?'

There was a chill in the pub's back room and the stench of its damp dinginess was even more overpowering than usual. Dylan sighed. 'It's always about the clothes with you, isn't it? Has it ever occurred to you that your vision for the band's look might not be the only thing going on in our lives?'

GJ bounced out of his chair and plugged his guitar into the amp, cranking up the volume. 'It's not just about the music, you know. Only bands that look right make it big.'

'Don't worry. Mum promised she'd bring my gear over since I was coming straight from work. Now, can we play? I'd really like to warm up before going on stage.'

'You're snarky today.' Linden laughed, rubbing a

smudge off his bass. He took a gulp of beer. What's going on to give you such a wedgie?'

'Never mind that. Let's do this.' Dylan grabbed a set of drumsticks from the top of the upright piano in the corner of the room and strode over to sit behind the kit. His foot tapped as he ran through the tunes in his head. He stretched out his shoulders and neck and did a drum roll. Linden grinned, picking out a bass line and Dylan fell into rhythm with him. Fingerpicking the intro over the top, GJ's body was loose as he moved in time to the backing. When the voice came, it cut through the emotional heartbeat with a clarity that sent shivers down Dylan's spine. Linden irritated the hell out of him, but his voice was incredible. Linden winked at him, soaking up the appreciation. GJ smiled and sank deeper into his knees. Dylan nodded in time with the music as Linden's voice soared and swooped, carrying him over the waves of emotion he was never able put into words.

As the song ended, a familiar voice rose over the top, clapping and shouting. Dylan grinned and did another drum roll.

'Sounding great, boys.' Dylan's mum manoeuvred her electric wheelchair through the doorway of the practise room and down the ramp. She beamed.

'Rachel!' GJ stretched his arms wide and strode over, bending to kiss her cheek. 'These are spectacular,' he said, fingering the brightly coloured filigree butterflies that rose on tall stalks from the back of her wheelchair. 'Where did you get them?'

She laughed, flushing slightly as he sat down next to her and crossed his legs, facing her. 'A friend made them for me. Aren't they pretty? How's that new boyfriend, GJ?'

GJ grimaced. 'He's gone. I'll tell you all about it over a drink later.'

'Come here,' Rachel spread her arms and he leaned in, laying his cheek against hers.

'Anyway, I'll always have you guys? Right?' GJ pulled back with a grin.

'Right.' Rachel beamed. 'And your adoring audience.'

Dylan walked over and Rachel tapped her cheek for a kiss.

He crouched down and kissed her on the end of her nose. Then he touched his cheek to hers.

'Your gig clothes are in the bag.' She smiled and inclined her head towards the back of the chair.

'Thanks for bringing my stuff, Mum.' He unhooked the bag and rifled through the clothes.

'No problem. You make yourself pretty. I don't know how you can bear wearing those beach clothes when it's so cold, but who am I to say.' She winked and pulled her woollen wrap closer round her shoulders. 'They're not beach clothes, Mum,' she said, putting on a deep voice that was impressively similar to Dylan's.

Dylan laughed. 'I know, I know, but it's boiling up there, particularly when the beat gets physical.'

Rachel smiled. 'Go and get changed. I'll claim my space at the bar before the place gets busy. Are you ready to go?'

'We certainly are.' Linden strode over and kissed Rachel's hand. We're always ready, Mrs McKenzie. GJ and I will move Dylan's kit through to the stage while he changes.'

'Is there any point in me reminding you to call me Rachel?'

'Nope, I can't switch now. Doesn't matter how old I get.'

'I'm sorry …' A musical voice came from the door.

Dylan looked around and his breath caught. The woman from the cottage leaned against the doorframe, smiling. Her eyes were bright and her long, pale-copper hair was looped over one shoulder in a loose plait. She had changed since he saw her this morning, swapping her loose trousers for a sheer, floaty dress over a vest top, leggings and Doc Martens.

She held up a poster. It was an advert for their band, Instantaneous Rock. There was a rip in one corner and a piece of Sellotape hung from another. Dylan had stuck the posters on all the lampposts along the main street a couple of days ago. He vaguely wondered which one this was.

'I'm looking for the gig?' she said, turning from Rachel to Dylan. 'I'm new so I'm not sure where I'm going.'

'You moved into the cottage on the main street.' Rachel turned her chair and wheeled over to the door. 'I saw the removal van. I was going to pop around and introduce myself, but you've beaten me to it. I'm Rachel and it's lovely to meet you.'

The woman smiled. 'Tabitha.' She walked over and held out her hand.

Rachel took it. 'Well, Tabitha, the boys will be playing soon. Why don't we get to know each other by the bar while we wait for the music to start?'

Tabitha. The name sent a thrill through Dylan. He would have to find out more about her from his mum later.

Tabitha tilted her head, watching Rachel for a moment, and then she smiled. 'I'd love to, thank you.' She stood back to allow Rachel through the door and then turned. For a moment, she held Dylan's gaze.

His face heated.

Linden chuckled.

Tabitha raised her eyebrows and then turned and walked out through the door, before shutting it firmly behind her.

Dylan leaned over, pretending to adjust his drum kit, hoping the guys wouldn't see the flush of his skin. This woman made him feel like an awkward teenager again, and he wasn't sure he liked it. But the thought of her watching him play set his heart beating fast.

When he straightened up they were still staring at him. Linden had his arms crossed, an amused smile on his face. GJ's lips were tight.

'Well, the new girl seems to have made an impact on you,' Linden said, sitting down and rocking his chair back on its legs. 'I've never seen you this flustered.'

'I'd love to chat, but that room is filling up.' Dylan stood and rested his drumsticks on the snare. 'I've warmed up enough. I'm going to get changed.'

The last thing Dylan heard before he slammed the door to the bathroom, was Linden's laughter.

3

DYLAN

'WELCOME, WELCOME,' BOB, THE LANDLORD, SHOUTED from the platform.

Backstage with Linden and GJ, Dylan rolled his shoulders, loosening up for the workout to come.

'It's time to welcome the band that needs no introduction! Wildley Forest's very own Instantaneous Rock! Show them some love, people!'

Nothing could spoil Dylan's mood once he was ready for a gig. He twirled a drumstick and strode onto the stage in his combat shorts and black tank top, the huge tiger tattooed on his upper arm visible to the audience. He could almost feel it growling and shifting as he took his place behind the drum kit. He tapped his foot, the rhythm already coursing through him like a heartbeat.

Linden picked up the mic. 'Good evening, Wildley Forest, we are back in our favourite place, ready to play for you. Can I hear it for Instantaneous Rock?' He put his hand to his ear and grinned as the audience cheered. 'Come on, you can do better than that.' They were louder this time. 'Now you're talking! Take it away, Dylan!'

Dylan started a quiet drumroll that built up to a pulsing crescendo. He nodded when Linden came in with the bass line, sending the music through people's bones and down into the floor through their feet. He saw them sway, felt the link the music created, pulling them all into the same bubble of energy. Riding the wave, he surfed Linden's song, GJ's guitar solo, and the rolling excitement of the audience. He kept going with the pulsing heartbeat that held them all together and allowed the others to soar.

Looking out into the room, he saw Tabitha sitting with his mum at the bar. All her reticence was gone. She stared at him, lips parted, following the movements of his arms as he caressed the drums, weaving a pulsing magic. The song drew to a close and she took a deep breath. Leaning forwards, she murmured something in Rachel's ear and then pulled back to look at her, eyebrows raised. His mum grinned, turned to the band and pointed directly at him. Adrenaline pumped through his system when Tabitha nodded and raised her eyebrows at whatever Rachel had said. The older woman threw her head back and laughed, reddening Tabitha's cheeks.

Dylan felt his own cheeks flush in response. Gritting his teeth, he played the intro to the next song too fast, ignoring GJ and Linden's furious looks.

Something caught Dylan's eye to the left of the audience, and he turned his head. He saw a flash of white, and then it vanished. He blinked. It couldn't be. One minute there was nothing there, the next, a white tiger was threading its way through the bodies on the dance floor towards the stage.

Dylan almost faltered. His heartbeat sped up. He wanted to scream, to shout to everyone to get out, but he was frozen on the stool, locked into the motion of the song. His foot kept hitting the pedal of the bass drum. His arms stayed loose, his wrists flexing as the sticks flew over the drumheads. How could his body be so finely tuned in this moment and so unresponsive to the fear pumping through his veins? He closed his eyes. When he opened them, the tiger was gone. Nobody else had noticed it. He shook his head, and then sought out Tabitha at the back of the room. Her eyes shone, warming him. He swallowed. He needed to get a grip. Ever since he'd laid eyes on Tabitha, the world had tilted. Her long, silky hair had wound its way around his heart and was reeling him in without words. She was so different and his steady, predictable life felt choking in its lack of possibility.

He was used to the girls crowding the stage, running their fingers over his tiger tattoo, watching his muscles flex while he played the drums. He liked the attention, but it always felt empty. Tabitha was different. He knew it. Did it mean *anything* that she was watching him?

She leaned over, whispering something in his mum's ear and smiling. Rachel threw her head back for a deep, belly laugh. For a moment, he felt transported across the room. His mum liked her. His heart rate increased while the women chatted, sipping their drinks as they watched him. His drumsticks matched the growing pace of his body, pushing the other band members out of their comfort zones.

'Dylan,' GJ said, 'what are you doing? I can't play that fast.' Linden frowned, watching GJ struggle with the intricate guitar solos while his bass line continued at a steadier pace. Dylan didn't care. The pulse was driving him forwards.

GJ began another guitar solo, but they were going so fast now that he stumbled over it, fingers falling over themselves in an attempt to keep up. He gritted his teeth and kept going, but the song was off now. His chords were out of time and jarred against Linden's melody. Exchanging looks and nods, GJ and Linden cut out a few verses of the song and went straight for the ending, forcing Dylan to wind it up.

'Get yourself a drink,' Linden hissed at him when they had finished, his hand over the microphone. 'I don't know what you've got going on over there, but this is a paid gig and we need to be professional. Leave your crap out of it and get your head back in the game. Do you hear me?'

Dylan nodded, not caring what Linden thought. He saw amusement on his mum's face and knew she had tracked everything. His mum always knew what was going on. She had an intuition that bowled him over and helped him understand the world in a way he knew his friends found inexplicable.

Balancing his drumsticks across the snare, he jumped off the stage leaving Linden and GJ to play a slow song. The people in the front row surged around him, swallowing him whole. He pushed his way to the back of the room, ignoring the hands that reached for him along the way. By the time he got to the bar, his mum had a pint of his favourite beer waiting for him on the table. He sat down, propping his legs up on the empty chair next to him and leaned back.

Tabitha eyed the tattoo on his shoulder and he instinctively flexed his muscles. Her lips twitched as though she was trying not to laugh.

He held out a hand. 'Dylan. It's lovely to meet you properly. I tried to introduce myself earlier outside your cottage, but I met your cat instead. She's beautiful.'

'Tabitha.' The woman nodded. '*I'm* Tabitha, my cat is Emily and she's not normally that accepting of strangers.'

Her eyes were on his tattoo.

'You can touch it if you like,' he said, moving his arm towards her. 'There's something so magical about tigers, isn't there?'

She nodded, not saying a word, but her finger drifted up to his bicep and traced the lines there. A shiver shot through him sending his heart racing. 'You like tigers.' It was more a statement than a question.

Dylan smiled. 'I do. He's my guardian.'

'From what?' Tabitha asked.

There was a shuffling in front of them. The crowds parted and Linden and GJ appeared. Linden's sculpted face was dark with anger as he stood, legs apart, hands on his hips in front of Dylan. 'What the hell was going on with you up there?' Girls hovered in the background, waiting for the chance to talk to him, but he ignored them.

'I can't help it if you can't keep up.'

'Can't keep up? You're supposed to *keep* time not blast right past it. What is wrong with you?'

'He was showing off,' GJ said through gritted teeth. He glared at Tabitha.

Tabitha raised her eyebrows, coughed, and then turned her gaze to the table, where she picked intently at the label on her bottle.

'Stop it!' Dylan hissed at the guys. 'You're embarrassing yourselves.'

'I'm embarrassing myself?' Linden asked. 'I'm not the one who trashed our performance, all because the new girl was watching!'

'Oh God,' Dylan closed his eyes, pinching the bridge of his nose with his fingers. 'Okay, you're embarrassing *me*. Please stop. I'm so sorry, Tabitha. They're not usually *this* bad.'

Tabitha stood up, looking at the men in front of her. She was small, but at that moment her presence loomed above them, making them seem tiny by comparison. 'Don't worry, I'm leaving. Good night, Rachel.' She strode over to the door without turning back. In a moment of silence, the door slammed behind her.

'What do you think you're playing at?' Dylan's voice was low and brittle. 'She's new here for God's sake.'

'So what?' GJ slammed a ten-pound note on the bar and held his hand out for a drink. 'She's messing with Instantaneous Rock.'

'Messing?' Dylan stood up, hands clenched into fists by his side. 'She came to watch us play. We're normally pleased to find new fans. That up there, that was all me. It wasn't her fault.'

Linden stepped towards him until they were nose to nose. His voice was low. 'Just remember: the band comes first. Tonight was going great until she arrived, but you've been jumpy ever since. I will not let her interfere and ruin everything.'

'Get over yourself, Linden.' Rachel's voice was sharp. 'Nobody's trying to interfere. Tabitha came to Wildley Forest to paint the tigers at the zoo. She wanted to open a ich, quite frankly, could bring trade into the village side. If people come from far afield to look at her art, they will spend money in the cafe; your mother's cafe, no less. She will be an asset to this village. So mind your manners and if you can't be kind and welcoming, keep your mouth shut. Now, are you going to play again, or should I just go home?'

Linden stepped back, closed his eyes and took a deep breath. When he looked at them again, his gaze was clearer. 'We are going to play, but this conversation is not finished.'

'Too right it's not.' Dylan slammed his drink down on the table, slopping beer everywhere. He got up without a word and strode up to the stage, settling in behind the drums.

Linden and GJ followed him up. GJ started a song Dylan could have played in his sleep, and he fumed as he drummed on autopilot.

A few songs later, Linden took the mic. 'For those of you who are new to Instantaneous Rock, let me introduce the boys. On guitar we have the cool, the fabulous GJ.' GJ launched into an elaborate riff, his fingers flying over the fretboard. Someone whistled, someone else whooped and there was a smattering of applause. 'At the back we have the tiger himself, did you see his tattoo? The fabulous Dylan McKenzie.'

Dylan launched into a drum solo, losing himself in the complex rhythms that flowed out of his drumsticks like an extension of his own heartbeat. He knew his sticks would be a blur. So for a moment he stopped, sticks in mid-air, allowing the silence to fall through the echoes of his own beats. Then he counted himself in and flew through the final riff. The crowd were silent for a moment, and then they roared.

Dylan stood up, raising his sticks into the air, and then shifted slightly so they could see his tattoo.

'Thank you, Dylan.' Linden rolled his eyes. 'He does love the spotlight, that one. And finally, I am Linden on bass and vocals. Wildley Forest, I give you, Instantaneous Rock.'

4

DYLAN

THE CLUB WAS DARK. THE BASS POUNDED THROUGH
Dylan's bones while he queued on the grand staircase in the
entrance hall. He paid, and then walked down the corridor
to the bar, peeling his feet off the sticky floor with each step.
The club was sweaty and dank, and he shuddered as the
stink of stale beer seeped into every pore of his skin. He
had no idea why he had come. He was furious with Linden
and GJ and wanted nothing to do with them. He had to get
better at saying no.

'Here.' GJ handed him a pint.

Dylan took a mouthful, nearly gagging when the
watered-down beer hit the back of his throat. 'Urgh, what *is*
that?'

GJ shrugged. 'It was on offer.'

'Great.' Dylan gave the glass a disgusted look.

'Well, you get in the next round then.' GJ rolled his eyes
and turned his back on Dylan.

'We should get a late-night gig here,' Linden frowned at
the DJ. 'We'd be a million times better than this.'

'You want to be working at this time of night?' GJ spread his arms wide. 'You'll have to do that one without me. Don't get me wrong, I love performing, but after a full day's work and a gig, I am *definitely* off the clock.'

'What about you Dylan, would you be up for it? A double act, maybe? Or will you be too busy chasing after your new girlfriend?'

Dylan's anger boiled. 'She is not my girlfriend and you know it.'

He turned his back on them and pushed his way to the bar. Linden had an unnerving instinct for which girls Dylan really liked and bulldozed his chances every time.

Ditching the watered-down pint, he ordered a bottle and a shot. Maybe oblivion would help. At the very least, he would forget this miserable evening. He downed the shot, ordered another and took a deep glug of beer. The alcohol warmed the edges of his consciousness and the racket in the club receded.

He wondered what it would take for him to leave them behind and start something new? He had locked himself into this band a decade ago and seemed unable to let it go.

He walked over to his friends, stumbling from the drink.

'Are you okay there, mate?' GJ suppressed a smile when Dylan gripped his arm. 'You seem a bit cooked.'

'Don't be an arse.' Dylan took another gulp of beer. 'I've had enough of your games.'

GJ's eyebrows shot up. 'Games? What games? You think Instantaneous Rock is a game?'

'No, I think it's a prison.'

Linden narrowed his eyes. 'Is it Wildley Forest that's a prison? The band? Or just us?'

'Don't you want to get out of the village? To build a place in the outside world? To be free to be yourself?'

Linden's tone was glacial. 'I have a place in the world. I don't need another.'

Dylan slammed his pint down on the table. 'I'm going to the loo. Make sure they don't clear away my drink.'

He felt their eyes boring into his back as he wove his way towards the toilet, looking for a moment alone. He had called these men friends for a lifetime, but really they were drinking buddies. They didn't know him much more than the fans who swarmed around the stage when he performed. They knew the Dylan they wanted to see, not the one that stood, isolated, below the surface. He paused in the hall outside the toilets and leaned against the wall, dropping his head back and closing his eyes. Anger threatened to swamp him.

He didn't know how long he'd stood there when a growl jerked him out of his reverie. His heart pounded as he opened his eyes. Shit. The white tiger was back. Its gaze was locked on him from the opposite end of the hall, and it was coming his way. He took a deep breath, pushing his hands into the wall to steady himself.

'It's not real,' he whispered. 'It can't be real.' A real tiger would have caused panic in the pub. Besides, he had been the only one to see it.

It growled again, louder this time, and moved silently towards him. He grunted, backing down the corridor, not taking his eyes off the tiger. The alcohol rolled through him and he tried to steady himself.

He hit the end of the hall. Shit. There was no exit. He turned, putting his back to the wall.

The tiger froze a mere foot away, rumbled again, and

then turned around and walked back down the hall.

'What the hell?' Dylan whispered.

He held his breath, watching it go. The moment it turned the corner he scrambled back down the hallway, lurched to the toilet letting the door bang against the wall, fell against the urinals and threw up, emptying his stomach.

When he had finished, he collapsed against the floor, leaning his forehead against the cold tiles.

'Dylan, are you okay?' GJ's voice was soft.

Dylan felt a gentle hand on his shoulder. 'No, I … did you see …?' Dylan's head pounded. He shook it, and then winced. 'Never mind. I'm drunk. Ignore me. I'm going home.' He climbed to his feet, picked up his jacket and pulled it on.

'How much have you actually had tonight?' GJ put a hand on his upper arm, steadying him.

'God knows.' Dylan dropped his head into his hands. 'I need to get out of here. I need fresh air.'

'I'll take you home. Let me prop you up.' GJ looped Dylan's arm over his shoulders, taking his weight, and dragged him out of the toilets and down the hall.

'About the new girl,' GJ said.

Dylan tensed. 'What about her?'

GJ's jaw was set, his shoulders raised towards his ears. His eyes narrowed.

Dylan sighed. 'Not tonight, mate. I haven't got it in me to have the same old arguments.'

GJ swallowed. 'I may not be as predictable as you think, drummer-boy.'

'Then what do you have against Tabitha?'

'Nothing, nothing at all.' GJ sighed and they headed out into the darkness of the cool night.

5

DYLAN

THERE DIDN'T SEEM TO BE ANY WAY TO MAKE THE COFFEE strong enough. Dylan ground more beans and tried again. Having personal access to an industrial coffee maker when you had a hangover was a major bonus of working in a cafe. His head pounded, his throat was dry as a desert and his stomach rolled like the Atlantic. He couldn't believe how drunk he had been, or that he had forgotten he was on the early shift.

The cafe was packed. It was a bright morning and the whole of Wildley Forest seemed to have turned out for coffee before the rain set in. The cosy space was rammed with people wrapped in thick winter coats and hats, despite the bright sunlight streaming through the windows. Dogs slept by their ankles. A roaring fire was lit in the front room and Dylan had been delivering warm scones with cream and jam to nearly every one of the wooden tables.

This was the bad side of working in a cafe. He wanted space to nurse his hangover. Instead, he got people and every one of those people wanted to chat with the local celebrity.

Dylan's phone rang. His mum's face flashed up on the screen. Swiping it to voicemail, he slipped out from behind the counter, leaving Cassandra to deal with the queue.

'Hey, Dylan,' a familiar voice called just as he reached the door.

He turned. Bob, the pub landlord, was coming towards him. 'I, erm, I just wanted to find out if everything was okay after last night? Things got a little, let's say, tense? I hope my star attraction isn't looking unstable?'

Dylan put on the most reassuring smile he could muster. 'It's all fine, just a bit of a domestic. Between you and me, I don't reckon Linden should have had that drink before the show. It makes him too confrontational. I'll make sure he doesn't do it again.'

Bob's eyebrows shot up. 'Yes, well. Please do. You're a great little band and I'd hate for you to lose the appeal you've worked so hard to build.'

Dylan's smile was so fake it was making his cheeks ache. 'Sorry, Bob, my mum's outside. I just need to let her in.'

'Of course! Tell her I'm sorry for delaying you.'

Dylan raised his hand in acknowledgement, and then ducked out the back door before anyone else could stop him.

His mum was waiting for him outside. 'Ready to help a gasping woman round to the back for her morning pick-me-up?' Rachel raised her eyebrows, suppressing a smile.

Dylan opened the side gate and she came through, moving faster than his hungover legs could carry him.

'It was a big night then?' she asked, when he caught up with her at the second gate.

Dylan gave a genuine smile for the first time that morning. 'Oh, you have no idea.'

'Actually, I do.' She laughed outright this time as he let her through to the back garden. Don't you remember me sitting by your bed with a bowl, a pint of water and paracetamol? I wasn't expecting you, but I guess you wanted to be looked after.'

'Sorry.' Dylan grimaced. 'That does make sense of my alarm being set. I assumed I had been uncharacteristically organised.' He opened the double doors at the back of the cafe and she wheeled up the ramp, sliding into her favourite space at the table next to the garden window. She put the *reserved* sign on the side and opened the newspaper he had left, folded and ready for her.

'Your regular?' he asked.

She nodded. 'But add a chocolate brownie please. I didn't get anywhere near enough sleep last night, so I need artificial energy.'

Dylan grimaced. 'My treat. I owe you that, at least.'

'At least!' Rachel propped up the newspaper and started reading.

Dylan found one of the biggest coffee cups they had, filled it almost to the brim with almond milk cappuccino and plated up a brownie. The hairs on his arms rose as the echo of a growl sent a spike of adrenaline through him. He looked up and his eyes widened. It was back.

The tiger prowled towards his mum, a low growl rumbling in its throat. 'It's not real,' he whispered to himself, but his certainty faded as it walked closer.

'Mum!' he yelled when it snaked around her chair. The whole cafe quietened, and everyone turned to look at him.

Someone giggled and he realised he was spilling coffee on the floor. He straightened his hand.

'Yes, darling?' She smiled, tilting her head.

Dylan stared, eyes wide as the cat walked a breath away from her.

'Is something wrong, sweetie?' She frowned.

'Dylan?' Cassandra said, touching his arm. He jumped. Wow, he'd forgotten she was there.

'Would you mind covering for a minute?' he asked her. 'I think I need to sit down.'

She nodded, but her forehead was creased with worry. She watched him for a moment, and then shook her head. 'Go on.' She turned to serve the next person in the queue.

His mum was still staring at him. 'What is happening to me,' he muttered. Putting the cake and drink onto a tray, he carried it over and slid onto the seat opposite her.

'What's wrong, Dylan?'

'Did you see anything strange a moment ago?'

'Strange?' Her forehead creased. 'Well you were acting oddly. Is everything okay?'

He sighed and leaned back in his chair. 'I think I'm just overtired.'

'Could you get a day off? Do something different? You could wander up to the zoo? Tabitha goes up there to sketch all the time. You might see her.'

'Mum, are you stirring?'

She smiled. 'I thought you might like a chance to get to know her without Linden and GJ watching.'

Dylan picked up her coffee and took a gulp, feeling it begin to light up his system. 'I might do that, thank you. What will I do when I move away and you're not there to give me a pep talk at breakfast?'

Rachel's jaw tightened, but she still smiled. 'You'll have to find your own coffee to drink. And you must have me learned by heart now. You won't need me for much longer.'

Dylan stood up and kissed her on the cheek 'I won't ever stop needing you, Mum.'

He did the rounds, picking up dirty crockery from the other tables. He avoided the front counter where Linden and GJ stood in the queue. He didn't have it in him to deal with them yet.

'Excuse me.' An unfamiliar voice brought him up short. He looked up to see an elegant woman dressed in black, a red and gold scarf arranged around her neck. Behind her, a man in beige chinos with a jumper slung around his shoulders stood tapping on his phone. 'Could you tell me where Tara McLoughlin's showroom is?'

'Tara McLoughlin?' Dylan frowned. 'Never heard of her.'

'She's the one who sold that painting for an obscene amount of money,' Cassandra said, from over his shoulder.

The woman pursed her lips in disapproval, but the man grinned. 'That's her,' he said, a note of pride in his voice.

'You've got the wrong place,' Cassandra said with a shrug. 'There aren't any artists here.'

'Maybe you should become better informed.' The woman sniffed, turned around and walked out. The man smirked, then followed.

'What about Tabitha?' Linden's voice was loud. 'Doesn't your new crush have an art showroom?'

Dylan turned to look at Linden. 'Yeah, but her name's Tabitha. These people were looking for Tara McLoughlin.'

Linden shrugged. 'I'm surprised you made it into work this morning, Dylan.'

'Have you just come to torment me? Because I assure you it's not necessary. My body is punishing me more than you ever could.' Dylan looked around the crowded shop. 'Coffee to go?'

'Not a chance, tiger boy,' Linden said. 'We'll sit with your mum.'

Dylan gave a curt nod. 'Sit down. I'll bring your drinks.'

He took a deep breath and tried to let go of his boiling irritation. Sleep had done nothing to soothe his anger at Linden or GJ.

He couldn't blame them for all that was wrong with his life. It wasn't their responsibility to make sure he lived his dreams, but they seemed to get in his way at every step and he was reaching the end of his patience. He watched them kiss his mum on the cheek, saw them chat and laugh with her, making her smile, bringing light into her eyes and a glow to her cheeks. She had clearly forgiven them for last night, but she was a better person than he was.

He grunted, heading to the counter to pour out coffee. Out of the corner of his eye he saw the tiger again, felt its growl deep in his own chest. He knew without looking that it was watching his friends and that it liked them even less than he did.

'I hear you,' he murmured under his breath. 'Where do you go when you're not here?' The tiger backed away, knocking into a display of tourist pamphlets. And then it was gone. He walked over, bent down and picked up a leaflet that had fallen to the ground. Wildley Forest Zoo. 'I think someone is trying to tell me something.' He shoved the leaflet in his pocket. 'Well, I could do with a day off.'

6

MAX

MAX POKED A STICK THROUGH THE BARS OF THE TIGERS' sleeping area, prodding the large male in the hindquarters.

The cat tensed and growled. He withdrew the stick and the cat relaxed.

'You don't like that, do you?' he said. 'Ursula wouldn't like it either. Did you know that? If you hadn't been given to me, she might have been your keeper. You would have liked that, wouldn't you?' He laughed and prodded the cat again. This time the animal pawed the ground and dropped into a crouch, peeling its lips away from its huge, curved teeth. 'That's right. Act like a proper tiger. She would have you all tame like a house cat, but I know what's best for you.' He got up close to the bars, put his face near the tiger, and growled.

The tiger put its ears back and swished its tail sharply from side to side.

Max felt his heart rate rise. His blood pumped through his system, lighting his body up like a bulb. He let out a deep breath and chuckled. The tiger backed away, not taking its eyes off Max. 'That's it. Keep those wild instincts up and running.'

The tiger growled, and then padded over to the locked door of its sleeping quarters.

A shiver ran down Max's spine. 'She's here isn't she?' he whispered. On a whim, he pulled the lever that allowed the enormous predator out into the enclosure. The cat turned to look at him, and then walked out through the door.

Max went into the small bathroom to the side of the keeper's space. He checked his reflection in the mirror from all angles, neatening his hair and pouting. 'She'd be lucky to have you,' he murmured to himself, pulling in his stomach and pumping up his biceps. 'Anyone would be lucky to have a guy like you.'

He nodded, let himself out of the keeper's room and walked up the hill on one side of the enclosure towards her usual spot. She wasn't there. He kept walking, looking around and peering through the enclosure.

The large male was on the other side near the fence. He was sitting, looking at a woman; a woman in floaty, wide legged trousers, drawn in at the ankle. The cat and the woman just stared at each other, unmoving.

'Not again.' Max rolled his eyes. Tabitha gave those beasts far too much attention. He had thought she came to the enclosure to see him, but he was becoming less sure. Of late, she seemed far more interested in the cats than in him. He thought he had made it clear he was interested. He turned around and made his way back to the keeper's room. He went to the fridge and got some chunks of meat. Dropping them through the bars into the cats' sleeping quarters, he spread them out, and gave a sharp blow on his whistle. A moment later, the tigers streaked into the room, going straight for the meat. Shutting the door to the outside enclosure, he locked them in and then let himself out into the fresh air. He straightened his shirt, his gaze on Tabitha. No problem: he could be more direct.

7

TABITHA

It was blustery, and Tabitha pulled her coat around her as she walked the empty path to the tiger enclosure. The wind whistled around her ears, and she slid on the mud. She heard the mournful cry of an exotic bird, followed by the rumbling grunt of a tiger. Reaching firm ground, she allowed her focus to drift, sinking into the sounds and scents of the zoo. She smelled the musk of a stable, the stench of manure and the tang of lunch being cooked in the cafe nearby. She almost went in for a coffee, but a growl caught her attention and pulled her straight to the heavy-mesh enclosure.

'Well hello, tiger,' she whispered, glad there was nobody else around. 'Where's your other half?' She peered into the bushes, looking for the female that shared the space. The male tipped his head back and yawned. Tabitha sat on the bench and pulled out her sketch book. She drew fast, catching the lines of the teeth and the huge jaw.

The sharp note of a whistle startled her and she looked up. The male was alert now, his focus trained on the bushes in front of the sleeping area. He stood up, stretched and then ran off in the direction of the sound.

Tabitha walked around the outside of the tiger enclosure, making noises in her throat that normally called the cats out. The undergrowth was thick on one side. High trees with tall, bare trunks reached up to the sky, surrounded by thick bushes and tall ferns. The edges of the enclosure were more open with a pool, a shelter and a high platform, all of which were empty.

Tabitha sighed. Her great plan only worked if she could find the tigers, but there was still benefit to be had in sketching the plants in the enclosure. Laying out a waterproof picnic blanket she settled down on the side of the hill that overlooked the tiger pool.

It was always a few degrees colder in the zoo than anywhere else, so she zipped up her long, quilted coat and poured herself a mug of hot coffee from her thermos. She stared into the enclosure, calling to the tigers with her mind. Nothing happened. She opened her sketchpad and her hand began to move over the page. Giving herself over to the rhythm of her art, she allowed her consciousness to drift.

She expected to find herself with the tigers, but instead she was in a cafe, looking into Dylan's face. Damn, why had she turned up here? He looked alarmed. He could definitely see her. How was this possible? She had wondered at the nightclub, but he'd been so drunk it had been hard to tell.

Wanting to give him space, she walked away.

'Mum!' The shout raised her hackles. She looked up and realised she was walking straight towards Rachel. Stopping in front of the woman's chair, she tilted her head as she watched her new friend. Would Rachel see her as well? But

34

the other woman didn't show any signs of recognition or alarm. Tabitha relaxed.

'Yes, darling?' Rachel smiled at Dylan and tilted her head.

Tabitha snaked past Rachel, focusing her attention on her human body back at the zoo, and willing herself back into consciousness.

She opened her eyes and took a deep breath. That had been too close. She would have to be more careful in future. She looked at the sketch. Instead of the tigers she had planned to draw, there was a portrait of Dylan. Her breath caught as she looked at the lines of his face. Why did he fascinate her? What made him different?

She turned the page, picked up her pencil and started drawing one of the tall, straight trees that rose out of the high enclosure, trying to hold her conscious attention on the lines of the branches and the high, straight trunk. She would not go back into trance. She would not go to Dylan again. The sun was shining and her focus wavered as her hand moved over the paper. She wondered where the tigers were. Surely it would be safe to search for them now?

And then she was back in the cafe. How would she ever be able to draw if she travelled to Dylan every time she went into a trance? He was talking to his friends, but he didn't seem happy. A growl vibrated through her chest and she pulled herself into check. She wouldn't let him see her this time.

'I hear you.' She felt the words form in the air around her. 'Where do you go when you're not here?' She watched him. He seemed to be waiting for an answer from her, but she backed away, knocking into a display.

'Who's that?' The voice was all wrong. It didn't sound

like Dylan. She looked around, but the room was already fading. 'Who's that?' the voice repeated.

Tabitha came back into full consciousness on the hill by the tiger enclosure. The sun had gone behind a cloud and she shivered. She looked up. Max stood over her, staring at her sketchbook. It didn't matter how many times she told Max she visited the zoo to draw the cats, he was convinced she came to see him and wouldn't leave her alone. She looked down. The portrait of Dylan was almost finished now. 'It's a friend.'

'That's Dylan.'

Tabitha sighed and shut her sketchbook. 'Yes.'

'How do you know him?'

'I saw him play last night.'

Max snorted. 'Oh, right. His trashy band.'

'You know him?' Tabitha asked.

'Everyone does. Those guys have lorded it around Wildley Forest for as long as I can remember. I was at school with Dylan. He was a big fish in a small pond even then.'

'I'll take it as a compliment to my craft that you recognise him so clearly.' Tabitha shoved her book into her bag. Where are the cats?'

'They're shut inside their sleeping quarters. Do you want to come and look? It will give you a new insight into what tigers are actually like.'

Tabitha hesitated. Max gave her the creeps, but she really wanted to see the tigers. 'Can I take pictures?'

'Of course.'

Tabitha pursed her lips.

'You'll be right up close,' Max said with a smile.

For the first time Tabitha saw a glint of something genuine in his eyes. She smiled back. 'Lead the way.'

8

Max put a key into the lock of an inconspicuous door at the side of the enclosure, opened it and ushered her in. 'Come on inside. I know it's not luxurious, but there's a comfortable chair you could sit in while you draw. And it's warm.'

His chest was puffed out and he had a huge grin on his face as he gestured towards the enormous male, which paced backwards and forwards in front of the bars. The cat yowled at them but didn't stop pacing.

Tabitha looked around the room. It was nicer than she had expected, but there was a general air of grubbiness. The once-white surfaces were a mottle of grey and yellow, and the flowery armchair in the corner was stained. But there was an overriding scent of bleach that gave the tired room a sanitised feel. Opposite the door, a wall of thick metal bars crossed to form small squares. On the other side, the large, male tiger paced.

Max turned on a fan heater in the corner of the room

and fired up the kettle. He nodded towards the armchair. 'Have a seat.'

Tabitha sank into the chair gratefully. She was starting to thaw and the scent of fresh coffee was sparking her system in anticipation.

She had a great view of the tigers. The male still paced, but the female lolled on the straw next to the wall. She hadn't taken her eyes off Max since they walked in.

Tabitha frowned. It was amazing to get this kind of view, but she hated seeing the cats cooped up like this. She pulled out her sketch book and started blocking out the lines.

Max handed her a coffee. It was stronger than she would have liked, but the heat warmed her freezing hands and defrosted her insides so she sipped it gratefully.

'Do I need a coaster?' she asked, inclining her head towards the chest of drawers next to her. Scruffy though it was, it was made of mahogany and could have been beautiful. She didn't want to damage it any further.

Max handed her a bit of cardboard and she grinned as she took it, put it on the dark surface and sat her coffee on top.

Max was as good as his word. He went into the small anteroom and didn't interrupt her at all. She could hear him banging around as he cleaned and tidied, heard the occasional curse followed by the crash of things falling off a shelf, but he left her alone.

Her hand flew across the page, bringing the tigers to life. She sang to herself, forcing her mind to stay on the job and remain present. As she moved into a more detailed layer, her mind shifted. She fought to remain alert as she drew, but the lull of her hand dragged her deeper into trance.

A tiger walked through the trees, moving silently across the twigs and dried leaves. It was relaxed but wild, and Tabitha kept herself insubstantial as it passed a breath away. At the last moment, it swung its head around, its yellow eyes boring into the space she inhabited. Had it seen her? As if in answer, it threw its head back and roared.

The sound of a van brought her back to the present. The female cat rose to her feet, a growl rumbling through her throat. Tabitha smiled. 'Don't worry, sweetie. We'll get you out of here somehow.'

Wildley Forest was a leading conservation zoo that regularly reintroduced animals to the wild and had established entire populations in areas where species had become extinct. But for some reason, the big cats were excluded from any such program and the only reason Tabitha could think of was Max. She looked up as he came back into the room, wondering what secrets were hidden beneath his tense, muscular frame. But he wasn't giving anything away.

'I've been meaning to ask,' Tabitha said, putting her pencil down and taking a few pictures with her phone. 'Is the zoo involved in any tiger conservation? I've been looking online and the tigers are the only animals not covered. Could these tigers ever be reintroduced to the wild?'

'No, but they can be bred.'

'And what happens to the cubs?' Tabitha stood, set her sketchpad on the seat of the chair, and walked nearer to the bars, studying the tigers.

'What's all this about, Tabitha?'

'I spend all this time drawing and painting the cats, and I'd like to give something back. That's why I moved here. I want to be close enough to visit regularly, but I'm keen to get involved with tiger conservation as well.'

Max shoved his hands in his pockets. 'That's why you come? Are those the only reasons?'

Tabitha frowned. 'What other reason would there be?'

Max flushed to his roots, but said nothing.

Tabitha looked at her watch. 'Oh, goodness. Is that the time? Thank you so much, Max, but I have a meeting in five minutes. I've made a great start though. I can continue this from home.'

'Come back after your meeting.'

Tabitha gave a tight smile. 'Thank you, but I need to open the shop. Maybe another time.' She slid her book into her bag and slipped past him and out the door.

9

TABITHA

TABITHA SAT BY THE WINDOW OF THE CAFETERIA, WATCHING a family cooing over the monkeys that swarmed across the trees in the large enclosure next to the children's play area. She loved seeing these tableaus of family life, even though they sparked her loneliness.

A tall woman in a black suit, a white shirt and flat, black ballet pumps walked into the cafe. She squinted into the bright autumn sunshine, scanning the expanse of empty tables. Smoothing a wayward strand of brown hair which had escaped the knot at the nape of her neck, she held her hand over her eyes to block out the glare. She wasn't wearing any make-up but, even at this time of year, she had a slight tan from working outdoors. Her gaze swept past Tabitha.

Tabitha stood up, straightening her clothes. She had dressed in skinny jeans and a knee length tunic, brightly coloured and clasped in at the waist with a wide belt. She did not look like she was here for a business meeting.

'Ursula?' Tabitha walked towards the woman, shoulders

back, both hands outstretched. She loved the flicker of surprise that flashed across the woman's eyes.

'Tara.' Ursula grasped them. I'm so honoured to meet you. I have been an admirer of yours for a long time.'

'That's very kind.' Tabitha smiled and gave Ursula's hands a squeeze.

Ursula took a deep breath then released it, allowing her shoulders to relax. 'Can I get you a coffee?'

'I'm good, thanks.' Tabitha let go of her hands and gestured at her reusable, bamboo cup. 'I've spent so much time here, they have it waiting for me when I arrive.' She winked.

Ursula laughed, sliding onto the bench opposite Tabitha's things. 'I think I've seen you around. You sketch near the tiger enclosure? I didn't realise who you were though. Max referred to you as Tabitha.'

Tabitha shrugged. 'I work as Tara. I live as Tabitha. I prefer to be anonymous and my public profile doesn't allow for that. My cover won't last long, but if you could help me preserve it for a while, I'd appreciate it.'

'Of course.' Ursula beamed. 'I'm so excited about our project. I've been pestering Max for his tiger conservation plans so I can work out where we can build and expand, and where we're working from scratch. I haven't received any information from him yet, but I will give you more detail as soon as I can.'

'Listen,' Tabitha leaned forwards, propping her elbows on her knees. 'Does Max have any interest in conservation at all? I keep asking him about it, but he's so evasive. Is he going to be a problem for us?'

'You don't trust him?'

Tabitha shrugged. 'I'm just not sure yet.'

Ursula sighed. 'I don't blame you. But if he doesn't engage in tiger conservation projects, he is not doing his job properly and I need to keep records of that. If he makes problems for you, please do let me know.'

Tabitha tilted her head and narrowed her eyes. She looked at Ursula, wondering how much she could trust the woman. She had always seemed very open on the phone, and genuinely excited about tiger conservation.

Ursula tilted her head. 'Is something wrong?'

Tabitha released a breath slowly. She had no idea whether or not this was a good idea, but it could be her only chance to do something. 'I can't really back any of this up, but I don't have a good feeling about Max. If you tell me what kind of evidence you need, I'll keep a look out.'

Ursula swallowed. 'I'm embarrassed to say my boss, Sophie, has a thing for Max. Unfortunately, he knows it. He flirts mercilessly with her and gets away with a ridiculous amount. But if you see any indication that he is obstructing our conservation efforts, or mistreating the cats, please do tell me.'

Tabitha nodded. 'I will. In the meantime, let's talk tiger territories. She opened the huge ring binder that sat next to her on the table. She handed Ursula a map, divided up into pale yellow sections. 'This one is in India. There's a large amount of agricultural land right next to a huge, but over-crowded reserve. We would be allowed to buy this to rewild. We would use native tree and plant species to expand the habitat, allowing the animals to roam further. The best bit is a stream that runs down one side. We would have water. I was hoping to find somewhere we could release our tigers, but the area is already overcrowded. I have a friend, though, who owns a very large and luxurious wildlife sanctuary. I will find out whether he has a home for two extra cats.'

Ursula poured over the map. 'This looks perfect for our project. I'm not sure about our tigers though. They have always lived in captivity. They wouldn't be suitable candidates for release.'

Tabitha shrugged. 'Then a sanctuary is an even better option. They'll have much more space than here, and they'll be in their proper habitat, but cared for.'

Ursula swallowed. 'I would need to persuade Sophie to let the tigers go. That's a big ask. They are one of the zoo's top draws.'

Tabitha leaned her chair back on its hind legs, folded her arms and raised an eyebrow. 'I know you'd lose valuable animals, but I can offer financial compensation, and the press coverage of the project would be awesome. I suggest we launch a fundraising effort to run alongside my own donation so we can keep developing the territory. I'd be happy to offer a painting. That should raise a large sum. The territory would be a long-term project for the zoo, would provide thirty-seven local people with job opportunities and education, and put you right up there in terms of tiger conservation. If that doesn't appeal, I guess I'm wasting my time here.'

'No!' Ursula let out a slow exhale. 'I'll make it work. Just give me some time to win Sophie over. And Max.'

Tabitha nodded. 'If you want to appeal to Max, you'll have to go through his ego.'

'Could you talk to him?'

'Huh.' Tabitha took a gulp of coffee. 'Max likes to educate the scatty artist. He doesn't take me seriously.'

Ursula frowned. 'You don't strike me as the kind of woman who would put up with that.'

Tabitha grinned. 'Sometimes it serves my purpose. He can think what he wants about me. I just want to draw the tigers and help them get back where they belong. I'm afraid Max is *your* problem.' Tabitha handed Ursula a small pile of paper. 'These are your copies of the proposal. Have a look, and then we can talk again. I need to know within ten days whether you're in.' Tabitha stood and picked up a satchel from the ground by her feet. 'You have my number and I'm by the tiger enclosure most days, so if you have any questions come and find me.'

Ursula stood up and held out her hand. A grin spread across her face. 'This is the most exciting project I've ever had the chance to work on. Thank you for coming to me. I promise I will do everything in my power to make it happen.'

Tabitha clasped the offered hand in both of her own. 'Just remember,' she said, holding Ursula's gaze. 'It's all about the tigers. Nothing else really matters.'

10

TABITHA

TABITHA GROANED AS SHE SPOTTED HER PARENTS SITTING IN their enormous car outside her house, the engine running. She jogged over and knocked on the window with her knuckles.

Her dad looked up, grinned and opened the window. 'There you are. We've been waiting for over an hour.'

'I hope you haven't had the engine running all that time?' Tabitha raised her eyebrows.

'If you'd been here, we wouldn't have had to,' her mum snapped, getting out of the car. 'I've been freezing in here.'

'Maybe tell me you're coming next time, and I'll make sure I'm ready and waiting.' Tabitha walked up the path to the cottage, unlocked the door, and stood back, holding it open to allow them in. She had been hoping to put them off until the house was finished. As it was, it was nearly done, but she knew they would notice every flaw.

Her mum looked around, her arms tightly folded. 'It's certainly different. Surely you have the money for some-thing better?'

Tabitha forced a smile. 'I have the money for whatever I want. *This is* what I want.'

'Well, it will do for a while, I suppose.' Her dad walked around, peering at the paintings on display. 'How many of these are taken?'

'About half,' Tabitha said with a shrug. 'I'll box those up within the next few days, and more are heading for a gallery in London at the end of the month. I'll just keep enough for my display here.'

'And is the plan working? Are you getting more done so close to the tigers?' He opened her sales log, which sat by the till and ran his finger down the columns.

Tabitha slammed the book shut, only just missing his fingers.

He gave her a look.

'I'm certainly not missing the long bus journey from my old place, but it's a bit soon to see that reflected in my accounts. I haven't even finished unpacking yet.'

'Never mind your father,' her mum said, putting a hand on her arm. 'Let's go upstairs. You can show me around and put the kettle on.'

Tabitha's gaze swept over the unfinished sketch on her easel. She had planned an afternoon of drawing and unpacking. Lovely as it was to see her parents, this would put everything back. Still, there was no choice now. 'Come on then,' she said, and held the door at the bottom of the stairs open.

Her father held back, his fingers straying to the sales book unconsciously.

'You too, dad,' she said, narrowing her eyes at him. 'This is my business and I'm running it very successfully. I don't need you checking up on me.'

He looked about to object, but she raised her eyebrows and he sighed. 'Okay then. A coffee wouldn't go amiss.' He walked over to her, pausing in front of her to pinch her cheek. 'You're grown up now, I guess.'

She batted his hand away. 'Yes, I am. Thank you for noticing.' She ushered him up the stairs and closed the door firmly behind them.

11

DYLAN

DYLAN WOKE TO A FAMILIAR SINKING DISAPPOINTMENT. HE blinked, trying to bring the room into focus. He was in his old room at his mum's house. For a moment, he couldn't remember why he wasn't at the flat, and then it all came back. He had been too irritated with his friends, and had come here to avoid them. He sighed, sat up and looked at his watch. His eyes focused on the date and a stab of excitement shot through him. He smiled. It was his day off. Ten minutes later, he was showered and dressed waiting for the kettle to boil.

'Why are you in such a rush? I thought you weren't going into work today.' Rachel yawned as she came into the kitchen, a blanket draped over her shoulders.

'I'm going up to the zoo.'

She grinned.

He smiled. 'Stop it. I need a day out. Will you be okay on your own?'

'Aren't I always?' She was silent for a moment and then

turned to him. 'You can't stay here looking after me forever, Dylan.'

'But it's always been the two of us. What would you do?'

'I'm a grown-up, sweetie. I was a grown-up before you arrived and I'll be a grown-up long after you've moved out. I adore you, you know that, but you're not the only one looking out for me. Go out and shine. You don't have to stick with Instantaneous Rock. If your dreams don't match theirs, break free. Show the world what Dylan McKenzie can do and get to know Tabitha.'

'Who said anything about Tabitha?'

Rachel suppressed a smile. 'Isn't she why you're going to the zoo? That girl is more than you could possibly imagine. I'm not surprised she has scared your friends off. They could never measure up to her and I bet they know it.'

'What do you mean?' Dylan leaned forwards, propping his elbows on the breakfast bar, looking his mum in the eye.

There was a pause. Rachel grinned. 'I get a good feeling about Tabitha and I know you do too or we wouldn't be having this conversation. Dylan, some people lift us up and some people drag us down. Give her a chance to show you which of those she is. And think about who and what you really want in your life. Now, go. Have some fun. You deserve it.'

Dylan laughed. He downed the last of his coffee then pulled on his coat. 'See you later?'

'Always.' Rachel winked and then turned and started tidying the kitchen, humming to herself as she worked.

DYLAN PAID FOR HIS TICKET AND ZIPPED UP HIS COAT. THIS was a stupid idea. What good would it do to see *these* tigers?

The cat he had seen was something different entirely. It was colder here than in the village and he wished he'd brought a scarf and gloves. Walking in through the gate, he paused to look at the penguins that were swimming around a huge glass tank near the entrance. There was a man standing in the middle of the water, throwing fish to them and their excitement was palpable.

He looked at his map, crossed the road and started walking up the path that would lead him to the tigers. There was hardly anyone here. In summer this place would be heaving. On sunny bank holidays there were queues right the way through the village, but today was neither sunny nor a bank holiday. The chill wind had a knife edge that cut through the too-thin coat Dylan was wearing. He ducked into a small shop to buy a hat and scarf. They only sold zoo merchandise, so he was now the proud owner of penguin mittens and a sloth hat. He zipped his jacket up. Warmer now, he felt as though he had the whole place to himself and breathed the cold, fresh air deep into his lungs.

A rumbling growl iced his blood. He frowned at the map, and then looked around him. He wondered what would happen if one of the big cats escaped their formidable enclosures. As much as he loved seeing the white tiger, he knew it wasn't real. He wouldn't want to see a solid, heavily muscled tiger stalking him. The unmistakable grunt of a big cat sent chills down his spine. The thick foliage in front of him was moving. He swallowed, trying to think clearly. There was no mystery to hearing a big cat. He was at the zoo, heading for the tiger enclosure. But the dread persisted.

After his dark thoughts, the tiger habitat was lush and surprisingly normal. He walked around the perimeter, peering in through the foliage but there was nothing obvious to see.

A movement caught his eye and he stopped. A tiger was lying in a lone patch of sunlight, its head twisted around to groom its gigantic flank. His heart sped up. The cat stopped, fixing him with its yellow stare.

'Well, hello there,' he said, glad he was alone. 'Have you seen any white tigers around?'

'We don't have any white tigers in Wildley Forest Zoo,' a voice said from behind him.

He turned. The man in front of him was familiar, but he couldn't place him.

'You've got to be kidding me,' the man said. He shook his head, turned and walked away.

'Wait,' Dylan called out, jogging to catch up. 'Is there a problem?'

The man stopped. He squared his shoulders and then turned around, his gaze flickering to the hill behind the tiger enclosure. Dylan followed his line of sight. A woman sat on the grass. She seemed to be writing, or drawing. There was something familiar about her. She looked up. Tabitha.

'Stay away from her.' The man glared at Dylan. 'She's working. She doesn't want to be interrupted.'

'You know her?' Dylan felt an odd spike of jealousy.

'I do. And I suggest you leave her alone.' The man walked away without waiting for an answer.

12

MAX

'BLOODY DYLAN!' MAX MUTTERED, PUTTING HIS FOOT down on the accelerator and ignoring the speed limit signs dotted around the zoo. He looked down at the crumpled drawing on the floor of the van. Dylan's face — or what had been sketched of it — peered up at him. She'd caught his likeness so well he felt as though the man was watching him and that just irritated him even more. What the hell did Tabitha see in him? He'd torn the picture out of the book when she'd got up to stand near the bars. He wondered how long it would take for her to realise it was gone.

A woman with a toddler wandered across the road. He leaned on his horn, startling her. She screamed and froze, forcing him to swerve around her.

Another woman on the pavement stared open-mouthed as he shot past. Ursula. Her face darkened in the rear-view mirror. Damn. That woman got everywhere.

His phone rang and he answered.

'Stop the car.' Ursula's voice was sharper than he'd heard it before. 'Stop now, or you're fired.'

'You can't fire me,' he snapped.

'Now.' Her voice was ice cold.

He pulled over to a bay on the left, rolled his window down, and sat with the engine running, waiting for her to catch up. She appeared at his window, her cheeks red.

'For God's sake, Max. You almost hit that child.' She leaned her hands on the ledge of the open window. 'I *can* fire you and I will if you don't get your act together. You're stretching my patience. Don't push me farther.'

He leaned towards her. 'And whose side do you think Sophie would take, eh?'

'What do you have on her, Max? What makes you so sure that she would ignore gross misconduct in order to keep you by her side?'

Max grinned.

Ursula frowned, scrutinising his face. 'Has something happened?'

'Nope.' Max tried to arrange his face into a conciliatory shape, whatever that was. 'I'm sorry I drove too fast, but I'm just trying to use my time efficiently.'

Ursula nodded, her lips pursed. 'Have you looked into the conservation information I gave you? We are making huge strides forward in other areas of the zoo, but lagging way behind with the tigers. We've been offered a uniquely exciting opportunity, but I need to establish where our conservation efforts are at the moment in order to pitch the case.'

'I haven't had a chance to look yet, sorry.'

Ursula closed her eyes. She took a deep breath and then let it out slowly. Opening her eyes again, she fixed Max with a hard stare. 'Get it done. I need a report on my desk in a week.'

'So soon?'

'It's been two months! Tiger conservation is a key part of your contract.'

Max gritted his teeth. 'Yes, of course.'

Ursula nodded. Standing up, she put her hands on her hips. 'I suggest you take some deep breaths. Get a drink or something. And stay away from the tigers for the rest of the day.' She nodded again, turned and walked away.

Max hit the button to shut the window, cut the engine and closed his eyes. He had a lot to lose if Ursula decided to be more attentive. He had to keep himself under better control. When had she given him that information on conservation? He had no recollection of it at all.

Firing up the engine, he drove slowly to the main management block, slid into a space and climbed out of the van. He punched in the entry code, and then turned to the pigeonholes on his left. His was packed to the top. He tugged out the envelopes and flicked through. There was an A4 envelope stuffed so full of paper that it was barely sealed shut. He went over to the coffee machine. The watery brown liquid that trickled into the thin plastic cup could barely be called coffee. Max winced at the nasty taste and threw the rest in the bin next to the machine. Sitting on the hard sofa, he pulled the paper out of the envelope.

He flicked through sheet after sheet of information on tiger conservation. There was some kind of map and a five-page letter from Ursula with suggestions, questions and a bold, underlined deadline in a week's time. Max shoved the paper to one side, unread, and rubbed his forehead. He was no good at this stuff. He was a hands-on kind of guy and had worked his way up to where he was now using charisma, posturing and a fair bit of bluff. Paperwork was absolutely not his thing.

He shoved the paper back into the envelope and bounded up the stairs, looking for the one card he had left.

'Come in.' Sophie's voice was sharp.

Max pushed the door open and flashed her his most charming smile. 'Can we talk?'

Sophie flushed and pushed her chair back. 'I could do with a break, actually. Let's get out of here and get some proper coffee before I scream at my paperwork.'

Max walked tall as they left the building, bathing in Sophie's reflected glory. He knew he would never reach the management heights she had achieved, but winning her over had been the next best thing and it gave him the ability to ignore Ursula when he needed to. He had no hope of ever winning *her* over.

The cafe in the entrance building was empty, so they ordered coffee and then sat at a discreet table in the corner.

'What's going on?' Sophie tilted her head.

'I could do with your help.'

Sophie's smile dropped. 'Talk.'

'Ursula's on the war path.'

'About what?'

Max grimaced. 'She wants my tiger conservation proposal in a week.'

'And?'

'There's no way I can come up with something that quickly. I'm flat out looking after the cats.'

Sophie raised her eyebrows. 'And yet you have time for coffee?'

Max coughed. 'Yeah, but I was working late last night.'

Sophie nodded. 'I get that, but big cat conservation is one of our key objectives for the year. Can you do it, or not?'

Max swallowed. Sophie had never failed to take his side before.

'Of course I can do it. I was just hoping to get an extension.'

'There is no give on Ursula's deadline. The best I can do is to offer my help, if you'd like it. Or, if you're really not able to fit it in alongside looking after the cats, I'll find someone to take over while you complete it.'

'No,' Max snapped.

Sophie raised her eyebrows.

'I mean, I don't need someone to take over, thank you.' He took a deep breath and leaned back, trying to look relaxed.

She watched him, eyebrows drawn together as though waiting for him to say something else.

He shifted in his seat.

'Fine.' She stood, reaching down to pick up her bag. 'If you'd like my help with the conservation plan let me know, but don't leave it until the last minute. I can't drop everything, no matter who is asking.' She knocked back the last of her coffee. 'Break over for me, and for you too. Show Ursula you're fit for this job.'

Max slumped as she strode out of the cafe. It didn't matter how fierce Sophie was with the rest of the staff, she had always been on his side. She had never said no to him before. He ran a hand through his hair. Life had been good a few days ago, but with Tabitha losing interest, Ursula getting on his case and now Sophie distancing herself, he was starting to feel very isolated. He slammed a palm down on the table and pushed himself up, allowing anger to flow through his veins, chasing out the pervasive burn of fear. He *would* find a way to turn this around.

13

DYLAN

'MAY I?' DYLAN GESTURED TO THE SPACE ON THE BLANKET next to Tabitha. She was sitting, cross legged, a sketchbook on her lap. 'Or would your boyfriend object?'

'My boyfriend?' Tabitha's eyebrows shot up.

'The tiger keeper. He warned me not to come over.'

Anger flashed across her face, but she covered it quickly. 'But you decided to come anyway?'

Dylan grinned. 'I figured if you wanted me to leave, you could tell me yourself.'

'I'm glad to hear it. And Max is not my boyfriend.' She moved her pencils out the way and nodded at the empty space on the blanket.

Dylan sat down, 'You're drawing the tigers?'

'That's the plan.'

Dylan picked a blade of grass and twirled it between his fingers. 'Not your boyfriend?'

'No.' She stood up, brushed herself off, and walked up to a glass panel, her sketch book and a pencil clutched in one hand.

'Look, there they are.' Tabitha pointed to a den next to the pond. 'They're sleeping.' She walked back up to the picnic blanket, sat down and started drawing.

She seemed more at home here in the outdoors hunched over her sketchbook. She looked up at the cats, frowning. Her eyes glazed over and then she looked back down and drew furiously before repeating the cycle. He smiled, watching her pause and tilt her head when the smaller tiger yawned and repositioned itself to get more comfortable. She mumbled to herself, holding a quiet conversation with the cats while she watched them, transfixed, leaning towards them as though they were domestic cats she could cuddle up to.

'I enjoyed your gig the other night.' Tabitha was watching him now.

Dylan grimaced. 'I'm sorry my friends were so rude. They're rather over-protective, and not fans of change. Where do you come from?'

'I don't come from far away. I was born in Wildley Town. My parents still live there, but I moved out a long time ago. Let's just say their idea of my future didn't match my own. I moved here for the tigers. I've been travelling miles by bus to sketch them, but now I can come every day and get involved in the zoo's conservation projects.'

Her hand flew over the page while she talked. He was mesmerised by the movement of her fingers, the fluidity of the lines and her focus on the creatures that were now padding around the enclosure. He saw a flash of white in amongst the bushes, and his eyes widened as the white tiger snaked through the enclosure with the yellow cats. He looked over at Tabitha, but she was completely absorbed in her sketch. The silence was only broken by the singing of a single bird and the hypnotic rhythm of Tabitha's pencil. The more he watched her, the more connected he felt to the nature around him; to the red kites that wheeled overhead, the tigers that prowled around the enclosure below, and the wallabies wandering free around the grounds. He heard the occasional elephant, cow or bird, but very little human noise and that brought him the peace he had been craving.

'You found each other then.'

Dylan turned around at the voice. The man from the tiger enclosure was standing on the path above him, hands on his hips, jaw tight. His hair was newly oiled and combed.

Tabitha sighed. 'What do you want, Max?'

'I told him you were working.'

'That's not all you told him, is it?' She glared at him, her lips compressed. 'He seems to have come away with the impression that we were involved, somehow.'

Max flushed. 'I didn't say that.'

Tabitha slammed her sketchbook shut.

Dylan stood up. They were almost the same height and, strong as this man clearly was, he was panting from the effort of walking up the hill. He had changed out of his overalls since Dylan saw him last and was neatly styled, his clothes artificially casual.

'You don't have a clue who I am, do you, Dylan McKenzie?' The man's voice was low, dangerous as the cats he cared for.

Dylan frowned. 'Should I? Have we met?'

'We were at school together. Apparently I was beneath your notice. I've seen you playing with Instantaneous Rock. You're a fraud, McKenzie, does your little girlfriend here know that?'

'Little girlfriend?' Tabitha smacked her sketchbook on

the ground and stood up. Her jaw was set, her hands planted on her hips. 'Do not talk down to me, Max. You don't know who or what you're dealing with.'

He smirked. 'I'm really scared now.'

A quiet growl came from somewhere. Dylan looked over one shoulder, and then the other, but there was nothing out of the ordinary and no sign of the white tiger.

Max was staring at Tabitha, who was glaring at him, her eyes catlike in her fury.

Dylan shook his head, unable to place the man. 'Listen, I'm sorry if I've insulted you. School was a long time ago. But please don't take your irritation at me out on Tabitha.'

'Max Sculter.' The man spat out the words from between clenched teeth. His eyes blazed. 'My name is Max Sculter. Ring any bells?'

Dylan took a deep breath. 'You look very different.'

'Not so easy to bully now, am I?'

'I don't remember picking on you.'

'Seriously? You terrorised the skinny kid in the corner. You liked to play the rockstar, charming every lost soul in the whole damn school apart from me, but you were a bully.'

'When? Give me an example.'

'Remember the sixth form dance? We'd all been looking forward to it for weeks. I'd been there for five minutes when someone *accidentally* spilled fish sauce all down my suit. Nobody would come near me for the rest of the evening.'

Dylan clenched his fists. His face flushed. 'That wasn't me. And whatever you think my friends may have done, *I* did not bully you.'

'It was your best friend, and you just stood by and let it

happen.' Max was pale now. He was breathing heavily, and his hands were clenched into fists at his side.

Dylan swallowed. 'What is this really about?'

'This!' Max pulled a wad of paper from his pocket and smoothed it out. Dylan found himself looking at a picture of himself. It was so lifelike; it was almost like looking in a mirror except that she had somehow made him look better than he had ever seen himself. Was this how he looked to her? His mouth went dry. He swallowed.

'Max, for God's sake,' Tabitha snapped, 'that's mine, and it's private.' She snatched the paper out of Max's hand and strode off down the hill.

'I don't know what you're so upset about,' Max yelled after her. 'You show your pictures all the time. I've done you a favour. He'll probably buy it now.'

She didn't turn around.

Max turned to Dylan and clenched his hands into fists 'Things were going well before you turned up.'

'Yeah, it seems like it.'

'Be careful, Dylan. Neither you, nor your mum, want me as an enemy.'

'Are you threatening my mum?' Dylan stepped closer. 'How low have you sunk, Max?'

Max bristled. He glared at Dylan, his hands clenched into fists at his sides. He took a deep breath and then stepped back. 'I'm not threatening anyone. I don't know what you mean.'

Dylan held up his hands. 'We're done here. Have a good day.' He turned and walked down the slope after Tabitha, ignoring the stream of swear words aimed at his back.

14

DYLAN PRETENDED NOT TO LOOK FOR TABITHA. THE SKY was becoming increasingly grey, and the air was heavy with moisture. The wind was biting and most of the animals were in their sleeping quarters. In the middle of the zoo he heard a strange, cat-like noise again, but the map didn't show any cats nearby. His adrenaline rose as the noise repeated, but there wasn't a person in sight to ask. He was completely alone.

He ducked into the zebra house when the rain started, leaning on the rail, trying not to breathe in too much of the ripe stench of dung. The zebra in front of him let out a familiar barking sound. Dylan chuckled and leaned back against the wooden wall of the shed. Here was the cat he had thought was on the loose.

It was so peaceful on this cold, drizzly day he felt as though he was the only person there. He felt free but, at the same time, the loneliness that always hovered at the edges of his awareness surged forwards. He spent his life surrounded by people, fending them off so they didn't notice his differentness. He was recognised everywhere he went in Wildley Forest Village, but nobody really saw him. His disguise was so absolute that he sometimes wondered who his real self was. Only his mother had ever seen him properly, but he had a growing hunch he might be able to add Tabitha to that short list.

He ran out into the rain, jogging over to see the flamingos, which were stomping their feet in the pond. At least *they* were enjoying the downpour. He sighed, it was time to go home and get dry.

He ran back to the entrance, trying to warm up. His clothes were soaked through and he was shivering, but he stood in the doorway to the shop, looking out at the expanse of grass, trees and enclosures, loathe to leave. He turned and walked into the shop, admiring the artwork, T shirts and cuddly toys, but there was nothing he needed and he had no excuse to spend his meagre pay.

A lone woman with scraped back blond hair was gathering leaflets together at the reception desk.

'Excuse me,' Dylan said, smiling in an attempt to smooth away her irritated expression. 'Do you have any jobs going?'

'Do you have experience?'

'Not with animals, but I work in the customer service industry. I'd be interested in anything: the cafe, the shop, something like that?'

'We have a vacancy in the children's Playbarn. Here.' She handed him a job description, an application form and a blue biro. 'Fill that in and give it back to me on your way out. You've nearly missed the deadline.'

Dylan sat down at a wooden table in the corner of the cafe. He started filling in the easy bits of the form first, padding it out to include as much of his customer service and team leadership experience as possible. He had no background with children, but he wasn't going to pretend. They could hire him, or they could hire someone else.

The same woman was there when he walked back to reception. He handed her the form with a smile, but she glared as she looked him up and down, and then took the piece of paper and started reading.

He was running out of reasons to stay. If the tiger didn't show up sooner or later, he'd have to leave.

Dylan wandered around the stacks of souvenirs, books and clothes. He picked up an iron sculpture of a tiger roaring and shivered. Turning, he saw the white tiger snaking between the displays. 'I wondered when you'd show up,' he murmured, trusting the animal would hear and understand.

The tiger grunted.

Dylan looked around now, wondering if the woman at reception would notice, but rather than screaming, she was walking towards him. He looked for the tiger, but it had disappeared.

'Do you have time for a chat now?' she said, raising her eyebrows.

'A chat?'

She held up his application. 'I'm doing the interviews. This is your only chance if you're actually interested in the job. Unless, of course, you'd rather shop?'

'No,' Dylan said quickly. 'Now is good.'

'We'll just chat in the cafe.' She gestured to the seating area at one side of the large shop. 'Order an espresso and whatever you'd like. Tell Samuel to put it on Sophie's tab. Then take a seat. I'll be with you in a minute.'

Dylan walked over to the coffee bar and smiled at the man behind the counter. 'One espresso and a cappuccino. Put it on — Uh ...' He gestured towards the woman, who was talking to someone by the reception desk. 'Her tab. Sophie?'

'Sure.' The man in the cafe nodded and turned around to work the espresso machine.

'What's it like working here?' Dylan asked. 'Do you enjoy it? Are they good people?'

'Meh.' The man shrugged. 'It's packed out or empty. But at least I'm not out in the rain or picking up rhino shit. It could be a lot worse. I'll bring them over when they're ready.'

Dylan nodded and sat at an empty table.

The woman strode over, a clipboard and fountain pen in her hand. She sat and started writing without looking at him. 'So, Dylan. Why do you want this job?'

Dylan took a measured breath. 'I need a change.'

'And our zoo is the place for you to figure things out?' She raised her eyebrows.

'Erm ... I have a lot of customer service experience from my job at the cafe.'

She was silent for a moment, watching him, her head tilted to one side. 'Your CV says you haven't worked with kids.'

'No.' He felt her focus drain away as she made a note on the clipboard.

Her smile was polite but detached. 'Thank you—'

'I'm in a band.' Crap. Why did he say that? He was desperate.

She looked up at him. 'And?'

'Dealing with the fans is like managing kids. Sometimes

there are hundreds of them, all at once. They can be angry, over excited or flat, and I have to pull them with me. It's my job to inspire them to feel better, to do better.'

'Hmm,' Sophie said, writing something down on the paper. 'That's very interesting.'

A woman walked into the café and Dylan's breath caught. Tabitha! He raised his hand. She nodded and started walking over to the table.

'You know her?' Sophie asked.

Dylan nodded.

The woman pursed her lips. 'Interesting,' she said again. 'I think that's everything. I have your contact details. I'll be in touch.' She stood up and gathered the papers together.

'It's nice to see you, Tara.' Sophie said, holding out a hand to Tabitha. 'I hope you've had a productive day?'

Tabitha shook it. 'Yes, thank you.'

Sophie nodded and walked back towards reception.

'Why did she call you Tara?' Dylan asked, suppressing a smile.

Tabitha rolled her eyes. 'She always does. How do you know Sophie?' She glanced over at the woman's retreating back.

'I don't, not yet, but maybe I will,' he said with a smile. 'I've just applied for a job.'

Tabitha's face lit up. 'Then maybe I'll see you around more often.'

'Are you heading back into Wildley Forest Village?' Dylan said. They started walking towards the door. 'Would you like to join me for dinner?'

'Well, that all depends.' Tabitha looked up at him, her eyes narrowed, her head cocked to one side. 'Will I have your friends to deal with? Because, to be honest, I've had enough drama for one day after Max's theatrics.'

'Nope, we're rehearsing later, but for now it's just mum and I. She'd be delighted if you came too. You've made yourself a fan.'

Tabitha's lips turned up. Her shoulders relaxed. 'The feeling's mutual, I assure you. I wish I was that close to my parents.'

'It sounds as though there's a story there?'

'Not really.' Tabitha spun around as a huge gust of wind caught in her hair. She tipped her head back and closed her eyes, smiling up at the sky. 'Isn't this weather gorgeous?'

Dylan laughed. 'I hadn't really thought about it like that. The rain didn't improve my trip to the zoo, if I'm honest.'

'Oh, but it did.' Tabitha grinned. 'You had the place virtually to yourself. Did you enjoy the zebras?'

'Were you watching me?' Dylan asked, narrowing his eyes. 'How did you know I was at the zebras?'

'Just a lucky guess.' She laughed. 'But my lucky guesses are usually right.'

15

THE SUN WAS SINKING BEHIND THE ROOFS, BATHING THE tiles with a glossy, orange glow when they walked down the main street in Wildley Forest Village.

'Is that Max?' Tabitha asked as she slowed down.

Rachel was outside her front gate. A tall, dark-haired man circled her wheelchair.

'And mum?' Dylan's eyes widened. 'Look at him crowding her.'

Dylan took off at a jog and put himself between Max and his mum. There was a whirring as the chair moved backwards. 'What's going on here?' Dylan pushed up his sleeves.

'I see the cavalry has arrived.' Max rolled his eyes.

'Do I need cavalry, Max?' Rachel asked, moving around Dylan on the pavement, but keeping the distance between her and Max. She tipped her head back to look him in the eye. 'You used to be such a lovely boy. Your mum is one of my closest friends.'

'You remember me?' he asked, doubt in his voice.

'Of course,' she said, frowning. 'I know you and Dylan didn't hit it off, but that doesn't mean I'd forget you. What's wrong, Max?'

'Nothing's wrong. I don't need your pity.' He walked backwards a few paces, and then spun and strode off down the street.

'That was strange,' Rachel murmured.

'That's the least of it,' Dylan grumbled under his breath.

Rachel frowned, her head tilted to one side. 'What do you mean? Max always used to be a nice boy. There must be something wrong.'

'I'm afraid that's pretty normal for him now.' Tabitha sighed. 'And Dylan's not Max's favourite person. Just take care around him, please?'

Rachel frowned again. 'Of course. I didn't know you knew him.'

'I've been sketching the tigers at the zoo for a while now. He's their keeper. I guess that doesn't mean much in itself, but I'm pretty sure he thinks I moved here to be closer to him. In fact, I'd had enough of that long bus journey to see the cats and I needed to be able to draw them in person more often.'

Rachel nodded, 'A pretty girl turns up at his enclosure every day. I can see why he might allow himself to become entranced by that idea. Still, I'm sure it will be easy enough to set things straight. Would you like to come inside, Tabitha? You could join us for dinner? The food is almost ready and there's plenty.'

Dylan grinned. 'Too late. I've already invited her.'

Rachel's face lit up and her eyes sparkled in the glare of the streetlamp. 'Great, give me ten minutes.' She winked, and then turned her chair back up the path and into the house.

Dylan rolled his eyes.

Tabitha looked down at the pavement, her cheeks flushed. She wasn't normally this easily embarrassed. Dylan was shaking up every corner of her normal.

Their hands were almost touching. She was acutely aware of the warmth coming from his body next to hers, of the prickles that ran over her skin where they almost brushed up against one another.

Tabitha cleared her throat and reached out, feeling the rough edges of the garden wall under her fingertips. 'Your mum's something special, you know? She gives people a chance.'

'I hear you.' Dylan held the gate open, letting Tabitha walk ahead of him up the path to the house. The door was standing part-way open and she could hear Rachel singing as Dylan swung it wide and stood back to let her through.

'You guys get settled,' Rachel called through to the hall. 'It's almost ready.'

16

THE ROOM WAS SO LIVED-IN COMPARED TO TABITHA'S DUSTY, half-unpacked cottage. The sofas were expansive and comfortable. The coffee tables were heaped with magazines and books, and the lush, purple curtains were drawn tightly closed against the darkening night. One corner of the room was dominated by a huge drum kit. A pair of black drumsticks had been left lying across the snare, and the music stand was stuffed with as much paper as it could reasonably take. Next to it, an acoustic guitar sat on a stand.

'Who plays the guitar?' Tabitha asked, running a finger along the wooden curve of the body.

'Me.' Dylan's voice was husky. 'I play the drums in the band, but I started the guitar first. I used to play along to CDs in my bedroom and then Mum got me lessons.'

'So why do you play the drums in the band?'

He shrugged. 'I love it. The drums create the heartbeat. They hold the music together, binding the different lines into a single entity. I feel the wholeness of the music when I play.'

Tabitha smiled. 'That's how I feel about my painting.'

'Do you always paint tigers?' Dylan picked up the guitar and sat down, resting the instrument on one thigh and plucking at the strings with his fingers while he turned the pegs to tune it.

'Not always, but mostly. Cats are my muse. I paint Emily too, my Siberian cat. You met her the other day.'

Dylan nodded. His eyes were hooded, his fingers beginning to pick out gentle rolling chords.

'She's a beautiful cat. Has she settled into her new home?'

Tabitha smiled. 'Emily's not like most cats. We have a strong bond. She knows when we're home, even if it's a new place. She won't leave me. Do you live here with your mum?'

'No,' Dylan smiled. 'I live with my friends, but I keep my instruments here because we live in a flat. There's no playing allowed. It's annoying but, luckily, Mum likes to listen to us play. In fact,' he looked at his phone, 'we're practicing here in a couple of hours.'

'Can I ask you a question?' Tabitha suppressed a smile.

Dylan raised his eyebrows.

'Why is the band called Instantaneous Rock?'

Dylan laughed, a belly laugh Tabitha hadn't heard before. 'We spent days trying to name the band, but we'd had enough. We came out of a science lesson where we'd been learning about Instantaneous Rock Transformations, and I commented that would be a good name for the band. That was it. It was all quite random in the end.'

Tabitha laughed. 'I love that. Do you sing as well?'

Dylan smiled. 'I do, but don't tell Linden I said that.'

'Will you sing for me?'

He looked down at the guitar, watching his fingers moving over the fretboard, plucking out notes and harmonies as he began to hum. Tabitha leaned back into the comfortable chair, allowing herself to relax for the first time in days. In this house, she felt safe.

The fire flickered in the grate next to Dylan, throwing light over his face. A lock of hair fell onto his forehead and worry lines that she hadn't realised he possessed had smoothed out. He closed his eyes and began to sing.

> *Dreaming of a place on the other side of here,*
> *Dreaming of a me that's only shadow.*
> *The road appears to lead away*
> *But always comes back home.*
> *The image shifts and fades*
> *And again, I'm alone.*

The words tugged at her heart and brought tears to her eyes. They reminded her of all the goodbyes she had mourned, all the futures she had seen dissolve. His voice was deep, husky. It sent shivers through her, opening her heart as she allowed herself to sink into the music.

Dylan's gaze locked with hers as he sang, the verses flowing from him like water. She felt emotion pouring from him and somehow knew he felt unable to express it outside of his music. She wondered what held him back. His mother was so open, so loving, she couldn't imagine what he might feel unable to tell her.

She felt her consciousness moving outside of her body, felt her tiger double begin to form. She knew the moment Dylan recognised it, saw his eyes widen, heard his breath catch. He looked over at her, wondering if she saw it, but she didn't react, didn't give anything away. Her tiger rubbed up against his legs while he played and she felt the shiver run through her own body. Felt the tingles in her skin as they touched. There was no separation, no division between her, the tiger, and the man who sang just for her.

As the song ended and the last note faded, Dylan sat perfectly still, his fingers just above the strings of the guitar. Tabitha felt the image of the tiger begin to disintegrate. She saw him watch the cat dissipate, sensing his disappointment. The two halves of herself merged as the song faded from the air, but the magic was still palpable.

Dylan put the guitar back on the stand.

'You have a beautiful voice,' Tabitha said. 'You should let your friends hear you.'

Dylan leaned back in the chair and sighed. 'Linden got there first. They're creatures of habit, that lot. It's hard to break cycles that have already been set in stone.'

'Nothing is ever set in stone,' Tabitha whispered, her voice resonating with something deeper than logic. 'The only given is change, and those who resist it ultimately have it forced upon them. Don't be that person. I'm sure your friends are great guys but they're trying to hold you static in a place that works for them, because you're always there for them. But where is the care for you?'

Dylan swallowed. 'How do you know this stuff? I mean, you're right, I know you are. But you've barely met them. How would you know?'

Tabitha shook her head. 'It's really not hard to spot. Did you write the song yourself?'

Dylan smiled, but seemed sad. 'I did, but it's been a while since I wrote anything new.'

The doorbell rang.

Dylan groaned. 'Damn. They're early.'

Tabitha sighed. She knew who was outside. She felt their chaotic energy as strongly as she could hear their aggressive banter. The atmosphere she and Dylan had created was crumbling, replaced by his anxiety about her meeting his friends. It wasn't the right time. The friction between these two realities was too much right now. She picked up her bag and coat, and walked past Dylan to the kitchen.

Rachel was wheeling back and forth with plates piled high with food. Tabitha put down her things and picked up a plate with each hand.

'Oh, thank you,' Rachel said. 'I may have gone a bit overboard.'

'It looks amazing. I'm so sorry I can't stay.'

'You can't?' Rachel's shoulders slumped. 'Why not?'

'Dylan's friends are here. Trust me, it's better this way. Another time?' She put the plates on the table and came back to lean on the worktop.

Rachel took Tabitha's hand. 'Don't let them drive you out.'

'Don't worry.' Tabitha smiled at Rachel, squeezing her hand. 'Emily, my cat, is waiting for me and I don't want her to get lonely.'

Loud voices came closer, and then the door to the hall opened.

The row silenced.

Linden and GJ stared at Tabitha, mouths open wide.

Tabitha owned the space. Her hair streamed around her shoulders, the gauzy fabric of her dress floating in the breeze from an open window. 'Excuse me,' she said, eyeing each of them in turn.

They stood, rooted. Then scrabbled out of the way. She stepped into the hall and then out of the door, held her hand up in a gesture of goodbye and walked off down the street.

Her heart sank as she walked away. She knew she was doing the right thing, but whatever it was that connected her to Dylan was trying to pull her back like a taut elastic band. She turned. He was standing outside his front door, his face dark, overshadowed in the evening light. His hands were shoved into his pockets. She felt the threads of energy he was sending out to her, sadness, hope and regret.

'We'll get our time,' she whispered, and then turned for home and Emily.

17

DYLAN

PUTTING ON HIS GIG WEAR, DYLAN FOCUSED INTO HIMSELF, looking for the creative heartbeat the band relied on. It was cold outside, but the chill on his bare legs would only be for a short time and the khaki combat shorts would give him freedom to move for the whole night. He began to sing as he rolled his shoulders and flexed his back. Playing the drums was a full body work out.

'Are you ready?' GJ shouted, banging repeatedly on his door.

'Cut that out. I have ten minutes yet,' Dylan snapped. Ever since seeing Tabitha yesterday, he had been questioning pretty much everything about his life. He could play the drums forever, but could he be happy playing local gigs with Instantaneous Rock for the rest of his life? Or did he have the talent to go further? He thought about the guitar sitting on the stand at his mum's. His friends had never even heard him play. They'd never heard him sing either. He'd been categorised as the drummer at the age of ten when they'd formed the band. Apparently, there was no space to experiment and switch things around.

He spent longer than usual styling his hair and making sure his stubble was the perfect length. He looked at his tattoo in the mirror, flexing his bicep to see the movement of the tiger. On cue, he heard a rumble behind him and turned to see the white tiger watching.

'What are you doing in there, Dylan? Applying your make-up?' Linden shouted.

Dylan heard muttering from the living room and then the front door banged.

The cat made a soft purring rumble and settled down on the floor.

'I know you can understand me, but I wish I could tell what you were thinking.' Dylan sat on the bed and leaned his elbows on his thighs. 'I have no idea what you are. Maybe you're my muse? My guardian come to life? Could Tabitha see you at Mum's yesterday? I couldn't help feeling there was a connection there somehow.'

The tiger got up, padded closer and then lay down again inches from his feet.

'I must be losing it. Not only am I seeing things, but I'm talking to them as well. God!' He stood up and pulled on his trainers.

'I'm ready,' he shouted, standing in the open door a moment too long, letting the tiger through. As it passed next to his legs it disintegrated, leaving an empty space next to him that sent chills up his spine. He made his way down the hallway to the front door.

'Linden's gone,' GJ said, pulling on his shoes. 'He needed to speak to Bob before the gig.'

'Thank goodness,' Dylan said, letting out his breath in a rush. 'I could do without any more aggro.'

'Ignore him.' GJ opened the front door. 'He's just jealous because he doesn't look as good as you. He knows everyone fancies the drummer.'

Dylan laughed. 'Don't let him hear you say that.' He picked up his drumsticks and strode through the door, not bothering with a coat.

'Dylan,' GJ said, keeping pace, 'I can tell something's wrong. Is it Linden? I know he's a nightmare, but you'll never understand how much your presence in the band means to *me*.'

'Well, thanks,' Dylan said. 'But you know I can't stay here just for you.'

GJ sighed. 'I know. Linden won't ever leave Wildley Forest and, if I'm honest, neither will I. I love gigging, but I enjoy my programming job too. I'm not going to give up a solid career for the chance at a dream I'm not good enough for. But you *are* good enough. You should do whatever you can to get yourself out there. Quit the cafe. Quit the band, but do me one favour. Don't forget me.'

Dylan gaped at GJ. Phrases were looping in his mind that were now spectacularly out of date. *GJ is suffocating. GJ will never grow up. GJ needs to get over himself. GJ will never get anywhere.* In a moment, the man in front of him had turned from a jealous schoolboy to a man with a solid career, who played gigs in his spare time and wanted the best for his friend. How had GJ grown up so much, while Dylan was still working in a job he hated, wishing someone would magic up opportunities for him? The only person bailing on his future was him.

GJ shuffled his feet and shrugged. 'I've always known you were the best of us. You just need to realise it yourself.'

Dylan swallowed and gave him a hug. 'You'll always be one of my best friends. Don't ever worry about that. And, thank you.'

GJ let out a breath and leaned against a lamp post. 'One of my friends is a producer. If you record a demo, I'd be happy to pass it on to him.'

'You've kept that quiet.' Dylan raised his eyebrows.

GJ shrugged. 'I didn't think you were ready.'

Dylan inclined his head. He probably hadn't been.

18

THE ATMOSPHERE IN THE PUB WAS INTOXICATING. THE ROOM was packed, voices were raised, and people were staggering around drunk already.

'Let's own this room before it owns us.' Dylan twirled his drumsticks then launched into a roll that set the crowd cheering. 'Give it to me, GJ!' he yelled over the sound of his own snare and whooped as GJ began a fast intro.

Linden kicked in a long, high note that had everyone screaming and then the song was on its way. Dylan sank into the feeling of the music, letting it carry him and holding it by turns. He had this. A moment of realisation had changed everything. It was up to him to make his life happen. He watched the guys playing as he held the music together, leading it, shaping it, holding them up as they surfed his rhythm.

He couldn't see Tabitha, but she would come. There was no way she could miss an evening as perfect as this one. He had no idea why he was so sure she would know. He didn't even have her phone number. Why didn't he have her phone number? He had been so absorbed every time he'd seen her, that he'd never managed to have such a sensible and real-world thought. Plus, she always turned up at the right moment. How did she do that?

The tiger snaked through the crowds and Dylan whooped again in greeting. It snarled and he laughed, rising even higher on the energy. He hadn't had a drop to drink. He didn't need it. The music would take him all the way. It was all the help he would ever need.

A heightened buzz hit Dylan with a force that almost winded him. The fizz started in his chest and flowed out to the tips of his fingers and toes. He looked around. The surging mass of people in front of him were indistinguishable for a moment, and then one face became clear. She stood in the middle of the room, her copper hair flowing loose and wavy over her fine-boned shoulders. The long, flared sleeves of her gauzy tunic lay low over the backs of her hands. She lifted one arm and twirled something between her fingers. It was an envelope.

Dylan's heart raced and his drumsticks ached to keep pace. He tried to hold back. He laughed at the alarm on Linden's face when he pushed the slow love song behind the bounds of anything reasonable, but he had the reins. None of them had the strength to fight his beat and he was taking them into euphoria.

'Again?' Linden shot him a furious look.

Dylan kept drumming. Linden barely registered.

'I said stop,' Linden shouted through a pause.

Dylan blinked. He faltered, the sticks skidding across the snare. Linden was staring right at him.

He stopped.

There was silence. The air was electric.

The crowd knew something was wrong.

'What the hell do you think you're doing?' Linden said from between gritted teeth.

Dylan slammed his drumsticks down on the snare, making it rattle. 'Making music.'

'Music?' Linden laughed. 'You just destroyed my song.'

'Your song?' Dylan asked. 'You didn't write it.'

'What's your problem, Dylan?' Linden pointed at Tabitha. 'Is it her? She's messed with your head. Things have gone to hell since she arrived.' He glared at her. 'Just leave us alone.'

Tabitha met Dylan's gaze, held up the envelope again and slid it onto the bar. Then she crossed the floor and walked out the door.

'Bloody hell, Linden,' Dylan said, standing up.

'Are you seriously chasing after her now?' Linden asked.

Dylan clenched his jaw.

'Just leave,' Linden said. 'Don't bother coming back. Ever.'

Dylan slid out from behind the drums and jumped off the stage.

'You hear me?' Linden yelled after him. 'This is it.'

Dylan gave a salute and made his way through the crowd and over to the bar. He grabbed the white envelope. The atmosphere in the room was thick, heavy and unmoving. Then someone started clapping, slowly, rhythmically. Another person joined, and then the whole room was applauding. Dylan's eyes widened at the sea of faces turned to him, smiling, their hands clapping out the rhythm of one of their songs. He gave a nod, and then made his way through the crowd to the door. The tiger stood there, a rumbling approval coming from its ribcage. He approached, and then stopped. If he continued through the door, he'd touch the tiger. It didn't move. It was waiting. He stepped forwards, his bare leg rubbing against the cat's fur. Dylan gasped. It was so soft and deep, so real. The cat met his gaze. There was an intelligence in its eyes that reached deep into his heart. It was … comforting. The tiger's eyes were familiar, but he couldn't remember why he knew them. 'Thank you,' he murmured. He blinked and the cat was gone.

He stepped through the door, hoping Tabitha would still be there. But the road was empty, orange lights from the street lamps glinting on the glossy damp of the pavements.

He looked down at the envelope in his hand. It had branding from the zoo on the front and his name and address in the middle. Feeling a stab of excitement, he tore it open and pulled out the bright, white paper. 'I'm delighted to say …' was as much as he read before his eyes blurred.

He closed them tight, and then read again. He read faster and faster, determined to take in every word, and then he started back at the beginning. Had Tabitha known what she was delivering? Had she known he was being offered the job? That he would be at the zoo five days a week from now on?

Knowing the guys would be at the pub for a while yet, Dylan headed to the flat. It was blissfully quiet when he let himself in. It was rare for him to have the place to himself, so he hoped the guys would stay and finish the gig. He dug around in his drawer for a pencil and some paper, sat down and began to pick at the guitar.

He'd brought it home the night before after playing for Tabitha. The chords formed in his mind and he opened to them, allowing the tune and the heartbeat to flow through him and out through his fingers.

The tiger moved around him as he sang, the words and melody coming to his lips from somewhere deep inside, somewhere waiting to be explored. The tiger was a doorway to something special, something powerful, an unformed version of himself. His heart swelled and images of Tabitha curled through his mind. He saw her drawing, saw her watching the tigers, standing in the audience. The notes flowed through him even faster now, the words gathering on the page in a way that had little to do with logical thought and everything to do with an outpouring of feeling that was so new to him, so powerful and authentic that a path opened up in his mind. He had a new job, the music was flowing and life was changing in front of his eyes.

19

THE DOOR SLAMMED OPEN, THE HANDLE RICOCHETING OFF the wall.

Dylan leapt up, guitar and songbook in hand, eyes wide as Linden strode into the room. 'For God's sake, Linden!' Dylan said through gritted teeth. He sat down, leaning the guitar up against the armchair and dropping his head into his hands, waiting for his heart to stop racing.

'You humiliated me today.' Linden stood over him, crowding him, his teeth clenched, eyes narrowed. 'You turned the audience against me.'

Dylan stood up, put a hand on Linden's chest and gave him a shove backwards. 'You did that all by yourself.'

'What were you playing before we came in?' GJ asked.

'It's nothing. Just a song I wrote.'

'You wrote a song?' Linden snorted. 'What do you know about writing songs?' He made a grab for the book.

Dylan jerked it away from Linden's hand. 'I've written songs before.'

88

Linden gaped. 'You have? Why won't you show me? Are you working with someone new?'

'It's for me,' Dylan said.

Linden let out a bark of laughter. 'So now you're a songwriter, singer, guitarist and drummer? He definitely doesn't need us anymore, GJ, not with all those talents.'

'Linden,' GJ said, his voice sharp. 'That's enough.'

'Just the thought of drummer-boy singing ...'

'Have you ever heard me sing, Linden?' Dylan said, his voice quiet. 'Do you have any idea what I'm good at?'

'You're not good at anything.' Linden leaned back against the wall. 'If you were, you wouldn't be sat at the back of a village band, going nowhere.'

'As are you.' Dylan took a step closer. His voice was soft, but rage was building from the centre of his chest, spreading through his body to his hands and brain. 'What makes you think you're any better?'

'I am at the front of the band. I'm the one the girls shout for.'

'You sing covers in a village pub.' Dylan balled his hands into fists, but held them rigid at his sides.

Linden got right up in his face. 'I *am* better than you.'

Dylan stepped back. He narrowed his eyes at Linden, and then punched him in the face.

Linden yelled and reeled back, clutching his jaw. 'You bastard!' he snarled, and then barrelled into Dylan head-first, winding him.

They flew across the room and crashed into the table. For a moment, Dylan lay back on the wooden surface trying to catch his breath before Linden grabbed him by the shirt and pulled him up. Dylan swung his arm round, dislodging Linden and then shoved him hard into the dining table.

'Urgh,' Linden groaned. He dragged himself up, clenching his fists at his sides and advanced on Dylan until they were nose to nose.

Dylan glared at him. They were equally matched and they both knew it.

Dylan didn't flinch. 'If you're so much better than me, replace me.'

'Maybe I will. You used to be inspired, but now you're dragging us down.' He shoved Dylan, who flailed for a moment, and then grabbed hold of Linden's hair as he fell. Dylan groaned as he landed hard on the edge of the armchair. The chair scooted backwards and dropped Dylan onto the floor, just as Linden crashed onto a flimsy wooden table, sending splinters flying.

'No,' Dylan yelled as his guitar toppled slowly.

GJ launched forwards, caught it, and then shoved it at Dylan. 'Stop it!' he yelled. 'Stop!'

Dylan and Linden froze. They had never seen GJ this angry before. His face was red, his eyes bulging. 'You are friends, for God's sake. We're all *supposed* to be friends.'

Linden pulled himself up and rolled his shoulders. Then he went out to the kitchen and came back with two bottles of beer. He handed one of them to GJ. 'You've been acting weird ever since Tabitha arrived,' he said, not looking at Dylan. 'She's addling your brain.'

'No!' Dylan rubbed a hand across his forehead. '*You* have been acting weird ever since Tabitha arrived. I'm not going my own way because of *her*, I'm going because you are so damn suffocating. You don't want anything to change. Ever. You have your cushy jobs and your evening gigs to make you feel like superstars, but what have I got? What in my life do you think is worth hanging on to?'

'Us!' Linden's voice was like ice. '*We* are worth hanging onto.'

Dylan eased himself up and massaged his bruised arm. His voice was quiet. 'If you were a real friend, you wouldn't try to stop me making something of myself. You wouldn't try to hold me stuck in this no-man's-land where I have nothing of my own. You would let me become myself.'

'Have I been holding you back too, Dylan?' GJ looked broken. He was pale, his eyes over-bright in the artificial light. 'I understand Linden has been a pain in the arse, I get that.'

'What?' Linden said. 'Where did that come from?'

'I get it,' GJ carried on. 'I get that you need something in your life to be about you and not him, or me. But Linden and I don't tell you what to do. You've always been free to follow your dreams. Why is it our fault that you haven't bothered?'

Dylan dropped his head into his hands. 'Please don't look at me like that,' he said to GJ.

'Like what?' GJ sounded tired, far older than his twenty-three years.

'Like I've kicked you in the nuts.'

'Well, maybe you have. And maybe I need to be given some time to feel the pain before I can get over it and move on. We made our choices; you've made yours and now we all have to live with them.'

'Oh God, you're still making it sound as though I've abandoned you all somehow. I've written a song. That doesn't mean we're not friends.'

'Yeah, maybe.' GJ grabbed his coat from the back of an armchair. 'Or maybe it's the beginning of the end.' He brushed something from his cheek, and then turned and went into his bedroom.

There was silence.

Dylan swallowed. He looked over at Linden, but the other man wouldn't meet his gaze. Snapping his guitar into its case, he grabbed the music book and his coat, and headed for the door. He reached for the handle.

'Dylan,' Linden said from behind him.

Dylan ignored him, jerked the door open and strode out of the flat before slamming it shut.

Outside, the air was biting.

Rage rolled through him as his legs pounded the pavement. It took hardly any time to reach his mum's house. He let himself in with the key and collapsed onto the sofa. It was still warm and the last embers in the fire were glowing. He kicked off his boots, curled up on the soft cushions and drifted off to sleep.

20

DYLAN

Dylan was walking through the mists. He heard the crack of a twig and turned, but all he could see was a blanket of thick, white fog. 'Is something out there?' he said. Nothing.

He kept walking but faster now. When he broke into the sunshine he let out a breath of relief and doubled over, leaning on his thighs to catch his breath.

There was a yowl.

Dylan turned.

A tiger padded out of the fog, the golden yellow of its fur shining bright in the sunlight. It stopped, staring at him.

Dylan held up his hands and moved slowly backwards. 'It's okay, I will leave you alone. Just let me go, please?'

The tiger sat down and watched as he backed away, step by slow step.

As the distance increased, Dylan started to breathe again. He was just about to turn when the tiger stood up and walked towards him.

He started to run. The tiger kept pace, not getting closer, but not dropping behind.

Dylan passed a fallen tree trunk that had been propped against a gate like a ramp. The tiger bounded up the trunk, and then paused at the top, eyeing him.

Dylan froze. He swallowed.

The cat bunched up its muscles, and leapt—

'I HAVE COFFEE FOR YOU.' HIS MUM'S VOICE CUT THROUGH the dream.

He forced his eyes open and swung his legs around, sitting up. 'Thanks.' His voice was unusually gravelly. Taking the cup, he sipped it, closing his eyes in appreciation.

'What are you doing here, Dylan? Has something happened?'

'I've fallen out with Linden. Can I stay here until I find a new place?'

'Of course. Is that all?'

'I have a new job.'

'Since when?'

'Today.' Dylan grinned and dug the letter out of his pocket. 'At the zoo.'

'You do?' Her face lit up. 'But you have no experience of working with animals!'

'I know. I'll be in the Playbarn, managing the people who look after the kids.'

'And less experience with children,' she said, but her eyes sparkled.

'I manage Linden, don't I?' he asked. 'Or at least I used to.'

'But what about your music?'

Dylan was silent for a moment. He wasn't sure he was

ready to share that he was composing, but he trusted his mum. 'I'm writing music again.'

'Dylan.' Rachel opened her arms. 'I'm so proud of you, darling.'

'You are?'

She nodded and hugged him.

He took a deep breath and closed his eyes, allowing the feeling of safety to wash over him.

21

TABITHA

TABITHA STOOD IN THE MIDDLE OF HER NEW GALLERY AND spun around, her arms out wide on either side of her. She had done it. It was her own. She was in control of her future at last. Walking over to the door with a huge smile on her face, she turned the sign in the window to 'open'. Allowing the nerves to prickle through her, she went to sit behind her easel, picking up her paintbrush.

She closed her eyes and took a deep breath, centring herself into the feeling of the tiger that was emerging on her page. There was a sketch in the book to her left, but she focused on the picture that was forming in her mind. She could see a tiger stalking through the trees, growling. The wind was blustery and the tall trees inside the zoo enclosure swayed as the tiger snaked past the base of first one, and then another. Tabitha shivered with foreboding, but she couldn't see any danger. She focused more, allowing her astral body to solidify into tiger form so she could walk alongside the powerful beast. She grunted and the tiger responded, comfortable with her familiar presence.

She reached her awareness out further, looking for the cause of the energetic disturbance, but there was nothing. Then the sky began to grow dark. The wind became stronger and the tigers started yowling. There was a rumble of thunder. The rain was coming down in sheets now and she could only see a foot or so in front of her nose. Where had this storm come from? Dread settled in the pit of her stomach, and then spread throughout her powerful body. She roared as the tree next to her creaked and groaned.

The tree tilted so slowly it took her a moment to realise what was happening. The creaking intensified as the tree was blown harder and harder. There was a loud crack. The tiger roared. For a moment there was silence, and then the tree began to fall. It bounced once as it hit the top of the enclosure on the side of the hill, but then it rested. Both tigers were there now, prowling the base of the tree, testing the wood with their paws. Tabitha walked in circles, trying to keep them away, but her astral body was thinning. The large tiger put one foot on the trunk and roared.

Tabitha gasped. Her eyes flew open and she clutched the side of her stool so hard her knuckles turned white. She could still feel the bite of the cold air, the lash of the rain and the excitement of the cats as their enclosure was breached.

It was bright outside the shop window. The sky above Wildley Forest was a clear blue, far brighter than they deserved on a mid-November day. What would lead Tabitha to dream up such a storm? She reached out her awareness to the tigers and couldn't pick up any distress. So where had she been? Where had that dream come from? And did it mean anything real?

She looked at the picture in front of her. A tall tree had

97

fallen against the top of the fence around the tiger enclosure. Dark, ominous clouds filled the page.

She went into the back, and then put the kettle on and
lit a candle. There was a bag of white sage smudging sticks
on the windowsill, and she pulled out a twig, lit it, blew out
the flame, and then breathed in the distinctive, musky scent
of the smoke. She walked around the shop, wafting the sage
into every corner, clearing any residual fear from her vision.

The bell on the door tinkled. 'Hello, is anyone here?'
Max stood in the wide-open doorway, looking around.
'Urgh, what is that smell?' he said, waving a hand in front
of his nose.

Tabitha sighed. 'What are you doing here?' She walked
out to the back and put the sage stick on a plate by the open
window. 'Why aren't you at work?'

'I swapped shifts. There's supposed to be a storm and
that can make the cats agitated. I'm going to go over later.
Wanna join me?'

Tabitha shook her head. 'I have plans for this evening.'

'Cancel them. The cats need you. I need you.'

'Don't be silly. The cats will be fine.' Tabitha sat behind
her easel and shut the sketchpad. She wasn't sure why, but
she didn't want Max seeing that particular picture.

Max walked over to her, 'Tabitha, you do something to
the tigers. I don't know what it is, but they're different when
you're there. I need you.'

She rolled her eyes. 'Thanks, Max. But I'm busy. I have
a list of commissions to fulfil and a shop to run.'

'This place? You can't make much selling paintings and
birthday cards. I could talk to Sophie about selling your
pictures in the shop. They could promote you as real home-
grown talent.'

'Thank you, but that's not necessary.'

Max scowled. 'I'm just trying to help.'

Tabitha sighed. 'I don't need your help, Max. I have a global audience, collectors constantly after originals, and I sell a lot of prints on my website.'

Max peered at a painting of a tiger mid-leap. It was impressionistic, with broad brushstrokes of orange, red and gold. 'Maybe I'll buy one. This one.'

'You can't afford it.'

Max bristled. 'How much is it?'

'That one is ten thousand pounds.' Tabitha kept her voice flat.

Max had a coughing fit. When he calmed down he was red faced. 'You'll never sell it at that price. It's tiny.'

'I've already sold it. It's waiting to be packaged up and couriered.'

Max's face turned an even darker red. He cleared his throat. 'What are you working on now?'

'I'm sorry, Max, but I don't have time to chat.'

'Oh come on, where's the harm?' He reached for the sketchbook on her easel.

Tabitha realised what he was doing too late. He grabbed the book and she lurched forwards, snatching at it. He swung it up high, holding it above her head as she tried to reach it.

'For God's sake, Max, give it back.'

Keeping it high above his head, he flicked through to find the last page used, and then turned his back on her and brought it down so he could look.

Tabitha slumped back on her chair.

Max glanced over his shoulder, eyebrows raised. 'You planning on breaking the tigers out?'

'Of course not.'

'Then why draw that?' he asked, pointing. His finger slid across the page, smudging the tiger.

Tabitha slammed her pencil down. 'What exactly do you want, Max?'

'I'm just trying to be a friend,' he said. 'You are new here, after all.'

Tabitha sighed. 'Thank you, Max, but I don't need feedback on my work. I know what I'm doing.'

'Everyone needs feedback though, right?' He grinned.

'Do you?' Tabitha raised her eyebrows. 'Do you need feedback on your work, Max?'

He flushed. A vein throbbed in his forehead.

Emily hissed at him. Her body fluffed out and her tail rose right up behind her as she crouched low and hissed again.

'Easy, tiger.' Max sneered.

The distraction broke his focus on Tabitha. He moved towards Emily, ducking fast to reach down and grab her. 'Aren't you the feisty one,' he said, holding her at arm's length. 'Just like your mama. I wonder how you'd fare against the tigers, eh? I bet you wouldn't be so fierce then, would you?'

'Give her to me.' Tabitha stood up and grabbed the cat from him. 'If anything happens to her, if she ends up anywhere near those tigers, I will come after you. I know how you treat those poor animals. I won't have that behaviour anywhere near my cat, or my home.'

'Okay, okay.' Max held up his hands. 'But just so you know, your attempt to sabotage me won't work.'

'My attempt to what?'

'You told someone you were worried about the tigers.

Who was it? Did you go straight to Sophie, or were you talking to Ursula?'

'And what if I did tell someone?'

His jaw was tight and he was breathing heavily. 'I'd hate for you to jeopardise your access to the cats. I've given you something special. Don't throw it away.'

There was a long moment of tense silence.

The front door slammed open with a bang, the glass rattling in the frame. Linden stood in the doorway. He glanced from her to Max.

'Look who it is!' Linden crowed. 'It's scrawny Max gone all brawny!'

Max turned chalk white then a flush began from his collar line.

'What are you doing here?' Tabitha asked.

Max cowered, his face bright red now. Tabitha wondered whether he knew he was wringing his hands.

Tabitha got up. She was tired of men, and these two in particular. She walked over to the door and opened it. 'Get out.'

'You heard the lady,' Linden said.

She looked Linden in the eye. 'You too.'

'You don't scare me,' Linden said.

'More fool you. I have more power in every cell of my body than you will ever have.'

Linden stared at her, open mouthed. 'Fine. I just came to tell you to stop messing with my boy, Dylan.'

'If he wants me to stay away from him, he can tell me himself.'

'*I'm* telling you.'

'Out.' Tabitha's voice was as quiet as a purr, but it had all the menace of a predator. Her heart soared as her tiger form shimmered into existence, prowling around the legs of the men in front of her, but she resisted the temptation to make it visible. The cat stopped in front of them, bared its teeth and growled.

Linden shuddered.

Max looked around him and scratched at his head. He rolled his shoulders as though dispelling a nasty dream.

The cat stalked, circling around the men.

Linden's head whipped to the side. 'Is something there? I thought I saw …'

'… out of the corner of my eye,' Max finished.

'And do you see anything now?' Tabitha tilted her head and watched them, not blinking.

'No,' Max's voice was more hesitant than she had ever heard it.

Linden gave his head an abrupt shake. 'Got to go,' he said, swinging the door open, and jumping down the step. 'See you.'

Max followed him out but paused on the step. 'See you at the zoo?'

Tabitha gave a strained smile. 'Of course. I'll be back to draw tomorrow, as always.'

His shoulders relaxed. He turned and walked down the path, waving as he went out onto the street.

She closed and locked the door behind them. 'What have I got myself into,' she murmured, sitting down behind her easel. Wildley Forest was supposed to be a quiet, contemplative place for her to create. Instead it was one drama after another.

She tried to send her awareness back to the tigers, but her mind wouldn't go that way. Instead she felt herself pulled towards the cafe in town. She sensed Dylan before she saw him. Prickles ran down one side of her body, calling her to turn in that direction. He was standing at the counter in the cafe, talking to a woman. She looked stunned, and then forced herself to smile and pulled Dylan into a hug that make Tabitha wince. She felt a tingle as the fur on her astral body stood up, felt her tail swish from side to side and a grumble from her chest. She snaked through the people, barely touching them, knowing that in her astral state she was not solid enough for anyone apart from Dylan to notice her.

Dylan was emotional. She could sense the pull of his energetic field fluctuating, sending out wave after wave of watery energy. She yowled at the discomfort coming from him, not able to identify a reason for it. He was in no danger. There was nothing that claws or teeth could solve. There was only the turmoil of a man on the verge of change. She wondered how long it would take him to embrace that change? Would it be fast enough for her, or would she miss the transformation? It all depended on how long she was able to stay in this community. She had been driven away before. Environments became too toxic for her to create in. People didn't understand her or her need for freedom and authenticity. They didn't understand that she wouldn't play the game in order to satisfy their pointless rules, or that she refused to make herself small and power-less. They didn't understand that she was a woman deep in her own power, a woman who knew how to access the depth of her own being, who knew how to tap into the mysteries of the world. As the tiger, she knew.

In her physical body, her fingers sketched while she watched him, the picture of Dylan springing from the page in vivid charcoal. His turmoil bled from every stroke as she poured her heart into expressing this moment in time that she didn't yet understand. Every moment of pain she helped him carry was a burden that weighed on her. She had learned to separate her energy from others when she travelled in tiger form. She had become an expert in protecting herself and moving right past other people's sadness, but with Dylan it was different. With Dylan the pull was so strong that his feelings dragged her into connection in a way she couldn't resist.

She watched him walk out of the cafe and stop on the street. He looked sad.

The tiger growled.

Dylan turned around. 'Hey, you,' he whispered so low that only she could hear. 'I wondered when you'd show up again.'

She walked over to him and rubbed her giant head against his leg. She knew he felt her fur, knew he felt the weight and pressure of her head, and she knew from his trembling that it meant something to him.

22

TABITHA STARED AT THE PICTURES. ONE CANVAS AND A sketch sat in front of her on the easel. The canvas was a vivid painting of a tiger standing on a fallen tree trunk and looking over the top of its enclosure boundary, ready to jump. The other was a charcoal image of Dylan.

The tiger was unsettling. Tabitha wished she knew how to drop back into the dream, but she could only travel at will in present time and she had no idea whether that other vision was a fantasy or some time in the future.

She stood up. The room span slightly and she gripped the side of the table. Putting away her paints, she went through to the kitchen, grabbed a sandwich from the fridge and ate it in a few bites. She gulped down a glass of water and focused on the feel of the solid floor under her feet, calling herself fully back into the present. She looked over at Emily. 'I know, I know. Time I got some fresh air. If I go now, I might be home before Max even gets into work.'

The fresh air called her back to earth as she walked along the main street out of Wildley Forest Village. The barn owl that lived on the tree outside her house screeched and she cooed back to it, waving her hand. Orange leaves blew along the path, swirling around her ankles. Maybe the cold was finally on the way. Autumn had been holding off, letting the sunshine stream in even though it was mid-November.

A cat raced across the road followed by a red cockapoo, barking furiously. A car's brakes screeched. It swerved, narrowly missing the dog.

Tabitha let out her breath in a rush. The dog was still racing around, agitated as it looked for the cat and its owner by turns. Tabitha crossed the street and then crouched down. 'Come here, my lovely,' she called. She made clicking noises with her tongue and found a cat treat in her coat pocket. 'Here you are, beautiful, come to Tabitha.' The dog hesitated for a moment, its head cocked on one side, and then it padded over and sat down in front of her, wagging its tail. Its tongue lolled out on one side as it panted, its big brown eyes fixed hopefully on Tabitha.

She held out the treat and the dog took it gently with its lips, not touching her fingers with its teeth at all. 'Aren't you a lovely, gentle doggy.' She caught hold of the lead that was trailing from its collar and started walking up the road in the direction it had come from.

'Percy, come. Percy, where are you? Come back now, please …' The voice was faint, but Tabitha followed it, breaking into a jog and watching with a smile as Percy's enthusiasm mounted. Soon he was pulling at his lead and she really had to run to keep up.

'Oh, thank goodness.' A woman spied her and smiled, dropping into a crouch and holding her arms out as Percy ran into them. She clutched him to her chest. 'He ran after that cat and pulled the lead right out of my hand. Where did you find him?'

'Just further down the road. The stars were in his favour today. The car managed to swerve around him. He's such a beautiful dog, so gentle and friendly.'

'Thank you,' the woman said, wiping a tear from her eye. 'He's normally so nervous around people. You must have a real knack with animals.'

Tabitha smiled. 'I'm pleased I was there for him. You go home and have a drink. You look like you could do with it. I suspect Percy could do with a big cuddle on the sofa too.'

She waved and walked on, smiling as the woman called more thanks down the road after her. She reached back to Percy with her mind, but he was happy, focused on searching for food along the side of the road, completely unscarred by his near-death experience.

The road up to the zoo was long and twisty, but Tabitha loved the young saplings that grew in the fields on either side and the long, yellow grass that surrounded them. The potential was so strong here that it never failed to warm her insides and remind her what a never-ending miracle life really was. A red kite wheeled overhead, and she wondered what little field animal might be hiding in the grass, trying not to become lunch.

'Tabitha.' The voice from behind her made her heart beat faster. She stopped, turning slowly. Dylan was running towards her, his dark-blond hair artfully mussed, his stubble a shade too long. He was dressed in the outfit she had seen him in at the cafe, a dark red shirt with indigo jeans and black boots. He looked ready for an evening drinks party, not the freezing, muddy conditions of the zoo.

'What are you doing here?' she asked, smiling.

'I assumed you knew?' he said, his grin widening. 'It was that letter you brought me at the pub. I'm the new manager at the Playbarn.'

A thrill of excitement shot through Tabitha. 'You got the job?'

'I did.'

'Will it still leave you time to work on your compositions?'

Dylan stopped walking. He frowned. 'How did you know I was composing again? Have the boys been shooting their mouths off?'

Tabitha's face flooded with warmth. She had been a tiger when she saw him composing. She wasn't supposed to know. 'Yes.' She took the offered way out. 'Linden was in my gallery earlier. He mentioned it.'

'I hope he didn't give you grief?' Dylan said, his frown deepening.

'Don't worry. Just a lot of prancing and posturing.'

'Sorry. I have no idea what his problem is at the moment.'

'I can look after myself.'

'I believe you, but everyone needs looking after some-times, whether they can do it themselves or not. Does *anyone* look after you, Tabitha?'

'Emily looks after me.'

'Your cat?' Dylan raised his eyebrows but didn't smile.

'My cat. I know she seems soft as anything, but she can be pretty edgy when she doesn't like someone and she's a shrewd judge of character. The owls outside the cottage keep an eye on me too. They guard my threshold.'

He laughed. 'You have it all worked out, I see, but it doesn't sound like you have much human companionship.'

'Are you after the job?'

'If I said yes, would that make me like Max?'

Tabitha smiled. 'I don't think you'll ever be like Max.'

'Thanks.'

She gestured up the hill to the entrance. 'Are you ready for your new job?'

Dylan grimaced. 'My new boss is pretty fierce.'

'Sophie? She's not really. She's an animal person and doesn't have much patience with people, so don't expect any new-boy favours, but she's kind and loyal. I like her. She'll never treat you unfairly or be underhand.'

'You're a good person, Tabitha. So many people judge and pigeon-hole everyone they meet. You don't do that.'

Tabitha shrugged. 'I don't see the point. I've been judged enough in my life to know it's a load of rubbish. People see me and they think ...' She tailed off. Her forehead creased into a frown; her lips pursed.'

'They think what?'

'They think I'm weird, mad, a witch, whatever their particular fear is. They see differentness and think it's a problem, not an opportunity.'

'What about me? Do you see my differentness?'

She smiled. 'I do. Right now you are change. You have so many beautiful colours around you, and some scared sludgy ones too. You are standing at a crossroads and I don't think either of us know which way you will go. That's exciting. Make the most of it.'

Dylan swallowed. 'Where did you learn to do that?'

'Do what?'

'Read people.'

Tabitha shrugged and shoved her hands in her pockets. 'I didn't. This is just the way I am.'

'You said people think you're a witch. Are you?'

'Would it matter if I was?'

'Everything about you matters, Tabitha. I want to know it all.'

Tabitha was silent for a moment. They were approaching the gate to the zoo so she slowed to a stop near a huge oak tree and leaned on the trunk, flattening her palms against the rough surface. 'I honestly have no idea. I am who I am and I don't need a label. I follow my own truth, listen to my own conscience and always try to be the best version of myself I can. I have a close connection with animals, particularly tigers and my cat, Emily. I have owls nesting in the tree outside my house wherever I live, and I love being in nature. I am always authentic, and I live in my own power. Does that make me a witch?'

Dylan grinned. 'I like that. I've lived with labels for so long I think I'd forgotten they were optional.'

Tabitha stared at him for a moment, and then her face broke into a smile wider than he'd ever seen it. 'Well then, maybe I *am* doing some good in Wildley Forest Village. I was beginning to think this move was a mistake. Come on, let's get inside. I have some sketching to do. I have a waiting list as long as my arm for paintings, and more than one of my customers are getting impatient.'

23

DYLAN

TABITHA WAS WAVED INTO THE ZOO BEFORE SHE'D EVEN GOT her membership card from her purse, but the man looked at Dylan with raised eyebrows. 'If you want a ticket, the desks are over there.'

'Thanks, but I'm the new Playbarn Manager.'

At that moment, Sophie strode through the shop and straight to the reception desk. 'Are you ready to begin?' she asked.

A thrill of excitement shot through Dylan. 'Yep. As ready as I'll ever be.' He undid the buttons on his cuffs and rolled up his sleeves. 'Show me where you need me.'

'Here,' Sophie handed him a pile of clothes. 'The toilets are over there. Go and change into your uniform and I'll take you over.'

Dylan came back out, straightening his bright blue polo shirt. The uniform was different to the one he had seen Max wearing, and the staff on reception and in the shop had yet another variation.

Sophie kept up a steady stream of information as they

walked across the grass to the Playbarn. The zoo had just opened and there were only a few visitors clutching coffee cups.

'The Playbarn opens an hour later than the zoo,' Sophie said, 'so you'll have a chance to meet your staff and look around.'

He pulled his shoulders back and plastered a big smile on his face as he walked through the door.

The people inside looked exhausted. They turned slowly, saw Sophie and every one of them straightened.

'Dylan is your new manager,' Sophie said without cracking a smile. 'Please will you show him the ropes.' She turned to Dylan. 'They'll get you started. If you have any questions, my direct line is here.' She handed him a business card, nodded and left.

TABITHA

'GOOD LUCK!' TABITHA CALLED OUT TO DYLAN, WAVING. He smiled and held up a hand, but he looked nervous and she chuckled as she strode out to the tiger enclosure.

With his new job, Dylan was walking deeper into her life. She couldn't help smiling when she thought about bumping into him at the zoo, but she would have to work harder to protect her anonymity. If he found out her other identity, her story would eat into her normal life. And she had worked hard to avoid that.

At the top of the hill above the tiger enclosure she looked around. There was nobody in sight and she smiled, filling her lungs with fresh, clean air. Spreading out her waterproof picnic blanket, she sat down and took out her sketchbook. She lined up the book and pencils on the rug in front of her, closing her eyes and feeling into the space around her. There was the hum and chaos of human interaction. Shouts and giggles threatened to break through her trance, but she distanced herself from them, looking for something deeper. Underneath the day trip wrapping, she found the normal, daily life of the zoo. She felt the keepers. They were focused on the animals in their care, distracted by home concerns. She felt the heady mix of excitement, happiness, exhaustion and turmoil coming from every corner of the zoo. Below that was the constant hum of the animals. She felt the tigers in the enclosure below her. They were frustrated and pent up and their aggression poured out of the enclosure. She wondered whether they were locked in their sleeping area again. Putting her pencil to the sketch pad in front of her, she allowed her awareness to snake through the trees and towards the night quarters. She felt her tiger-self manifest more strongly as she walked through the enclosure towards the door, sensing the other cats' frustration build to a boil.

The door to the sleeping quarters slid up and the first tiger charged out. Its ears were back, its body low to the ground. Why was it so riled? It could only be Max.

Her white-tiger-self dropped into a defensive crouch and met the aggression of the male head-on. Her human-self drew while the white tiger roared, rearing up high and showing her massive bulk to warn the cat off. She snarled, her long teeth bared and then swiped at the male. He yowled and recoiled. Up on her hind legs, she swiped at the cat again as it pounced, fighting for dominance.

'What is that tiger doing? It's fighting with itself!'

Tabitha heard the child's voice as though it were travelling through water, but it served to pull her back to her body and she felt herself ground, felt the hard earth beneath her. She opened her eyes.

The tiger was looking around, growling and sniffing the grass by its feet.

'Look at it now, Mummy,' the voice said, breaking into giggles. 'Isn't it strange? Do tigers always do that?'

Tabitha tuned out the chatter and focused on watching the cats from a distance. She forced her tiger form to recede so the cats could no longer see it. She had no idea why she was a tiger when she astral travelled, but even as a young child her parents had seen a white-striped kitten running around the house when she was drawing. She was almost positive they had never worked out it was her.

She felt Max's energy before she saw him, and slammed her sketchbook shut as he sat on the blanket next to her. 'Don't you have to feed the cats? Or put enrichment activities in their cage?' she said, turning to look at him. This was her time; sacred space where she only had to think about drawing and connecting with the cats. This was her power time, her renewal. All Max did was drain her with his insecurity and creepy attempts to win her over.

'I wanted to see you.'

Tabitha sighed. 'That's flattering, thank you, but I need to concentrate on my commission right now.'

'A commission?' Max's forehead creased. 'What kind of commission?'

'A painting of the tigers.'

'My tigers?'

Tabitha gritted her teeth. She had humoured Max day after day in an attempt to make things easy when she visited, but he was monopolising more and more of her time and she was falling behind. 'They are not *your* tigers. You are *their* keeper.'

'A little tetchy today, aren't we?'

'Do I need to remind you to keep a respectful distance, Max?'

'Wow.' He got to his feet. 'I was just being nice.'

She picked up her sketch book and pencils, and folded up her blanket. 'I'm going to say this one last time. Leave me alone.' She walked away without turning back. She felt his gaze on her back but didn't care.

Desperate for some quiet, she wandered the paths looking for a place to settle. The lion enclosure was heaving with families and the meerkats nearby were also mobbed. It was only at the rhino enclosure, at the far side of the zoo, that she was able to find any peace. With its wide sweep and exposed windy space, it was largely empty except for an occasional car driving past.

Tabitha's pencil flew over the sketch pad, creating the images she saw in her mind. Two men fighting in sheet rain with a dark, stormy sky overhead. A tree, fallen against the side of the tiger enclosure. A tiger walking up the fallen tree branch. A tiger on the wrong side of the fence. The images flew so fast through her mind and she filled the book with sketches, dotting back and forth between them as the images shifted and morphed. An hour later, she slammed her sketchbook shut. 'No,' she muttered from between gritted teeth. 'No more.' She had no reason to believe these images were anything to worry about and she certainly couldn't take them to Max or the zoo authorities. She formed a wall in her mind and pushed the pictures to the other side, blocking their intrusion. Tucking the sketchbook under her coat, she headed for the exit.

24

DYLAN

By the end of the day, Dylan was frazzled and exhausted. The noise and chaos in the Playbarn had exceeded his expectations so drastically he was starting to wonder what he had let himself in for and how quickly he could transfer into some other position. He regularly managed packed pubs full of drunk fans storming the stage, but the revolving door of shouting and screaming children had done him in. They had three children with minor cuts and bruises and one mum who put in a complaint after her child was hit in the face by a toddler.

The light was fading when Dylan finally locked the door. The visitors had gone and there wasn't a keeper to be seen. He wandered over to the tigers, allowing the fresh air to flow through his system, easing his headache. He looked automatically up to the hill behind the enclosure, but Tabitha wasn't there.

A voice froze him in his tracks.

'Come on, you're a predator for God's sake. Show me your teeth. Or do I have to come in there and make you?'

Max was standing in the exclusion zone between the public area and the tiger's enclosure. Two massive cats were pacing on the other side of the fence. He poked his fingers through the boundary, pushing them into a thickly furred flank. The tiger leapt away and then dropped into a crouch, snarling, its long teeth bared.

'That's better.'

Dylan stepped back, putting a leafy, green bush between him and Max. Taking out his phone, he pulled up a search engine. A battery alert flashed up. He closed it, and then typed 'Tiger Keepers' into the search bar.

'We never enter the enclosure with the cats …' the first interview said. 'In a good zoo, no keepers are ever allowed into enclosures with large predators,' said another. He looked up Wildley Forest Zoo and scoured the website for details. He typed 'tiger keeper in enclosure' into the search bar, but there were no results. He tried again with lion and one heading came up.

INQUIRY LAUNCHED INTO LION KEEPER ACCIDENT

Yesterday our lion keeper, Samantha Cooper, was injured whilst setting up enrichment activities in the lions' enclosure. We are relieved to report that Samantha is stable and will make a full recovery. Samantha is an experienced keeper who has looked after large predators for many years. It is currently unclear how the lions were able to enter the enclosure with her. The zoo policy is to keep a secure barrier between predators and keepers at all times and Samantha was expert at maintaining protocol. A full inquiry is being held into what happened, and the zoo will take all appropriate action to ensure that it is never repeated.

He looked up at Max who was now leaning against the fence, his shoulder eye-wateringly close to the enormous predators. One of the tigers growled, but Max just laughed.

Dylan opened the camera on his phone. The battery light flashed up again, and then the phone went dead. 'Damn,' he muttered to himself. He pressed the on button again. Nothing.

Max bent down and picked up a large stick. He poked it through the fence and prodded the larger cat. It leapt back with a growl, and then turned and launched at the fence.

Max lurched backwards, vaulting over the visitor rail as the tiger's weight impacted the heavy fence. He bent double and laughed until he was gasping for air.

Dylan watched him, stunned. He hadn't warmed to Max and he knew the man hated him, but he had assumed he would love the animals in his care.

He turned and walked back to the Playbarn, letting himself in and locking the door behind him. He went through to his tiny office, shut the door and picked up the phone. Sophie's card was propped up on his computer screen. Taking a deep breath, he dialled.

'What do you want,' she said, picking up on the first ring.

'I need to log a potential issue with one of the keepers.'

'Seriously? You've only been here a day.'

'I went over to see the tigers after I'd locked up, and the keeper was behaving very strangely. I thought you'd want to know.'

She sighed. 'Did you recognise the keeper?'

'I did. His name is Max.'

'And what exactly do you think you saw?'

'I *know* I saw him interacting very closely with two angry tigers. I saw him poke them with a stick, *and* with his fingers, and I heard him threaten to go into the cage with them.'

Silence.

'No members of staff are allowed in enclosures with large predators,' Sophie said, her voice clipped. 'Max is a very experienced keeper. You must have misunderstood.'

Dylan sighed. 'He was in the exclusion zone between the tigers and the public. He goaded them until one charged at the fence, and he only just vaulted over the handrail in time.'

'Did you get a picture, or a video?'

'No, my phone ran out of battery.'

'Convenient.' Sophie's voice was pure acid. 'I know Max winds people up, but that's a huge accusation you're making, and I suggest you don't go down that road unless you can back up your story. We're a community here. If you think you can waltz in and target established members of staff with false claims, you are not in the right place.'

'I wouldn't dream of making a false claim,' Dylan said, his voice clipped. 'But I would have thought you might want to investigate an allegation of animal abuse, rather than rebutting it.'

'I suggest you watch your tone. And if you insist on pushing these ridiculous accusations, find proof before you call me again.' She hung up.

Dylan closed his eyes and took deep breaths.

Maybe he *was* in the wrong place if this was how they worked here. He would give it a week. No more.

25

DYLAN

Dylan was drenched. The rain was drumming hard on the pavement at his feet, bouncing on the tarmac and adding to the growing number of puddles. His thin coat was soaked through.

The road was empty of people as he ran for his mum's house, unable to face meeting up with Linden at home. He looked in his pockets for a key, and then swore, realising he'd left it at home.

He pounded on the door with his fists, and then waited as quiet footsteps padded towards the door instead of the hum of his mum's wheelchair. Dylan frowned. Who was there?

The door opened. Tabitha stood in the doorway, her copper hair damp, her huge eyes wide and bright. 'Dylan,' she said, stepping back. 'Come in out of the rain. Have you walked all the way from the zoo?'

Dylan hadn't realised how cold he was until he stepped into the warmth of his mum's hall.

'Dylan? Is that you? I wasn't expecting you.' Rachel

wheeled towards him from the kitchen. 'Why don't you have a shower and get changed before you drip any more weather on my floor.'

'Sorry,' Dylan murmured, not looking away from Tabitha. She looked so relaxed here in his childhood home. Her pale skin shone with vitality in the warm light of the hall, her large, blue eyes glinting. Her lips curved into a smile.

'Sorry, he murmured again, and then inched past her, trying not to drip water on her clothes. As he brushed against her arm, the warmth of her skin was a shock to his system. He fought to keep his breathing steady, knowing his mum was watching him, but he saw his surprise mirrored in the widening of Tabitha's eyes.

'Come on, Tabitha, let's get the kettle on and we can all sit down for a drink when Dylan is warm and dry.' Rachel's voice was so normal it jarred against Dylan's sensitised nerves.

Tabitha licked her lips, and then walked past him into the kitchen, her hips swaying. She turned as she reached the kitchen workshop, her gaze locking with his one more time before his mum shoved him down the hall to his room.

'Go on,' she whispered furiously. 'Tabitha isn't going anywhere, but you're soaked and cold. Your hands are shaking. Get in the shower, warm up, put on some dry clothes and I promise Tabitha will still be here when you get back.'

He reached the bathroom in two strides and pulled off his top and trousers, slamming the door behind him. He cranked up the shower head as far as he could take it, allowing the steaming water to pound onto his aching back. It had been such a strange day, so full of elation and challenge. One day in the job and he'd probably blown it already. Why hadn't he kept his mouth shut about Max? He leaned his head against the shower. If he managed to keep this job, it was certainly not going to be ordinary.

Warm at last, he climbed out of the shower and dried off. He sprinted across the hall in a towel, ducked into his old room and threw open the wardrobe. It was mainly full of his mum's things now, but he kept a few clothes there for moments like this. Pulling on his favourite of the two outfits, he combed his hair and made his way to the kitchen.

Tabitha was sitting at the table opposite Rachel, nursing a large mug of coffee and laughing. Dylan leaned against the doorframe, taking a moment to watch her in this unguarded moment. She turned around and smiled at him, pushing back the chair next to her and filling a large mug with steaming, black coffee.

'How was your first day?' Rachel asked, tilting her head and smiling.

'It was … interesting.' He took a sip of coffee, and then pushed out the chair next to him, propping his legs on the seat. 'I saw Max,' he said, letting out a long breath. 'He thought he was on his own, and he was poking the cats through the bars and threatening to go in there with them.'

Tabitha's eyes widened. 'That's not good. Can you report it?'

Dylan sighed 'I've already logged my concerns with Sophie, but she accused me of making trouble on my first day. Unfortunately, my phone ran out of battery so I couldn't get any pictures or video. Without that, she's not going to listen to me.'

Tabitha frowned. 'I'll let Ursula know. This is just the kind of thing she's after, although I'm not sure she'll be able to do much without evidence either. Thank you, though.

You did the right thing, whether Sophie appreciated it or not.'

Dylan nodded. 'Although, if he goes into the cage like he threatened, I'm pretty sure the cats will look after themselves.'

Rachel gaped. 'Go into the cage with them? Are you serious?'

Tabitha rolled her eyes. 'It wouldn't surprise me. He's so hot-headed.'

'It sounds like you have some plotting to do,' Rachel said with an attempt at a smile, but Dylan could see she was troubled. 'I'm going to leave you to it. I have a film I've been dying to watch, so I'll head to bed and enjoy it in comfort. Please help yourself to food, light a fire and make yourselves comfortable. Dylan, are you staying here tonight?'

'Do you mind? I don't want to see Linden at the moment.'

Rachel nodded. 'Your bed is made up. Sleep tight my darlings.' There was silence as she left the room.

Tabitha shifted in her chair.

Dylan swallowed then cleared his throat. 'Would you like a proper drink? Mum always has a good supply of gin in the cupboard.'

'I'd love one, thank you.' Tabitha smiled.

Dylan went out to the kitchen and came back with two glasses filled with clear liquid. He handed one to Tabitha. 'Do you mind if I ask what's going on between you and Max?'

There was a pause. Tabitha flushed. 'Nothing's going on.

Dylan put her drink on the table in front of her. 'I know

he wants me to stay away from you, but do *you* want me around?'

'Would I still be here if I didn't?'

Dylan let out his breath, feeling his chest relax. 'Do you want *Max* around you?'

Tabitha sighed. 'No. At least not in the way you mean. Max is okay when he's not trying to make moves on me, but when he is, he's as much of a predator as the tigers he cares for. I do want to be around the tigers and he is their keeper, so I don't burn my bridges. But believe me, I can look after myself and I know how to deal with predators.'

Dylan blinked. For a moment he had thought the tiger was snaking around Tabitha's chair, but it flickered out like a candle being snuffed out. 'Shall we go through to the living room? I wouldn't say no to a fire after that soaking.'

Tabitha followed him to the other room and sat down on the sofa, her legs curled up underneath her. She sipped her gin and tonic in silence and watched him build the fire. He felt her gaze on his back and his heart rate rose. Finishing, he dusted off his hands and sat on the sofa next to her. She was so close, but the distance between them felt insurmountable. As she stared into the fire they might as well have been in different worlds.

The silence stretched out.

'How's the painting going?' he asked, grasping for something to say.

She frowned, pursing her lips. 'That question is more loaded than you intended, I think.'

Silence.

'Maybe I can help you figure things out?' Dylan's voice was rough and he coughed to clear his throat.

Tabitha sighed. 'I'm supposed to be working on a huge

commission and I really can't afford to be late with it. But every time I sit down to paint I see images in my mind and I know I have to draw them.'

'What kind of images?' Dylan leaned forwards. There was a weird tension about her, as though she was crouched, ready to pounce. It filled him with expectation.

She reached into her satchel, pulled out a sketchbook and handed it to Dylan.

Dylan took the book and started leafing through. At first there were pictures of the tigers, pages and pages of them. Then he turned the next sheet and froze. His own eyes stared at him from the page. He gasped. 'How did you make me look so ...'

Tabitha frowned. She tilted her head and looked at him through narrow eyes. 'That's how you look when you play the drums. That's the light that shines out of your entire body. Haven't you seen it before?'

Dylan shook his head, not sure what to say. 'Could I ... buy this?'

'No. Have it. She took the book and carefully detached the picture. 'I shouldn't really have drawn you without permission, so it's yours anyway. Keep going. You haven't got to the pictures I was talking about.'

He turned the page and found an action sketch of him wrestling with another man. His head was being forced around so that he could see his own profile, twisted in a grimace. The other man was furious. His teeth were bared in a snarl as he pushed his face into Dylan's space. It was Max.

'You've been seeing *this* image?'

'Repeatedly. I see it when I'm asleep. I see it when I'm drawing. It pops into my head when I'm walking along the street. I can't shake the feeling that something is coming, and it has to do with you and Max.'

Dylan closed the book. 'It's just a bad dream. It isn't real. Max is a bully, but I can take care of myself.'

Tabitha sighed. 'I'm sure you can, but you're a good guy. Max has no scruples. He is all about winning. Nothing else matters.'

'What makes you so sure this is real?'

Tabitha shifted in her seat. She untucked her legs and sat up, dropping her head into her hands. 'I don't know. But these visions won't let go of me.'

Dylan looked at her. 'Do you have other visions?'

'Like what?'

Dylan took a deep breath and let it out slowly. He couldn't shake the feeling that she might understand, he just hoped he wasn't about to make a fool of himself. 'Do you ever see a white tiger walking around Wildley Forest Village?'

Tabitha frowned. 'It sounds as though you do?'

Disappointment settled in Dylan's chest. 'Oh, no. It's nothing.'

Tabitha leaned forwards, resting her elbows on her thighs. 'You shouldn't dismiss it. Visions exist to tell us something, even if it's not immediately clear what the message is. Tell me about your tiger.'

Dylan's shoulders relaxed and he leaned back on the sofa. 'I've been seeing her more and more, but nobody else notices. She can't be real, but I don't know what she is, or where she comes from.'

'How do you know it's a she?'

'I just know.'

'You don't think she's real?' Tabitha's eyes were wide.

Dylan couldn't help thinking there was a right answer to this question, but he wasn't sure what it was. 'Well, that's not quite right. She's real, but a real what? She's not a flesh-and-blood tiger. She's not a ghost either. I've touched her and she's solid and warm, but other times she vanishes into thin air. I don't know what to make of her.'

'Is she frightening?' Tabitha's voice was soft, quiet.

'Not since the first time. I feel a connection to her, as though she's my muse, or something. That sounds stupid, doesn't it?'

'Not to me.' Tabitha smiled. Her face was alight with something that hadn't been there a moment ago. Whatever test had been set, he had obviously passed.

She took the sketch book and started leafing through the pictures. 'Is this her?'

Dylan's breath caught in his throat. The tiger looking at him from the page was achingly familiar. The expression in the wise eyes was so human it was hard to believe she was an animal at all. He swallowed. 'That's her. You *do* see her too?'

Tabitha laughed. 'In a manner of speaking.' She seemed to find this funny and he wasn't sure why. But her smile warmed his insides, beginning to thaw the isolation that had set in when the gulf widened between him and his friends.

'I know that tiger well. You can be certain she's looking out for you.'

Dylan felt a flutter in his chest. Tabitha's leg was very close to his now. One small movement and there was just a breath between them. He felt air tingling across his skin. His sense of her was so strong and familiar that he couldn't imagine ever letting her walk away. He thought of nothing but her. The life he had lived for so long suddenly looked brutally empty.

'Tabitha,' he said, his voice hoarse.

She just looked at him and held his gaze, her eyes huge, liquid pools of turquoise blue. Her lips were parted, her chest rising and falling with each breath. She reached up, paused, her hand in mid-air, and then brushed away a copper strand of hair. 'So why are you running away from Linden?' she asked, leaning back on the chair.

Dylan swallowed. 'We had a row, a fight, even. I need to move out. Things aren't working anymore.'

Tabitha paled. 'I hope you weren't arguing about me.'

Dylan sighed. 'Don't pay any attention to them. I'd rather spend time with you any day.'

Tabitha shook her head. 'I won't get between you and your friends. They irritate you because you love them. You think they're holding you back from the career you want, but what if it's not their fault? What if it's always been fear that has got in your way and they're just a convenient scapegoat? Do you really think they'd stop you going after your dreams?'

Dylan frowned. 'How do you know all that? We've never talked about my career.'

Tabitha flushed, pulled on her shoes and stood up. 'Never mind.'

'Please don't go!' Dylan leapt up and put a hand on her arm.

She turned to look at him.

He let out the breath he had been holding. 'You saw how angry Linden was.'

Tabitha shrugged. 'I saw a man who felt humiliated on stage. I saw him lashing out because he was embarrassed. I saw a group of guys who have built their identity around a band, and who know that one of the members is going to leave them because he's too good to stay. I saw their fear at what they would become without you, at whether they could ever be good enough without your heartbeat lighting them up and holding them together. I saw men who are hanging onto the last vestiges of boyhood, because guess what? It's bloody hard to become an adult and all of us get angry at some point when we are pushed to rise to the challenge.'

Dylan stared at her, his eyes wide. He swallowed. 'But why would they treat you the way they did?'

'Because they looked at me and couldn't make sense of what they saw. They knew I was different, but they didn't understand it and that scared them.'

Dylan shook his head. 'How do you know all this stuff?'

Tabitha smiled, but her eyes were sad. 'Because they're right: I am different. I see things other people haven't learned to recognise. Let's just say I have a lot in common with your tiger.'

Dylan stepped towards her. They were standing so close now that the air hummed between them. He reached up one hand, paused, and then touched her cheek with the tips of his fingers. Tingles ran up his arm from the contact and a shiver ran through him. Her skin was warm and unbelievably soft. He could hear his own breathing mingle with hers, could feel their heartbeats in sync though they were barely touching. Her lips were full and parted. He began to lean in, and then reached out one hand and found the tips of her fingers with his own.

'No.' Tabitha stepped away, breaking the contact. 'Your friends matter. I won't be the reason you lose them. You can mend this, and then there will be other moments.' She turned away, walked out through the living room door and into the hall. She reached up to the hooks, took down her raincoat and pulled it on.

'Please, Tabitha?' Dylan's voice was rough.

She turned to look at him, her eyes filled with compassion. She walked back, reached up and stroked his cheek.

He leaned into her touch, allowing his eyes to close.

'You'll thank me for this, one day,' she said, and then she turned, opened the door and walked down the ramp, closing the door firmly behind her.

26

TABITHA

TABITHA TOOK A DEEP BREATH AND FORCED HERSELF INTO stillness. She lit a candle and a stick of white sage, and then picked up her sketchbook and pencil and settled into the armchair in the corner of the showroom.

Closing her eyes, she took a few deep breaths. She felt the moment her consciousness lifted from her body. The familiar freedom sank through her, releasing her mind and her awareness to wander. Still conscious of her body, and of her hand ready to sketch, she allowed herself to float, pulled by a connection to Dylan she didn't yet understand.

The moment she thought of Dylan, she was in front of him. She watched him say goodbye to his mum, walk to a flat in the middle of the village, and put a key in the lock.

He took a deep breath, and then walked in.

Tabitha slipped past him into the flat, her feline form as fluid as mist.

The chatter stopped when Linden and GJ turned and saw who was standing in the doorway.

'You came back!' GJ's joy was infectious. Even Linden managed a tight smile.

Dylan let out the breath he had been holding. 'I need a drink. Can I get you both a beer?' He walked through to the kitchen, his shoulders slumping as he reached into the fridge for the bottles.

Tabitha followed.

He reached out, touching her fur with his fingertips. 'I am so pleased to see you here,' he said under his breath.

Tabitha rubbed her head up against his leg, allowing herself to become more solid. She felt his stress ease.

Back in the living room, they clinked their bottles together, trying to pretend everything was normal. Their meaningless prattle was of little interest to Tabitha in her astral state. She wanted to hear Dylan's voice and he seemed too zoned out to oblige. Starting to feel restless, she felt a growl rumble in her chest. Dylan looked up and held her gaze. His lips twitched as he watched her and she snaked towards him, focusing on her tiger form becoming real enough for him to touch. GJ shivered when she walked past him. Dylan's eyebrows rose, but GJ gave no other indication he had seen anything unusual.

'Are you listening to a word I'm saying?' Linden said, sounding exasperated.

Dylan held Tabitha's gaze for a moment longer, before turning to Linden. 'No, sorry. My mind was elsewhere.'

Linden stared at him, mouth open. 'You do like her?'

'Of course. You knew that, right? That's why you've been worrying at both of us. That's why you apparently hate her and can't bear for us to have a mere conversation. If she hadn't been special, you wouldn't have cared enough to make a fuss. You have a life, Linden, and a career. I want that. I want to have more than Instantaneous Rock and a casual job. A friend would support me in that.

Silence.

Tabitha walked over to Dylan and lay down on his feet. She knew he could see and feel her clearly, no matter how blind his friends were.

Linden was red-faced. His hands were bunched into fists at his side. His chest puffed out in anger, but he said nothing. He didn't move.

'He's right.' GJ's voice was quiet, but firm. 'And he's right about the music too. This has to stop. Dylan was always a better musician than either of us, but we've never given him enough of a chance to shine. He's amazing at the drums, but have you ever heard him play the guitar? Or sing? I'd love to hear your new song, Dylan.'

'That isn't for the band.' Dylan shoved his hands in his pockets and stepped back, further away from the guys. 'That's a personal project.'

'I know,' GJ nodded. 'But if you're ready to share, I'd love to hear.'

Dylan looked at Linden.

Tabitha growled.

Linden shivered, looking behind him and around his feet. 'Go on then, sing.'

Dylan nodded. He took his guitar out of the case, sat down on the arm of one of the chairs and tuned the strings.

GJ leaned back in his armchair, closing his eyes and smiling as Dylan began picking out the chords.

The room was so still. Tabitha's form wavered. She floated on the ether, blending into the vibrations of Dylan's music, which felt like home in a way so profound that she didn't know how to orientate herself anymore. His voice was deep, smooth and resonate, filling the room with the sound of his body and soul.

> *Dreaming of a place on the other side of here,*
> *Dreaming of a me that's only shadow.*
> *The road appears to lead away*
> *But always comes back home.*
> *The image shifts and fades*
> *And again, I'm alone.*

As he sang verse after verse, he created harmonics that carried Tabitha higher, swirling through a fairground ride of sensation. When he stopped, there was silence so potent she could still hear the sound ringing around her.

GJ sat forwards, elbows on his knees, his lips parted and eyes wide as he stared at Dylan.

'You're right,' Linden said, his voice rough. 'You deserve more than Instantaneous Rock can offer.'

Dylan took a deep breath. He closed his eyes for a moment, and then opened them. 'You have no idea what that means to me.'

'What are you going to do?' Linden jumped up and started pacing. 'You'll need to record that. Do you have any others?'

'You've changed your tune,' Dylan said, shaking his head in wonder.

'I was trying to protect you. I don't trust Tabitha. But that was all you. *That* is something I'm ready to put my faith in.' Linden opened his arms wide. 'Come here. You're a dark horse, I'll give you that. But you're our dark horse.'

Dylan stood up and walked into Linden's embrace.

They slapped each other on the back, and then stepped away.

GJ was grinning wide. Tabitha felt the joy emanating from him and moved closer, allowing their energy to touch. He shivered again, but his smile broadened.

Dylan settled into a chair, more relaxed than she had ever seen him.

Tabitha felt the pull of her body and allowed her energy to respond to the magnetic tug.

At home in the gallery, she flicked through the pictures she had sketched while she travelled as a tiger. There was a stand-off between Dylan and Linden, Dylan playing the guitar and a picture of the guys relaxing around the fire. They were all nice, all held the tension and release she had witnessed in the room, but there was something missing. She felt it tugging at her consciousness. Standing up, she walked over to the window and peered outside. She couldn't shake the feeling that someone was watching her. With a shudder, she shut the blinds, blocking out the darkness that seemed strangely ominous.

Walking over to the front door, she opened it wide and stood on the step.

The barn owl screeched from the tree outside her front door and she answered back, the connection strengthened by her recent astral journey. Emily ran towards her, brushing up against her ankles and then dashing into the warmth of the shop. There was a rustle in the bushes.

'If you're out there, please show yourself,' Tabitha said, her voice as commanding as she could make it. A fox ran out of the bush and across the path. Emily hissed, but didn't move. Tabitha went back inside, shut the door and locked it before pulling the heavy curtain over it to keep in the warmth.

Stopping at the desk, she ran a finger over the plans for the reserve in India. She had been dreaming of this for so long and she would make it happen, with or without Wildley Forest Zoo. The large stretch of land to one side of an established reserve was currently farmland, but with access to water through the middle, they could rewild it into a beautiful habitat full of native plant and animal life.

Taking her notebook and pencils, she started sketching as the image grew in her mind. She saw the gnarled branches, the ground lined with leaves and the sun shining through the undergrowth. A tiger walked towards her, its lean body rippling with muscle. She made herself less substantial, fading into the undergrowth as the cat walked past. It stopped for a moment and stared right at her.

Tabitha lost herself in those eyes. They were so different to the cats at the zoo. The intelligent wildness of its gaze shivered through her, as the cat grunted, and then walked past.

She opened her eyes. Releasing the tigers from the zoo into her own reserve had been part of her dream, and she had been prepared to fight for it. But she would make a new dream. Ursula was right. Her tigers needed a different world to the one inhabited by cats that had been born into the wild.

Tabitha made a cup of tea, picked up her candle and made her way up the steep, curving staircase to her bedroom. It was a mess upstairs, so she straightened it up, singing while she began to weave positive energy into the room, focusing into her own purpose and putting up shields to keep her space clear.

She sat on the bed, stretching her legs out in front of her and closing her eyes. Familiar images started flickering through her mind and she shivered. She opened the book and started to draw. Dylan and Max fighting. A storm. A tree toppled against the side of the tiger enclosure. A tiger, its teeth bared, a rumbling growl coming from between drawn-back lips as it stood its ground in the sheeting rain and brutal wind.

She saw herself shimmer and her tiger form detached. She stared in wonder at the cat she knew so intimately, but so rarely saw. She watched the power of her feline body as it grew more and more solid, the muscles flexing beneath the white, striped fur, the growl rumbling from inside the enormous ribcage. Even knowing it was her own consciousness, she shivered.

The yellow tiger moved towards her astral form, slowly at first, and then at a run. She roared, rearing up on her back legs as the two huge beasts met head-on, swiping with giant paws.

Tabitha jerked and opened her eyes, almost feeling the heavy impact of the other cat. Her breath was short and she gasped for air. Tears streamed down her face, but she had no idea why. She put the notebook down, went through to the tiny bathroom and splashed water on her face. She leaned on the sink, looking at herself in the mirror and touched the dark circles under her eyes. She looked so pale. Her copper hair hung in curtains that made her eyes look even bigger than normal, and gave her a haunted look. She shook her head, went back into the bedroom and lay on the bed. Every time she closed her eyes, the images started up again, around and around on the backs of her eyelids. She shook her head again, trying to force some sense into her brain.

Pulling herself up, she turned on the TV, willing there to be something that would distract her. The news flashed up. A woman with dark, curly hair was standing on a road, with trees bending severely in the wind behind her.

These storms sweeping Europe are showing no signs of slowing. Rather, they are building in strength and speed every day. There is a good chance they will take a different course over the Atlantic, but if they do head towards the UK we need to be prepared to batten down the hatches and secure everything that isn't bolted down. So far, these storms have brought chaos, destruction and even loss of life, and they are only getting stronger. The advice is to monitor the weather forecast closely and adjust your plans if the course of this storm doesn't alter.

Tabitha frowned. She picked up her sketch book and looked at the pictures again. In the image of the men fighting, the trees were bent right over to the side from the force of the wind. She looked back at the television screen. The image was alarmingly similar.

Emily jumped up onto the bed, meowing and settling onto Tabitha's lap.

'It's okay, sweetheart, I'm not going anywhere,' she said, stroking the white, striped cat. 'Whatever happens, you and I are in this together.'

27

DYLAN

DYLAN WENT INTO WORK EARLY THE NEXT MORNING, wanting to get some time to explore the office properly before the staff came in.

It was still dark and there was an icy drizzle as he walked through the gates. He pulled his jacket tighter around him. The shop and cafe weren't open yet, so he went straight across the grass to the Playbarn. Slipping the key into the lock, he pulled across the sliding door, and then froze. There was a growl behind him.

He turned, expecting to see the white tiger, but there was nothing there.

There was another growl.

Dylan frowned, and then on impulse he pulled the glass door shut, locked it again, and went over to the tiger enclosure. He paused a few metres away and listened. Max's voice carried on the wind.

Dylan took out his phone and walked quietly up to the fence.

If anyone was up to facing-off to a tiger, Max probably

had a fair chance. He stood inside the enclosure, tall and broad, his bulging muscles on show in spite of the cold. He threw a chunk of meat and the two tigers pounced on it, but he still held the rest of the bucket of food. He had turned away from the cats now and was talking to someone on the other side of the enclosure.

Who could possibly be here this early?

The sun was coming up and Dylan squinted in the pale, early-morning light. The tigers had finished the meat and were prowling, their eyes flicking up towards the figure in the cage. Dylan peered through the enclosure and his breath caught. A familiar face was frowning at Max through the bars. Her long, copper hair flowed around the shoulders of her black hoody and her arms moved fluidly as she gesticulated from the other side of the enclosure, her movements becoming more and more urgent.

The large male dropped low to the ground and moved silently towards Max, its ears laid back.

Tabitha carried on pointing, but Max didn't turn. She looked up and caught Dylan's eye.

'Hey,' Dylan called, trying to keep his voice level to avoid spooking the cat further. It froze, turned to look at him, and then continued its approach. The man ignored him.

'Max,' Dylan yelled. 'Look behind you.'

Max didn't turn.

The tiger charged soundlessly.

'Help!' Dylan yelled, his voice over-loud in the silence, but there was no reply. Dylan's gaze was fixed on Max who was now turning, too slowly. Max roared when he saw the tiger, dropped the bucket of food and swung a thick wooden pole around to catch the tiger full against the body. The cat recoiled, but immediately dropped back into a crouch.

Tabitha turned and walked away, not looking back. She crested the hill and disappeared into the early morning shadows.

Max held the stick in front of him now, his face white as he backed slowly towards the safety door in the enclosure, leaving the bucket of meat behind. Both tigers leapt at the bucket. The male got there first and growled at the female. She flattened her ears and turned to Max. The tiger moved towards him again. Max's gaze was fixed on her, but he was still too far from the safety door. He turned to the spot where Tabitha had been, just for a moment. It was a moment too long. The tiger launched at him. Max turned back, and then screamed as he realised the cat was almost on him, teeth bared.

A second roar cut through the air and the tiger was knocked flying. The white tiger had materialised out of nowhere. It landed, flexing its muscled legs and crouching close to the ground, baring its teeth at the yellow cat, a growl rumbling in its throat.

'Come on,' Dylan yelled, running to the safety cage. 'Get out while you can.'

Max closed the distance, swung the door wide and threw himself in. He slammed the door shut and slumped against the wire barrier, letting his head lol back as he drew in strangled breaths.

'That's not far enough.' Dylan crouched down as close as he could get to the cage. The female was prowling around the metal barrier, her head low as she pawed at the fence. Max yelled and jolted forwards as her claws raked his back through the wire.

He turned, crawling on his hands and knees to the outside exit of the cage. He pulled the lever, forcing himself upright an.d dragged himself out, securing the door firmly behind him. Swaying, he staggered to the final gate and let himself out into the public area.

Dylan looked back at the cats. The white tiger had gone.

'Don't worry, mate. I'll call an ambulance.' Dylan turned on his phone.

'No,' Max gasped. 'Don't. I just need a minute. I know what I'm doing.'

'Come on, you've just been attacked by a tiger. You must need a tetanus shot, at least,' Dylan pleaded.

'I'm fine.' Max pulled himself up to standing, gritting his teeth and closing his eyes against the pain.

'Don't be ridiculous, Max. He's just trying to help.'

Dylan turned. 'Tabitha!'

She smiled. 'He would have been killed if it wasn't for you. You did a good thing.'

'I would not.' Max grimaced. There was a huge rip down the outside leg of his trousers and the back of his shirt was shredded. The edges were tinged with blood.

'You need help.'

'I know what I'm doing,' Max said from between gritted teeth. 'I can handle a bit of a scratch without it being an emergency.'

'You shouldn't have been in there with them, Max. You know that.' Tabitha stared him down, refusing to look away.

In the end, Max was the one who turned to look at the ground. 'I can manage myself.'

'But your boss …'

'Don't get her involved. I don't need to be micromanaged. Tabitha, go and draw your picture. Dylan, I assume you're here to work? I'm going to get myself cleaned up.'

Max almost disguised his limp as he strode off. Dylan heard a van door slam, and then the roar of an engine.

Dylan took a ragged breath. 'Are you okay?' he said to Tabitha.

She nodded, but the colour had leached from her face. 'I think I'm done here for the day.'

'But the zoo hasn't even opened.'

She nodded. 'Max invited me to come early, to see the tigers as I'd never seen them before. Well he was right about that. And I don't ever want to see them that way again. I don't suppose you got any pictures or video with that, did you?' She gestured to his phone.

With a sinking feeling, Dylan raised up the device. It was open on the camera, but he hadn't taken a single picture. 'I meant to. It all moved so fast.'

'Take a moment.' Tabitha put a hand on his arm. 'You look shocked.'

'Thanks.' Dylan nodded. 'I'll do that before the Playbarn mayhem starts.'

28

MAX

Fury drove Max hard as he pounded the empty road around the zoo. His life had been perfect. He had the best job, the respect of management, access to the tigers, and Tabitha always there to be grateful when he offered himself. Now everything had gone to shit. Why did Dylan have to get a job here? Dylan, of all people? And why did he pop up at the worst possible moments? Max had spent a lifetime trying to leave his school days behind, and now all that old humiliation was following him around in the most maddening way.

After a couple of circuits of the zoo, he pulled in next to the tiger enclosure, hoping Dylan had gone. He got out of the van, wincing at the pain in his back, and then went round to the van doors for his large metal prod.

'Max?'

He knew that voice. Ursula. Throwing the prod back into the van before she could see it, he slammed the doors and brushed the mud off his clothes. Thank goodness he had found time to change out of this morning's ripped and bloody uniform.

'Can I help you?' he said, standing just close enough to make her uncomfortable.

'I hope so. We've had another complaint about you. I had hoped you might tone things down after last time.'

Max frowned. 'A complaint? What was it this time?'

'It was from a member of staff.'

'Who?'

'I can't tell you that.'

He stepped closer. He was well into her personal space now. 'Oh, I think you can.'

She looked at him, standing tall, shoulders back, her hands on her hips. Her face was bare of make-up and dark circles ringed her eyes. Her cheeks were chalk white in the early morning light.

'Is that right?' Ursula tipped her head back so she was looking down her nose at him despite being six inches shorter. 'Is that beer I can smell on your breath? You shouldn't be around the cats if you've been drinking.'

'It was from last night,' he said from between gritted teeth. 'I am completely sober.'

'You'd better be, because I'm watching you.' Ursula folded her arms. 'I will be checking up on you and checking again. I don't know what you're playing at, but I don't trust you and I know you're not treating those animals right. I know you haven't started that conservation report. I know you think you have Sophie in your pocket, but even she can't get you out of this. Things are about to change, Max. You can either get on board, or walk.'

Max swallowed. How had she seen so completely

through him when he knew so little about her? 'I don't know what you're talking about.'

'Yes you do. And soon, so will I.' She stepped around him. He shifted, meaning to barge her with his shoulder but somehow, she moved fluidly out of the way and then walked off towards the management offices.

'Damn,' he whispered under his breath, loosening the collar of his shirt. The constriction was almost physical. The zoo had never enforced the conservation clause before. He growled low in his throat, sending the sound out into the enclosure.

An answering growl came from the bushes. The huge, yellow male stalked out, ears flat and lips pulled back from his enormous canines in a snarl. He grunted. The smaller, female walked up beside him. She went right up to the bars, tipped her head back and roared. The sound sent shivers down his spine, spiking his adrenaline and making him feel alive. This was why he did it. This was what made him real. This was what he was fighting for.

29

DYLAN

Dylan went straight to the recording studio after work. It wasn't what he had imagined. He had always pictured a huge, glossy building with famous people wandering around and brainstorming creative ideas on ultra-modern sofas. This place was scruffy and downtrodden. It wasn't anywhere near as clean as he wanted it to be, but the equipment was top of the range and the studio was entirely soundproofed. Dylan supposed nobody would know what conditions he had put up with as long as the track came out well.

There was one technician in the control room. He looked up when Dylan came in, and then pointed at the door to the soundproofed room. 'You go in there. Nod when you're ready and start to sing. We'll take it from there.'

'I have a number of lines to record: voice, drums and guitar. I was told we could do them all?'

'There's a drum kit in there. Do you have everything else?'

Dylan held up his guitar and gave an uncertain smile. He pushed the door open and walked through, shutting it behind him. He leaned against the wall. Taking a deep breath, he let the silence envelop him. He closed his eyes, ignoring the man on the other side of the glass. This was his moment, his time to create.

Dylan started singing, but his voice was cold, and cracked in a number of places. He coughed and tried again, over-conscious of the man on the other side of the glass.

He turned away from the microphone, putting his back to the technician. 'Damn,' he muttered to himself. There didn't need to be any pressure. That guy was the only person who could hear and Dylan performed to more people every weekend at the pub. But somehow this was different. These songs were so personal and raw and his voice was so much more emotionally revealing than the drums.

The drums. Of course. He would start there. Dylan moved to the kit. The tension drained out of his shoulders as his sticks flew over the drumheads, creating a heartbeat for the melody. This was where he was supposed to be.

When the last beat faded, he took out his guitar and tuned it. Picking out the chords, he closed his eyes and allowed the sound to lull him. It was so familiar, so comforting and normal, and his confidence grew. He felt the pulse of the chords behind the drums, the melody and the harmonics vibrating from the melting pot of sounds that swarmed around him.

A growl from the corner of the room made him turn. He smiled as the white tiger shimmered into sight, snaking through the room. She settled on his feet and he felt warmth flood him. A grin spread over his face. He nodded to the man on the other side of the screen and started again. This time the vocals flowed from him like water. He felt his awareness expand out of his body, watched himself sing with the tiger sitting at his feet. He saw her energy, a bright, golden shimmer that surrounded her and undulated as she shifted. He heard her yowl and the energetic vibrations toned alongside his music. From this vantage point, his song had changed. He heard the overtones and harmonics, felt them trigger something deep in his bones.

The man on the other side of the glass was watching him with a rapt expression. When the final note rang out into silence, the man took off his headphones and nodded. He came to the door and held out a memory stick. 'Hats off to you, mate. That was rockin'.'

'Thanks.' Dylan smiled and pulled his coat on. He crouched down to put his guitar into the solid case, and slid his drumsticks into a pocket in the lid. Now the euphoria had left, he felt drained. He raised his hand in a wave, and then went out into the cold air and shut the door behind him.

The chill gave him just enough energy to get home. The flat was blissfully empty when he arrived, and he curled into bed, blacking out the moment his head hit the pillow.

30

DYLAN

A RINGING FORCED ITS WAY INTO DYLAN'S CONSCIOUSNESS. He pushed it back, eluded it, did his best to ignore and escape from it. The more he tried, the louder it became, dragging him back into irritatingly clear consciousness.

He grabbed his phone from the bedside table and hit answer. 'Hello?' he croaked, his voice still thick with sleep.

'Hello darling, did I wake you up?'

'Yes. What do you want, Mum? I'm in the middle of a really important nap.'

She laughed. 'I've just been talking to a friend. Her tenants have moved out and the flat has just been refurbished. Do you still want your own place?'

Dylan sat bolt upright. 'Where is it?'

'It's here in Wildley Forest Village, at the zoo end near Tabitha's cottage.'

Dylan swallowed. 'Do you know what the rent is?'

'I've got the details here. Would you like me to email them over? it's fully accessible, so if you'd like to look, we could go together. My friend is here with me now and she could take us straight away.'

'Yes, please send them over. Give me ten minutes to look, and then I'll call you back when I'm a bit more awake.'

Dylan leapt out of bed and ran through to the bathroom. In the shower he let the water pour over him, washing away the last shreds of sleep. A new place. His own place, where he could compose, rest and invite Tabitha over.

Once out of the shower, he pulled on a smart pair of jeans and a shirt in an attempt to look like a responsible tenant, and then powered up his laptop. There was an email from his mum with an attachment. His heart pounded as he waited for it to download. Would he be able to afford it? Was it in a fit state? The rent was high, but just about manageable on his new salary. If he could get solo gigs and sell some albums, so much the better. The pictures showed a modern, neutral flat that he could make his own really quickly. The block was boxy and unattractive from the outside, but he could live with that in exchange for space and privacy.

He dialled his mum. 'Is she still there? I can't imagine this will stay vacant for long.'

'She is.' Rachel sounded excited. 'The last tenant was a wheelchair user, so it's already been adapted. There won't be many opportunities like this. Can you meet us in the main street?'

Five minutes later, Dylan was standing outside the tea shop.

'Over here,' his mum called, waving her arm in the air, a familiar woman by her side.

'This is Valerie,' Rachel said, her face flushing slightly. 'She's a big fan of your music.'

'Thank you.' Dylan shook Valerie's outstretched hand and smiled. 'It's lovely to meet a new friend of my mum's. How do you guys know each other?'

'Oh, through this and that,' his mum said, not meeting his eye.

'We've known each other for a while, and I have been keeping an eye out for a flat for you.' Valerie's smile was sincere. 'How ready are you to move?' she asked, reaching out and lacing her fingers through Rachel's as they set off down the street.

'If it's a match I can move straight away.'

Valerie smiled and gestured over the road. Dylan couldn't help noticing that she crossed where the curb dropped without being asked or reminded.

'So where's this flat?' he asked, following them over.

'It's not far, thank goodness.' Rachel shivered. 'I don't think I can take much more of this cold.'

'Make sure you're not on your own over the next few days. There are big storms coming.' Valerie frowned.

'Nothing would keep me from Mum if she needed me,' Dylan said, his voice sharp. 'It would take more than a storm to keep me away.'

Valerie nodded and let out her breath. 'Good. I hope you know how lucky you are to have a mum like Rachel.'

Dylan looked at Valerie, his eyes narrowed. 'I do. I tell her so most days. That's why she's so conceited.' He winked at Rachel. 'I'm also very protective. Did she tell you that?'

'Behave, Dylan.' Rachel wagged her finger. 'You may be a grown up, but I can still tell you off.'

Dylan kissed the top of her head. 'And I'm sure you

always will, particularly if I rent a flat where you can get in the front door any time you like. Are you going to show us around, Valerie?'

'This way.' She smiled, meeting his gaze head-on. 'See, there's a ramp up to the entrance and a good, wide front door. It's this ground floor flat.' She held open the main door and Rachel went first. Dylan followed, looking around.

There was a beautiful, open hall area. It was easily big enough for his mum to get inside, turn around and go into any of the rooms, including the spacious bathroom which was already fitted with rails. The floor was wooden and it gleamed in the sparkling glow of the spotlights. The whole flat smelled of lemons. The off-white walls were newly painted, and the living room had double doors that opened onto a large terrace area with a ramp. All the rooms were far bigger than Dylan had expected, and the fireplace looked real.

'What's the catch?' He looked at Valerie, trying to read her. 'Why can I afford this? I've looked at others and, believe me, unless there's a hidden catch somewhere, this should not be within my reach.'

Valerie held his gaze. 'Rachel is my friend. You are her son.'

Dylan gaped. 'And you'd lose out on rent for our sake?'

'Valerie has been there for me,' Rachel spoke up. 'She understands.'

Valerie sat on one of the sofas and propped one ankle up on her other thigh. 'Listen, My dad was in a wheelchair for years. I get it. Plus, I can afford to lose a little loose change if it makes Rachel happy. It's worth it.'

Dylan looked at Rachel again. She was defiant, her chin tilted up and her eyes too bright, but he could see the tear that was moments away from dropping from her eyelash to her cheek. Valerie was right. He had always wanted to take his mum into his home, but he'd never stopped to wonder how much it meant to her. He could see in her eyes now how much she had sacrificed, silently, when he took that pokey upstairs flat. 'Thank you. I would love to take you up on your kind offer. And if you ever need a musician for a party, or whatever, let me know. It'll be on the house, anytime.'

Valerie beamed.

'Dylan, would you have a look in the bag on the back of my chair please?' Rachel inclined her head to the side.

'In here?' Dylan asked, and she nodded as he reached into the carrier. 'Ah, I see. I don't suppose you have any glasses, do you?' he asked Valerie, holding up a bottle of sparkling wine.

Valerie went to the cupboard and pulled out three glasses, while Dylan popped the cork and poured.

'Here's to home,' he said, holding out his glass so Rachel could clink hers against it.

'Here's to home,' she said.

Dylan nodded and took a sip. He opened the door to the terrace wide. A screech from the tree on the other side of the road called his attention to the little cottage opposite. It was Tabitha's. Emily was on the windowsill on the inside of the shop looking directly at him. She jumped down. Moments later, Tabitha came to the window.

Dylan raised his hand. His heart was pounding.

Tabitha brushed a strand of hair from her eyes, and then waved to him before disappearing back into the room.

'Listen, I think that's my friend's house over the road.

Do you mind if I just go and say hello?' he said, turning back to the women.

Valerie handed him a key. 'I'll get the paperwork sorted, but move in whenever you like. There's no point in holding things up. I hope you're happy here.'

'Thank you, Valerie.' Dylan grasped her hand. 'You're a kind woman. I am so pleased my mother has a friend like you. It's good to know there are other people looking out for her.'

Rachel tutted. 'You talk about me as though I'm not a badass superhero.' She knocked back the rest of her wine and wheeled over to the door. 'I may not be able to walk, but I have other talents you mere mortals can only dream of. Take the rest of that bottle with you, Dylan, I'm sure Tab would love a glass.'

31

DYLAN

DYLAN PAUSED AT TABITHA'S FRONT GATE. THERE WAS A sign saying *Shop Open*, but the door itself was firmly closed. The owl shrieked. He looked up, hoping to see it, but it was buried deep in the foliage. He held up a hand, paused, and then wrapped his knuckles against the wooden door.

He heard footsteps, a meow and then the door swung open.

Reality shifted as Dylan looked at the woman in front of him. She was possessed by a wild beauty. She shone, from her bright copper hair to her bare feet and glinting, white toenails. Her full lips spread into a slow smile and her eyes shone bright turquoise.

She held out one fine-boned hand, her crystal bracelets clinking together on her wrist. 'Dylan, come on in.' She stood back to let him pass.

'I'm your new neighbour,' he said, stepping inside and breathing into the warmth of the small room. 'I just accepted a flat over the road. When I saw you at the window, I thought I'd come and say hello.'

'I thought you'd made up with your friends?'

Dylan frowned. 'How did you know that? I haven't seen you since.'

She flushed and shook her head. 'Never mind.'

'Regardless, you were right. We have made up, I recorded a demo today, and Mum's friend offered me a beautiful flat for absurdly low rent. Not many days come this good.'

The tension dropped out of her shoulders and she smiled. 'Well then, it sounds like we should celebrate!'

'The bubbles are on Mum.' He held out the bottle.

There were only ceramic mugs this time. Tabitha poured the bubbling liquid and handed him the larger cup. Their fingertips brushed and his heart sped, his breath catching in his throat.

Tabitha took her cup and sat on the floor, leaning against the wall, her legs doubled up in front of her.

'Do you mind if I look?' Dylan asked, gesturing at the pictures that lined the walls.

'Please do. They are for sale, after all.'

The walls were covered with images of tigers. Most were impressionistic watercolours, the lines and colours showing a movement and life that took his breath away. 'How do you do that,' he said, reaching towards a blue and purple image of two tigers fighting. 'You've used fantastical colours, but somehow it's more real than a photograph.'

Tabitha smiled. 'Thank you. That one was a commission. I'll be posting it in the next day or two, but I wanted to show it first.'

'Do you do a lot of commissions?'

'Yes. That's how I live. I'm known for painting tigers, so people come to me from all over the world. I have a waiting list two pages long and it takes me weeks to complete one large painting. The other pictures, the sketches, the pastel drawings, those are for the love of it. They still make me money, but not enough to survive on.'

Dylan stopped in front of a small pastel drawing of a white tiger. She was baring her teeth at the onlooker, her turquoise-blue eyes furious. A flicker of red and orange surrounded her pale, striped form. 'This is her,' he whispered. This is my tiger.'

Tabitha swallowed. 'I'd forgotten you would recognise her.'

'Why does she look so angry?'

'It was Max,' Tabitha whispered. 'He was threatening me. That was how I felt.'

There was silence.

Dylan tried to process what she had said. *That was how she had felt.* How did that relate to the tiger? 'Are you saying …?'

'Yes,' Tabitha whispered. She stood up. She held his gaze without flinching, but her hand shook slightly as she reached out and steadied herself on the table.

'The tiger is your feelings? That can't be. I wouldn't be able to see her if that was true.'

'She isn't just my feelings. She is me. When I draw or paint, I astral project. I send my awareness outside of my body, and I can travel where I want without physical limitation. But when I do that, I don't look like me. Instead I appear as a white tiger. I have always had a huge affinity with cats. They are my family. I feel closer to the cats than to people a lot of the time.'

'So all those times I've been with the tiger you have been watching me?' Dylan stared at Tabitha. She was pale.

She gripped the back of her chair so tightly that her knuckles had turned white.

'I'm sorry. I didn't mean to pry, but every time I started drawing, I was with you. Sometimes I can control it, other times not. You send me spinning. I've always been like this, but with you I am at the mercy of something I don't understand. Images tangle in my head, past, present and future, and I don't know what's what. I don't know what's real, and what's just fear. And I don't know why you are so important, why you haunt my every moment, waking and sleeping. My sketchbook is full of pictures of you, because every time I close my eyes, you are there. Whenever I sit down to draw or paint I have to fight to stay in my body, and it stops me drawing the cats, because I draw what I see when I travel. I know you're probably going to hate me now, but something is going on between us. I can't pretend to know what it is, but it's definitely important and it's definitely real.'

She stopped speaking, tilted her chin in the air and glared at Dylan, daring him to disagree.

Dylan stared at her. She couldn't be. How could that be possible? Images flashed through his mind. The tiger in his mum's living room, the tiger in the recording studio. Where else had she been? 'I need to go.'

'Dylan,' Tabitha said, her voice choked.

He shook his head. 'I'll see you later.' The door stuck for a moment, but he yanked it and it swung open, hard. He stumbled over the doorstep and then he was out in the fresh air, pounding towards home.

32

TABITHA

TABITHA STARED AT THE SHUT DOOR. WHY HAD SHE TOLD him? This was why she didn't let herself get close to people. They never understood.

She wouldn't ever forget the hurt and embarrassment in his eyes before he shut down. She was ready for him to be angry, was expecting him to shout and stamp his feet. She wasn't ready for him to retreat.

She locked the door and put her paints away. She didn't have the heart to work now. Pouring herself a cup of tea, she grabbed her cardigan and went upstairs to the bedroom, calling Emily through the door at the bottom of the stairs and shutting the shop out of her mind.

Upstairs, she stood at the window and looked at the flats opposite. There was a light on in one downstairs flat. She could see Rachel in there and another woman. There was no sign of Dylan. She pulled the curtains tightly closed, shutting the world out. Pulling back the duvet, she climbed in and made space for Emily.

Tabitha leaned back but the moment her consciousness

drifted, she pulled herself up. Reaching for the remote, she turned on the TV and flicked through the channels. There was nothing she wanted to watch, so she settled on a property programme, hoping it wouldn't give her any inclination to roam in tiger form.

An hour later it was still far too early for bed. She would normally have been downstairs painting, but that was off limits until she could learn to control her travelling. Something was brewing. It fizzed through every nerve in her body. She needed to paint. She needed to see what was coming, but she would not intrude on Dylan again.

There was a crash from outside.

Emily leapt off the bed and ran to the door. She hissed and her tail puffed up straight behind her.

'What is it, sweetheart? Tabitha climbed out of bed and peered out the window. Max stood in the now-dim light of her garden path.

The owl shrieked.

Emily hissed again, louder this time. She jumped back up onto the bed and stood on the edge, glaring out the window.

Tabitha opened the window and leaned out. 'What is it, Max? I'm not up for visitors now and the shop is closed.'

'I'm not here as a customer. Please let me in?'

'No. Not today. I'm sorry.'

'But I *really* need to talk to you.'

'You'd better talk quickly then.'

Max sighed so loudly Tabitha could hear it from the upstairs window.

'Max, are you drunk?'

'Drunk? Don't be ridiculous,' he said too loudly. 'I have

to drink far more than *that* to get drunk. Will you be at the zoo tomorrow?'

She allowed her gaze to flick up to the flats over the road. The ground-floor flat was dark now. She breathed out in relief. 'Probably not. Whatever it is, tell me from there.'

Max shifted from one foot to another. 'Look, I was hoping to do a better job of things than that. Could we maybe go to dinner? I have a table booked.'

'No.' She sighed. 'I'm not interested. Find yourself a normal woman, Max. I am not what you imagine.'

'A *normal* woman? What's that supposed to mean?' He took a swig from a bottle she hadn't noticed before.

'Never mind.' Tabitha shook her head. 'I'm not the woman for you.'

'You're wrong.' His voice cracked. He stepped closer to the front door and rattled the handle. 'Whatever you are is right for me. You're the only one who understands me.'

'No,' she said, putting her hands up in front of her. 'You're making that up. I don't understand you at all.'

'But, Tabitha …'

Tabitha shook her head. 'Go home. Sober up. I'm going in now.'

'No—'

She shut the window. She was just about to draw the curtains when she saw a movement on the other side of the road near the flats. She squinted through the darkness.

Max turned, looked around and then turned back to her.

She pulled the curtains tight and stood leaning against the wall. Here she was in a brand-new village and already she was surrounded by strife. The man she liked thought she was either deluded or a stalker. The man she didn't like was obsessed with her.

Emily wrapped herself around her ankles, purring. 'It's not my fault, Emily,' she whispered. 'I have to believe that. I am just an agent of change.' She repeated the mantra she had used her whole life when things started going wrong. 'But it isn't always easy, Em.' She buried her face in Emily's fur and the tears began to fall.

33

DYLAN

'SHE TOLD YOU TO LEAVE.' DYLAN CLENCHED HIS HANDS into fists as he walked up Tabitha's garden path. Max was standing in front of the door, rattling it in an attempt to get in. 'She said she didn't want visitors tonight.'

'So what are you doing here, drummer boy?' Max hissed.

'I was over the road when I heard her talking to you out the window.' Dylan flexed his muscles, knowing how the tiger on his bicep would shift and snarl. 'I'm sorry you felt bullied at school, but that does not give you the right to bully others. Tabitha has done nothing but support you, but now she has asked you for something in return. She has asked for space and privacy. Move on.'

Max looked him up and down with a sneer. 'Are you looking for a fight, drummer boy? Think you can take on a big tiger keeper with those delicate musician hands of yours? Oh so soft the hands of a drummer, right? You don't want to bash them up, do you? Trust me, your claws and teeth are puny compared to what I'm used to. I've been charged by a full-grown tiger. Do you really think a tattoo is going to frighten me?'

'No,' Dylan said, his heart beating faster. 'But if you've got any sense, *she* will.'

Max turned to the left, and then yelped and leapt backwards as the enormous white tiger stepped out into the open. He tripped and landed heavily on the path. 'Shit, where did that come from?' He scooted backwards, his breathing ragged.

The tiger growled and followed him.

'Oh my God, it's going to eat me.' Max scrambled to his feet, grabbing onto a tree trunk as he swayed, struggling to find his balance. 'What do we do now?'

'You're asking me?' Dylan kept his voice low. He had no idea how he was supposed to react with a tiger on the loose, but he was determined not to give Tabitha away. He had to fake the fear he didn't feel. 'I've seen you in the cage with tigers at the zoo. Surely *you* know what to do?'

'You saw how that played out.' Max reached up and yanked a branch down from the tree outside Tabitha's house. The crack sent a shudder through Dylan. The barn owl screeched and rose into the air in a flurry of white feathers. Max yanked the branch down further and tugged it off the tree, holding it as a barrier between himself and the tiger. 'I can't believe I'm holding off a grown-arse tiger with a twig. Could tonight get any worse?' He walked backwards one step at a time.

Dylan fell in behind him as they backed down the path towards Tabitha's front door.

'God knows where this creature has come from,' Max muttered as he edged backwards. 'It's glorious. If I can nail this cat for the zoo, Sophie will be bound to back off on that conservation project.'

The tiger peeled her lips back from her lethal ivory teeth, dropped into a hunting crouch and snarled.

'What do we do? What do we do?' Max yelled.

'Just breathe.' Dylan swallowed. Even knowing the cat was no danger, his heart was racing.

'Oh bloody hell,' Max moaned. He dropped the branch as he reached Tabitha's door and started hammering on the thick wood. 'Tabitha, Tabitha, help me!' he yelled.

Silence.

'God, she must really hate me.' Max's voice was high-pitched now. 'Tabitha!'

He hammered on the door again.

'She can't hear you, Max. She's probably got head-phones on, or something. We can get out of this ourselves. Come on.' Dylan reached down and picked up the branch. 'This way.' Dylan tugged on Max's sleeve.

The tiger was between them and the gate, but there was a low wall on the right-hand side that was small enough for them to step over. Dylan backed towards it. Max stood frozen for a moment, and then followed, walking back-wards, his eyes on the tiger.

Max swallowed. 'Please tell me you have a plan?'

'Breathe, and just keep coming this way to the wall.'

'A wall *that* size isn't going to stop a fully grown tiger.' Max's breath was coming in gasps now.

The cat shifted as they moved, positioning herself between Max and the front door, allowing the men a clear route out of the front garden. The low rumble continued from her chest, and her blue eyes blazed.

Max stepped over the wall. 'Come on,' he said from between gritted teeth.

'I'm going to close the gate,' Dylan said, moving back into the garden.

The tiger watched him from her place in front of the door.

'It's okay,' Dylan murmured, reaching the gate. 'Tabitha is safe from us. You can go now.' He slipped through the opening and closed the gate firmly behind him.

The cat stopped growling and settled down in front of the door, its blue eyes gleaming in the light of the streetlamp.

Max stood frozen on the street.

'Come on,' Dylan said, as he drew level. 'Let's get out of here before she decides to go walkabout again.'

'I can't believe you went back in there.' Max shoved his hands in his pockets, his shoulders rising up towards his ears.

'She looks calmer now it's shut.' Dylan knew how ridiculous that sounded. 'Let's go to Mum's house. She's just down the road.'

Max was silent.

'Max, did you hear me?'

'You go to your mum's.'

'What are you going to do?'

Max turned to face Dylan, a strange glint in his eyes. 'There's a tiger on the loose.' He grinned. 'I'm going to do my civic duty. That tiger will be mine by the morning.'

Pulling out his phone, he dialled and then walked off in the opposite direction.

Dylan stared after him. He knew the tiger wouldn't hurt Max, but Tabitha was certainly in danger. He walked slowly back towards her house, hoping to catch a glimpse of the large cat still on the doorstep, but it was gone.

'At least Max won't find her now,' he said to himself, but he couldn't deny the sinking feeling in his stomach as he realised he wasn't going to see her either.

He was still reeling from Tabitha's revelation and seeing her, teeth bared, tensed to pounce, hadn't made it any easier. He wasn't sure whether he was relieved or disappointed that she didn't follow them down the road. He felt embarrassed at having been seen in his most private moments, and disappointed that he didn't have the muse he had come to rely on. Most of all, he felt he had lost a friend. Since the tiger had walked into his life, he had made bigger changes than he thought possible. He still had a long way to go if he was going to realise his dreams and he wasn't sure he wanted to do it without her.

Max clearly hadn't known Tabitha's secret. He could still see the fear in the man's face when he had seen the tiger, had felt a stab of exhilaration that this man, for all his big-cat knowledge, could not recognise that she was more than she seemed.

Dylan turned, looking back down the street. He squinted into the shadows, hoping the tiger had been following him. There was no sign of her and deep down he wasn't surprised. He had shamed her: shamed her for being what she was and for telling the truth about it. He had shamed her for taking an interest in him, for being there every time he needed her. She wouldn't cross that boundary uninvited again.

34

TABITHA

TABITHA OPENED HER EYES. THE TIGER'S SNARL WAS mirrored on her own face. She stood up and went to the cupboard above her wardrobe, pulling out a box of tea lights and lighting a stick of sage. She arranged the candles and wafted sage smoke into the corners of the room, trying to recreate the usual calm atmosphere, but it didn't stop the churning in her stomach. If she could have got through the entrance gates to the zoo, she would have left right away to see the tigers. They always restored her peace.

Her only other route to them was her art. She needed to travel and run with the tigers, but she couldn't risk visiting Dylan. She was trapped.

'What am I going to do?' she murmured to herself, watching the smoke curl up from the sage stick in her hand and fill the room with its spicy scent. She felt herself discon- necting from her body and tried to fight it. Her mind was already drifting to Dylan and she knew that in a moment she would be by his side. She couldn't let go.

She heard a roar in her mind, felt the tug of the cats

and her legs went weak. She put the sage on a plate on the bedside table and then lay down as her head began to spin. She wouldn't close her eyes. She had to stay at home.

The roar in her mind was louder now and she felt her feline form detach and start prowling around the room. She forced her eyes to stay open and saw the room from two perspectives, but her conscious mind was shutting down and she knew she couldn't stop it.

She felt Dylan's thoughts for a moment, knew he was thinking of her, and then mentally slammed the door shut between them.

She was outside on the pavement, the path cold and slick beneath the strength and sureness of her pads. She moved silently out of the front garden, enjoying the strength in her heavily muscled body. The owl shrieked in the tree behind her and she growled in response. She turned onto the road up to the zoo, focusing on the pull of the tigers and yowling, letting the air into her lungs. The damp, musky smell of the undergrowth mixed with the more distant scent of caged animals, straw and dung. She took a giant leap over the gate and bunched her muscles to take the impact of the landing. It took her moments to reach the enclosure. Inside the cage, she manifested fully, taking on her most solid form. She walked around the perimeter, yowling and growling a greeting, and then turned at the low rumble behind her. The male tiger stood there, crouched low, teeth bared. She dropped into a matching stance.

For a moment there was stand-off, and then the male loosened his body and walked towards her, rubbing his gigantic head against her side. She yowled in response, before setting off around the perimeter with him at her side. When everything was falling apart, there was always this.

35

MAX

Max let himself into the zoo. It was quiet apart from the night-time calls of the animals and the hooting of an owl. He walked across the grass, grateful to be alone. He hated how insecure he felt around Dylan, hated the way the memories rushed back every time he saw his smarmy face. The humiliation was too close to the surface. He needed his tigers. With them he felt strong and powerful. He had the most vicious creatures in the whole zoo under his control. The only power was in strength and he would never be weak again. He would never allow anyone to bully or hold power over him for as long as he lived. Not again.

He got out his phone and dialled Sophie's number. This would be his moment of glory. He walked around the outside of the cage, listening to the phone ring out. Clicking his fingers, he called to the cats, knowing they were always on the lookout for him. He knew they hated him. He kept them locked up when they wanted to be free. He confined them in their tiny sleeping quarters when they wanted to smell the damp, fresh air and stalk the cage for intruders. He came into their territory when they wanted him gone. But he was also their provider. He brought their food. He liked to imagine them facing a hungry future if they hurt him.

'Max? Is everything okay?' There was no curtness in Sophie's voice now. He smiled.

'It will be. I've just had an encounter with a tiger.'

She sighed. 'Oh God, what have you done this time?'

'Not that kind of encounter,' he said, pushing back his irritation. He would not let his anger get the better of him when there was so much at stake. 'This tiger was in Wildley Forest *Village*.'

Silence.

'Sorry? I must have misheard.'

'You didn't.' Max smiled. 'There is a huge white tiger loose in Wildley Forest Village and we need to catch it. If we act now, we could keep it. Think of the visitors a white tiger would ...' He froze. A movement on the other side of the cage had caught his eye. Two tigers were walking next to the fence on the opposite side of the enclosure. The male sent a familiar thrill of dread through him, spiking his adrenaline and waking up his body. It was the other cat who froze him in place. It was enormous. The thick, white pelt gleamed in the moonlight as it moved shoulder to shoulder with the male. It turned to Max, its turquoise eyes tracking him until the last moment. Max forced his breathing to steady. Shit. Had it followed him? Or had someone actually caught it that quickly? Only half an hour ago that tiger had been eyeballing him with teeth bared. How had it got here so fast? And how had it got into that cage?

'Loose in the village?' Sophie's voice was high-pitched now. 'Have you called someone?'

'I'm calling you.' His tiger walked past him, snarling as it met his gaze. Behind it, the huge white cat kept pace. 'But then I guess you already knew.'

'What do you mean? You're not making sense.'

'Ah, we're playing that game are we? You catch the tiger, release it straight into my enclosure without a word to me, and then claim *I'm* not making sense?'

A heavy blast of wind caught him off balance. He looked up to the sky. The clouds were thick and dark, and the heaviness in the air made him shiver. Max forced his breathing to steady, tracking the cats with his gaze. The male turned a corner, the white cat followed, and then shimmered out of existence.

'Shit.' Max's heart was hammering now. What *was* that? Had he imagined it?

'Max, are you okay?' Sophie sounded worried.

He jogged around the cage, looking for the tiger. It wasn't there.

'Max, talk to me. Are you okay? Are you drunk?' She was getting angry now.

'Maybe I am drunk,' he said, almost to himself. 'That would explain things.'

'Max, is there a tiger?'

He stopped running, doubled over and took a few deep breaths. When he straightened, he looked into the enclosure again. The male stood right in front of him, staring him down. But there was no white tiger.

'No,' he whispered. 'There is no tiger.'

'Well then for God's sake, get out of that zoo, go home and get to bed. Sleep off whatever weird cocktail you've been drinking and don't come in tomorrow unless you're fit for work.' She hung up.

'No, no, no, no, no!' Max shook his head over and over again. Was he losing it? No, Dylan had seen it too. It must have been there. What the hell was going on?

36

DYLAN

DYLAN FELT LIKE DEATH WHEN HE WALKED TO WORK THE next morning. He was still replaying his conversation with Tabitha over and over in his mind. Her house was shut up tight, the closed sign firmly in place and the curtains drawn. He lingered outside the gate wanting to speak to her, but what would he say? The owl began to shriek over and over again and he couldn't help feeling it was some kind of warning. Whether it was aimed at him or Tabitha he had no idea.

Walking away from her house felt like a betrayal, but there had been no welcome in those cold blue tiger eyes last night.

The zoo was eerily empty. Freezing mist muffled the sound so that Dylan felt completely alone. The Playbarn was deserted, manned only by the minimum number of staff, all of whom were nursing coffees, glum looks on their faces.

There was a crack of thunder. He got up and walked over to the window. The fog had cleared. Heavy clouds were forming, but the wind was carrying them fast. He saw a single group of visitors looking up at the sky and hurrying towards the Playbarn, bundling their kids inside. He welcomed them, fixed on their wristbands and sent them off to the play equipment while the parents bought drinks and cake. There was nobody outside now and a light drizzle was starting to fall. As he watched, a single, bundled figure came up the path from the entrance. The way she walked looked familiar. Dylan opened the door and slipped outside for a better view.

She was almost past the Playbarn when she turned.

'Tabitha,' he yelled. He started jogging, but she just sped up.

He stopped, a weight dropping in his stomach. What had he done?

She turned one more time. From closer he could see how pale she looked, could see the dark circles under her eyes. She looked haunted.

He watched her hurry towards the tiger enclosure, her thick coat clutched around her middle, heavy boots laced high over skinny jeans. He imagined her huddling inside the covered area with her sketchbook and wondered whether the tigers would come out to give her something to draw. Maybe she had ways to call to them? Maybe she would project her tiger form and they would come out to see her? Did it even work like that?

He couldn't see her at all now. He peered through the picture windows into the Playbarn. It was still quiet in there. He ducked over to the tigers, but there was no visible life in the cage. He could see Tabitha sitting on the hill, but she obviously didn't want to speak to him, so he walked around to the cats' sleeping quarters, hoping to catch a moment with Max. There was nobody around. He knocked on the door to Max's room.

Silence.

With a sigh, he walked back around the enclosure. Tabitha was still on the hill. She was sitting down now, her head bent in concentration. He wished he could project his awareness like she could, so he could watch over her while she drew.

Was it possible that she had been watching over him, rather than prying? If he had her abilities, he would have been at her side right now, he had no doubt about that.

He felt a drop of rain on his cheek, and moments later the deluge started. Tabitha gathered up her things and then ran for a shelter on the side of the hill.

Dylan ran for the Playbarn.

'Boss?' a voice called from the doorway. 'There's been an accident.'

Dylan sighed. Max and Tabitha would have to wait.

37

HE HAD WALKED AWAY FROM HER, AND NOW HE WAS THERE every time she turned around. Tabitha sat on a bench in the small hillside shelter by the tiger enclosure. The wooden sides did little to block out the chill wind, icy air or pounding rain. The damp was sinking into her bones and joints, clouding her mind. She wanted to travel, felt the pull of the tigers who were so close but out of sight. But she couldn't. There was no way to make sure she wouldn't end up with Dylan in the Playbarn, and she would not risk him looking at her like that again.

'Tabitha!'

The yell shocked her from her thoughts.

Max was breathing heavily as he pushed his dripping hood back. The run up the hill had tired him out. 'Why don't you come inside? Surely you'd rather draw in the warm rather than staying out here in this?' He spread his arms wide.

'Oh, you have no idea.' Tabitha closed her eyes for a moment, clutching her hands together so he wouldn't notice that they were shaking with cold. 'But I know how this story ends. If I come in, you will take that as an indication that I'm interested in something more, and I'm just not. I would love to be your friend, Max. Not many people understand my attachment to the tigers and we share that, in some way. But I'm not ever going to be more to you than that.'

Max licked his lips. 'Listen, I know I've been like that before. I understand why you're wary. But I won't do that anymore. If you come out of the cold I will stay out of the tiger enclosure and I'll leave you alone to draw. I promise I won't bother you.'

Tabitha looked at him. She wasn't sure why, but she had a hunch he was speaking the truth for once. Plus, she was starting to lose all feeling in her fingers. She nodded, stood up and gathered her things.

'Come on, let's run,' Max said, and dashed off down the hill.

The door to Max's room was standing open when Tabitha reached it and she ducked inside. Tabitha shuddered. The room had been grubby last time, but now it was filthy. Dirt smeared the walls. Flies swarmed around a cupboard in one corner and a large tub of red meat that sat on a metal table in the middle of the room.

Max gestured to the armchair. 'You sit down and draw. I'll be through there.'

He went into the ante room, and Tabitha settled into the armchair, brushing at the arms. It was dirtier than last time, but at least she was warm.

She took out her drawing book and a pencil, and then looked at the tigers and started sketching. The female came to the bars and yowled, tilting her head as she watched

Tabitha. 'Do you remember me?' Tabitha whispered. 'Do you remember the friend who runs with you in your cage?'

She started drawing, taking down the lines of the cat's face and the curve of its shoulder. Humming, she allowed herself to sink into the repetition and focus.

She was outside. The storm had progressed from a light rain into a sheeting downpour. Max prowled, a gun held in front of him. She had no idea whether it held darts or bullets, but his face was deathly pale, his eyes flashing with fire. 'Where are you?' he yelled, looking around in every direction. 'I know it's me you want, so come out and get me.' She moved closer, trying to understand what he meant, what he was afraid of. She spun around at the roar that came from behind her and saw an enormous white tiger running towards her, felt the recognition in its gaze. She knew that tiger was expecting her, that it remembered standing where she did now, watching what was to come. They roared in unison, and Max pointed his gun at the white tiger. 'No!' she screamed as the bang went off—

The sound jerked her out of the storm and over to the play barn. Dylan was standing outside the door where she had seen him last. She had no idea whether she was back in the present or still in the premonition but, either way, she could not be near Dylan. She turned and walked away.

Tabitha jerked awake. The tigers on the page had been joined by another, bigger than the two in front of her. The huge, white beast snarled, teeth bared as it stared out of the page.

'Was it in here?' Max's voice was sharp from behind her. 'I've been looking for it all day but there's been no sign. I saw it, right in there with my tigers last night. I saw it with my own eyes before it faded away. I am not going crazy.'

'A white tiger?' Tabitha said, trying to sound surprised. 'Has the zoo got a new cat?'

Max narrowed his eyes at her. 'That's what I'd like to know, but I can't get any straight answers. You've drawn a very accurate portrayal for someone who knows nothing about it.'

Tabitha sighed. 'I draw tigers for a living, Max. I'd be worried if it wasn't accurate. For a while I used to visit a zoo with a white tiger, and I remember her down to the tiniest detail.'

Max nodded, but he didn't look convinced. 'If you do see a white cat in there, please will you tell me? Something is going on and I don't understand it. I saw it outside your front door, and then in the enclosure. Dylan saw it too. I'm not making this up.'

Tabitha snapped her book shut. 'I'll tell you if I see anything you should know about.

Max grinned. 'Do you want to feed them?'

'Can I?'

He handed her a long pair of filthy metal pincers with a chunk of meat at one end. 'Hold it through the bars.'

Tabitha took the tongs. The huge, male tiger rumbled as she walked towards the cage, smiling and humming. 'Here you are, my beautiful,' she murmured as she poked the meat through the thick metal bars. 'Eat up.'

The tiger watched her for a moment, and then took the meat from the pincers. A thrill shot through Tabitha. 'He took it!' She went back to the bucket and looked at Max. 'Can I do another?'

He grinned and nodded. 'Amazing, right?'

She smiled and grabbed another chunk of meat.

The smaller tiger had come to the bars now, but the male wasn't keen to give up the space and turned to snarl at her. She grunted and swiped at the larger cat with her paw.

The male roared. The hair on the back of Tabitha's neck rose as the sound echoed in the enclosed space. The smaller cat retreated, padding over to the back of the cage, growling as it paced.

'Are they usually like this?' Tabitha whispered.

'They don't like being shut up in here together. Don't worry about it. They're tigers. They're aggressive. They fight.' He shrugged his shoulders.

'Max?' A voice called from outside.

'Damn. That's my boss. Stay here. I'll head her off. Don't come out, whatever happens. I'm not supposed to bring guests in here.' He slipped out through the door, barely opening it.

Tabitha turned back to the tigers. The male yowled, and then lay down, rubbing its ears against the bars. The female moved forwards from behind and met no opposition. 'Well, well. Are you happier without Max here?' Tabitha gripped another piece of meat with the pincers. She poked it through the bars and the second tiger took it, making appreciative rumbles. 'It's not very nice in here is it. That must drive you wild.' She poked another piece of meat through the bars. 'I think there might actually be something rotting in here.' She put the pincers down and opened the cupboard surrounded by flies. The rancid stench of rotten meat and the powdery smell of mould caught her in the face. Right at the back, in the corner, was a shifting black cloud. Tabitha shuddered. She found a second pair of pincers, filthier than the first, and prodded it. A swarm of flies flew up and out. Backing away, she shielded her face and then peered back just in time to see the slimy mass before it was covered again. There were more dead flies lying on the floor of the cupboard around it, alongside filthy metal utensils and a mouldy sandwich. Tabitha clapped her hand over her nose and mouth, bile rising in her throat.

Fighting the urge to heave, she took out her phone and snapped some pictures, before slamming the door shut. She took more shots of the blood and dirt on the wall.

'No wonder it stinks in here.'

The door to the room swung open wide. She spun around, slipping her phone back into her pocket.

'Panic averted.' Max leered, puffing up his chest. 'She's gone.'

'They're a lot more relaxed,' Tabitha said. But when she turned around, the tigers were face to face, snarling, their tails swishing.

'Relaxed, eh? I hate to think what you'd classify as stressed!' Max laughed. 'Don't worry. Skirmishes and stand-offs are normal. Stand back, I'll deal with this.' Max strode into the corner of the room and gripped a long, thick wooden pole. He approached the cage, knees bent, a snarl on his face. The cats paid no attention.

Poking the stick through the bars he shoved the larger cat hard in the ribs. The tiger snarled, falling away from Max and then dropping low and stalking back towards the bars.

'Stop!' Tabitha grabbed for the pole. 'You're hurting him.'

'He's a big boy, he can take it.' Max laughed.

'I'd like to go now,' Tabitha said, walking towards the door.

'But you just got here,' Max said.

She put her hand on the doorknob.

'Don't leave.' Max reached across, blocking the exit.

Tabitha felt a rush of anger. A tiger growled, baring its

teeth. 'Are you threatening me, Max?' she asked, her voice low. 'That would be a bad idea.' She stared at him, focusing her anger in his direction. She drew deep within, connecting to her feline self. Her energy pulsed and she felt a rush of strength. She heard the echo of a growl and didn't know whether she had made the sound herself, or whether it was the cats in the cage behind her.

She saw the flaring energy of Max's adrenaline as he stared her down, and saw the moment he realised she was not going to be intimidated.

He withdrew his arm and stepped backwards. 'I was only joking. I'm sorry you took my silliness as anything else. I'm very respectful of women.'

'Of course you are.' Tabitha tried not to roll her eyes. She had never met anyone less respectful than Max.

'Will you be careful?' Max frowned. 'There's something up with the weather right now and there's a storm on the way. The cats are behaving erratically too.'

Tabitha nodded. 'I'll be careful. Please let me out.'

Max stepped back and she slipped out of the room before he could say more. Pulling her scarf up over her head she hunched her shoulders and bent into the cold wind. There was a strange scent on the air, but she couldn't quite place it. Hurrying past the Playbarn, she refused to turn, but felt Dylan's gaze on her at every step. The white tiger fought to get out, but she kept her caged, hoping that the message she was ignoring wasn't going to bring disaster.

38

DYLAN WATCHED TABITHA GO. SHE STARED AHEAD, refusing to look at the Playbarn. His chest felt tight as her back retreated into the returning mist. How did he end up here? For a moment, he had seen the potential for a different future. Had he really blown it in one, stupid moment?

He swallowed past the lump in his throat. Her face stared back at him in his mind. He wanted to run after her, but last time that hadn't paid off. Besides, there were hours left to get through before home time.

The day dragged, but eventually the light failed. There was nobody in the Playbarn now. Dylan checked his watch. He walked around, picking up old, used cups, tiny socks and the odd jacket. He added the clothes to the lost property box behind the desk and put the cups in the bin. The cleaners would be in later, so that would do for now. He checked his watch again. One minute to go. He went to the coat hooks and pulled on his jacket, standing the collar up and zipping it all the way. He looked around. 'Are you guys ready to go?'

There were only two members of staff left and they filed past him, coats and hats already in place. He locked the door behind him, pulled his phone out of his pocket and dialled.

'Is everything alright?' his mum asked, without saying hello.

'I've messed up. Are you home?'

Twenty minutes later, he was at his mum's kitchen table nursing a hot cup of tea.

'So what happened?' Rachel wheeled up to the table, her own cup in one hand. 'I thought things were going well with Tabitha?'

'I blew it. She told me something intimate and I freaked out. I walked out and left her alone. She hasn't spoken to me since. She's barely looked at me.'

'What did she tell you? No, I'm sorry. Pretend I didn't ask that. Whatever she told you, is it bad enough to make you want to walk away?'

'Not at all.' Dylan dropped his head into his hands. 'It freaked me out a bit, but I get it now.'

'Have you told her?'

'She hasn't given me a chance.'

'Of course she hasn't.' Rachel leaned forwards. 'You rejected her and that hurts. Tabitha is different to most people. She's used to being treated with suspicion. She expects to be shown the door and you obliged. She will avoid you now to escape being hurt again. She's probably wondering why she relaxed her guard and let you in.'

'How do you know all of this?' Dylan shook his head.

'Some of it she told me. Some of it is just human

nature. You've got to win her trust again. Show her how you really feel.'

'I don't know how.'

'Of course you do. You've had plenty of girlfriends before.'

'None of them were Tabitha. None of them meant anything compared to her.'

Rachel smiled. 'Tell her that. Show her you're worth taking a risk for.'

Dylan looked at his mum for a few moments, and then grinned. 'You're a genius. I know exactly what to do. Thank you, Mum.'

Dylan hummed as he walked back to the old flat, a tune starting to build in his mind. He took the stairs up to the front door two at a time and threw it open.

39

DYLAN

THE FLAT WAS SILENT. DYLAN WASN'T SURE WHETHER HE was relieved or disappointed that he would have to wait to tell the guys he was moving out. He wondered what they were doing. There had been a time when he would have known, when he would have been going to join them the moment he got back from work. It had been a long time since they had been that close, but Dylan still felt sad to be letting it go.

He thought back to what Tabitha had said. They were a part of who he was. Was that still true? He had spent years convincing himself that he had moved beyond them. He had stopped identifying with anything in this village except Tabitha, the tigers and his mum. But where did he exist now in this strange world he was unearthing?

He went to his bedroom, packed his guitar and manuscript books and put together an overnight bag, some bedsheets and a towel. The flat was furnished and the kitchen was fully stocked so that would do for now. The place was silent. He pulled his case out of his room, the

squeaking of the wheels eating into the last bit of equilib-
rium he had. He got out through the front door, carried the
case down the stairs and then went out into the cold. It was
pouring. He put his guitar down, pulled up his collar and
put his head down into the rain. There was nothing he
could do right now. He had patched things up with Linden
and GJ, but he had no idea whether that would last. Right
now, he would get home and begin again.

His hands were so cold he had to fumble to get the key
into the lock, but inside the flat was toasty warm. Valerie
must have left the heating on for him when she locked up.
He kicked his shoes off and hung his soaking wet coat up on
the hook in the hall. Not wanting to start out with a dirty
floor, he picked up the case and carried it through to the
bedroom. The bed wasn't made up, but there was a duvet
and a number of pillows. He went over to the window and
looked out into the rain-drenched darkness. The light
glinted on the drops of water that littered the outside of the
window. Over the road, Tabitha's house was all shut up
tight, only slivers of light glinting between the pulled
curtains. He heard the screech of the barn owl, and
wondered, not for the first time, whether the bird had some
strange way of communicating with Tabitha.

He went through to the bathroom and peeled off his
clothes before getting into the shower. The water was piping
hot and the pounding spray began to beat some feeling
back into his freezing cold muscles. He wasn't sure how
much of the tension was the cold, and how much was the
fear that flooded his body. He had just changed everything.
He had walked away from his friends and moved to a job he
knew virtually nothing about. The steps that had seemed
exciting before felt terrifying alone in a new flat at night. He

wished he hadn't offended Tabitha. He wished she had given him the chance to explain, but now all he was left with was his fear, and the opportunity to put things right.

He towelled off and then pulled on a pair of joggers, before getting out his guitar and sitting on the bed.

The melody was already forming in his mind and he picked out the chords on the guitar while he began to hum. The first lines came fast and he grabbed the manuscript paper, scribbling them down in pencil before he lost them. The words weren't any harder. The need to express himself was so raw, so urgent, that words tumbled from him and onto the page as he picked at the strings and sang line after line.

An hour later, the song was burned into his heart from the pain that poured through him and into the words. He sang it one more time, hoping to make it a little better, but there wasn't even one note he wanted to change.

The rain had stopped now and a full moon was peeking through the clouds. He went into the bedroom and opened the wardrobe. He hadn't brought many clothes, but there was a pair of low-slung jeans and a tank top that were presentable. He pulled them on, leaving his arms bare in spite of the cold. If Tabitha deigned to come to the window, he wanted her to see the tiger move across his arm, to remember that their connection was deeper than either of them had yet understood. He tuned his guitar again, shoved the flat keys in his pocket and headed out into the moonlit street.

There was still a crack of light between Tabitha's curtains. He went through her gate, waving a hand at the owl, which shrieked in welcome, or warning. 'Tabitha,' he called out, hoping she would come to the window. In response, he heard a growl. The white tiger stepped out from between the trees to his right.

He gasped, the thrill of danger crackling like lightening over his skin. All sense of the tiger as an ally was gone. Instead, the rumbling growl was ominous. She prowled closer, her belly slung close to the ground, her lips peeled back from enormous canines.

Forcing the fear back, Dylan began to play, his fingers picking out the chords. The tiger stilled and stopped snarling, her face relaxing into the beauty he remembered.

Dylan's voice cracked, but he began to sing, pouring his emotion into the music rather than letting himself break. He opened his heart wide, allowing everything he had held back to flood from him and surround the tiger.

> *Stripes in the Moonlight*
> *Silent paws on glassy ground*
> *Eyes flash in the darkness*
> *Eyes flash and my heart drowns.*
>
> *You shatter my defences*
> *You fill my heart with fire*
> *With you I am creation*
> *With you I find my wild.*
>
> *But when the shadow fades,*
> *My world is small and dark*
> *I can't find my way forward*
> *I can't light my inner spark*
>
> *Wild Shadow you consume me*
> *With your flames that burn so bright.*

Come back to me my tiger
Come back to me my light.

Wild Shadow

He swallowed. The turquoise blue eyes of the tiger held him captive, their intense human familiarity filling him with a grief that threatened to overwhelm him.

As the harmonics from the last chord faded, Dylan lifted the guitar slowly to avoid spooking the cat and unhooked the strap from around his shoulders. He put it on the grass and then walked closer. He held his hands open in front of him as he moved smoothly, not breaking eye contact until he was just inches away. She tilted her head, watching him, but still poised to pounce or flee. Slowly, he reached out one hand and held it there, open.

The tiger looked at him, perfectly still. Then it moved forwards, sniffed his hand and faded into blackness.

Dylan let out a choked sob. He staggered backwards and grabbed his guitar from the grass, clutching it to his chest. There was no sign of the cat now, no movement in the bushes, no growling. He had poured his heart out to her, and she had walked away.

The front door clicked. Tabitha stood there in joggers and a hoodie. Her eyes were bloodshot, her hair was pulled back into a ponytail and her feet were cosied up in thick fluffy socks. He had never seen her look so normal, or so vulnerable.

She leaned on the door frame and said nothing.

'I'm so sorry, Tabitha.' Dylan walked towards her as though approaching the tiger she had been a moment before. 'Please forgive me. I miss you. I miss your tiger.'

She shook her head. 'I understand you don't want to be watched. I get it. I have never chosen to watch you but, I travel when I draw or paint. It's part of my process and inspiration. Right now I'm trying so hard to stay under conscious control that I can't create. I have commissions and looming deadlines. I can't afford to have you in my head, Dylan. I can't afford to have you coming to my door and singing songs, however beautiful they might be. I have to forget you. I'm sorry.' She stepped back and shut the door, leaving him outside, alone.

Dylan stared, stunned. 'Tabitha,' he shouted, rushing up to the door, too late, and banging on it. 'Please, hear me out.'

Her voice travelled through the wood and stone. 'I am respecting your boundaries, Dylan. Please do the same for me. I am trying very hard not to travel to you as a tiger but, to do that, I need you out of my head and out of my life.'

There was no sound of doors banging, no shouting, nothing. But Dylan felt a wall come down between them more resolute than anything he had ever experienced. It stole the breath from his lungs, left him gasping on the path outside a frosty front door.

His guitar was icy to touch, but his insides were so frozen he couldn't find the energy to care. Tabitha was gone.

40

DYLAN SET UP IN THE SOUND STUDIO, ADJUSTING THE drums, and tuning his guitar. He turned it over in his hands, inspecting it for any signs of stress after its stint in the cold the night before. It was as perfect as ever.

For some reason, the studio didn't seem as bad the second time around. Dylan wasn't sure whether that was because he'd got used to the dinginess, or because he didn't have the energy to care.

The strange wall dividing him from Tabitha had zapped him of energy for anything other than his music. He went to work, got on with his routine, but he was only half there. He wondered if this was how Tabitha felt when she travelled. It was only music that breathed life back into his frozen chest. When he sang and played, he poured all the pain and loss into sound and for a moment there was light.

The technician was looking down, doing something on the desk in front of him.

Dylan took a deep breath. He had been in recording

studios before, but this time was different. He wasn't just creating something to sell, he was recording his soul.

'Ready?' he said.

The man looked up and raised a hand in acknowledgement.

'I'll start with the rhythm track,' Dylan called into the microphone. The technician nodded and flicked some switches.

He sat down at the drum kit and allowed himself to fall into the music, feeling the pulse flow from his fingers, through his sticks and into the drums. This was his place, his home. This was how he grounded into the earth and made life real. No matter how much he loved playing his guitar and singing, the drums were the beating pulse of his soul and would always call him back no matter how far he strayed.

He swapped his drumsticks for a set of brushes. The sound was soft, gentle and it lulled him as he heard the song in his head, opening him up to the emotions that dripped off every word. He felt the tug of the song building towards that final line, the moment he gave voice to the storm that was building inside him. As the last beats faded, he put the brushes down and stood up, turning his back to the technician and trying to block out the dingy room as he gave himself a moment to settle.

Turning around, he walked over to the microphone, reduced the height and sat on a chair in front of it, pointing it directly at his acoustic guitar. 'I'll record the guitar now, mate,' he said. The man nodded and flicked some switches.

Dylan put the headphones back on, and as the drumbeat started he began to pick out the chords, losing himself in the flowing current of notes that surged around him, carrying him forwards on the wash of his own outpouring of grief.

He imagined the man in the recording booth to be Tabitha. He pictured her face staring at him through the window, absorbing every emotion he poured from his soul. He imagined her understanding the message he sent through every note he played, reading the vibration of his grief in the movement of the strings. He closed his eyes and her image became clearer until he was sure she would be there when he opened them. Her presence was so strong that he almost felt the soft brush of fur against his leg. He wanted to open his eyes, but couldn't bear to risk losing the illusion so he kept them tightly closed until the last note had faded away.

Dylan opened his eyes. There was no tiger. The man in the booth looked up for a moment, and then bent his head over his work. The room was as dirty and dingy as it had always been and the smell of mould was just as bad.

Dylan sighed. This place was soulless and the music was breaking his heart wide open. The combination of emptiness and overwhelm was so acute he wanted to run.

'I'm ready for the last track. Is everything okay at your end?' he said into the microphone.

The man looked up and raised a hand. 'All good. Don't worry about anything at this end.'

Dylan put down the guitar. Adrenaline raced through his system as he raised the microphone and stood in front of it. He closed his eyes and pictured everything he wanted to leave behind. He saw it drifting away and focused on an image of Tabitha walking towards him. He remembered the last time he'd been here, the tiger in the room with him, his muse. This time the room was vast in its emptiness. He tried to connect with the tiger, to summon it, but he met a blank emptiness that left him hollow.

As the music started again, Dylan began to sing. With every note, he pictured Tabitha coming towards him. He sent out his intention, his hopes, his call for a better future. He sang with his heart and with his soul, allowing the vibrations to combine into something new. The music swirled around him, expanding his chest, his body, setting his nerves tingling.

He opened his eyes. There was still no tiger. A heaviness descended in his chest, but he pushed it back. He would play her the song before he gave up hope.

The man in the booth was staring at him, lips parted. He nodded.

Dylan nodded back. Something had happened while he sang. As he recognised the grudging respect in the man's eyes, he finally realised how little it meant. There was only one person who mattered now.

He recorded the rest of the songs, packed up his instruments and headed through the door to the booth. 'When can I get the final mix?'

'I can have it ready for you tomorrow.'

Tomorrow. That gave him one day to get ready before life began again.

41

DYLAN

THE PUB WAS LOCKED, BUT DYLAN BANGED ON THE DOOR. He waited, and then banged again.

'Alright, alright, keep your hair on,' a voice shouted from the other side of the wooden door. 'Give me a chance to find my keys.'

The door opened. 'Dylan!' Bob, the landlord, frowned and rubbed his forehead. 'What's so important you couldn't wait until opening?'

'Sorry, Bob. I wondered if you had any spots for a gig, soon?'

'You're in tonight, aren't you? I have you boys down for eight o'clock.'

Dylan took a deep breath. 'I'm looking for a solo gig.'

'Solo?' Bob frowned and tilted his head to one side. 'On the drums?'

Dylan flushed. 'No, I also play the guitar and sing my own songs.'

'Do you now?' Bob's eyebrows shot up. 'Well … you'd

better come on in. I was just making a cuppa. Would you like anything?'

The pub stank of stale beer. The wooden floor was sticky and Dylan wrinkled his nose as he followed Bob into his living quarters.

'So you've finally left the band? I wondered when that would happen.'

'You did?'

Bob tilted his head. 'It seems that everyone but you knows how good you are. Take a seat.' He got an extra teacup from a glass-fronted cabinet. The cups were bone china with wavy edges. They had gold rims and pink roses painted around the outside. He poured from a matching teapot and added milk from the jug.

The scene was so at odds with the musty, out-of-hours pub that Dylan had to suppress a laugh.

Bob grinned. 'Same rules as normal. You start at 8 p.m. Drinks are included as long as you're playing, but afterwards you're a paying customer just like everyone else.'

Dylan let out a sigh of relief. 'Great. When?'

'Tomorrow.'

Adrenaline shot through him. 'Tomorrow? That's too soon. Do you have anything in a week or two?'

'It's tomorrow or wait seven months. We're booked.'

Dylan took a deep breath and then nodded.

Bob held out his hand.

Dylan took it. Bob's handshake was weaker than normal. His bones felt frail under the skin. He looked at the man, eyes narrowed. He had known Bob his whole life. He had always been a fixture behind this bar and it had never occurred to Dylan that he might be getting old. But looking with detached eyes he realised Bob's grey hair was thinning.

His skin was more wrinkled and slightly translucent. Bob had become old while Dylan had rushed around pretending to be a small-time star. Time was passing and he had only just realised it was possible to miss his chance.

Dylan downed the cup of tea. 'Thanks, Bob. I'll see you tonight.'

The older man nodded. 'I'll see you later. Now, I have to start getting the bar ready. It takes me longer than it used to. Not really an old man's job, lugging kegs of beer around.'

'Is there anything you'd like me to carry for you?' Dylan asked, and saw the relief on Bob's face.

'You're a good boy, you know that?' he said, getting up and opening the door to the cellar. 'It's down here.'

An hour later Dylan was back at his old flat. He held up his fist in front of the door, paused, and then knocked.

The door swung open. GJ grinned, 'Dylan, you're here!' He stepped back to allow Dylan through and then slouched into an old, faded armchair. 'Why did you knock?'

Dylan smiled sheepishly as he sat on the edge of the sofa. 'I have some news. I've found a flat. It's on the ground floor and Mum will be able to visit me there. I'm sorry it's so sudden.'

GJ's eyebrows shot up. 'You're moving out? Wow, well I guess it was bound to happen sooner or later.'

Relief flooded Dylan. 'I guess so. You're not annoyed?'

GJ sighed. 'You know how I feel, Dylan. You should chase your dreams, but don't forget us. We love you, man, we want you in our lives. You're part of the gang, and as much as we have to grow up, we don't want to lose *this*.'

'Fair play.' Dylan nodded. 'So, there's a gig tonight?'

'You say that as though you're not coming.' GJ frowned.

'I wasn't sure whether you'd still want me to.'

'You have to come.' GJ's eyes were pleading. 'Linden thinks he's all that, but he's all pretty face and voice. Neither of us have the musical knowhow to make this work without you.'

'Of course you do,' Dylan said. 'You just need to have faith in yourselves. You can't just give up because I'm leaving.'

GJ shrugged and opened another bottle of beer. 'Whatever happens further down the road, you're here now and we have tonight. Let's make this our last blow-out gig.'

Dylan looked at him for a moment. GJ was pale. There were new creases on his forehead and at the corners of his mouth. This was the guy who had told Dylan to go for his dreams, who had said he would always have his back. He wasn't asking for much.

'In that case, of course I'll be there. But, listen. There's something you need to know.' Dylan gripped his bottle, peeling off the label, not meeting GJ's eyes. 'I'm doing another gig, tomorrow night. A solo gig.'

'Yeah? That's great news!' GJ's face lit up. 'Where do I get a ticket?'

'It's at the pub. Eight o'clock. Just turn up. It's free, but it would be great to know there's a friendly face in the audience.'

GJ held out a hand. 'Just don't forget us when you're famous, okay?'

Dylan grasped it and let out a sigh of relief. 'Never. We'll always be friends.'

42

DYLAN

'WOULD YOU LIKE ONE MORE?' LINDEN YELLED TO THE SEA of people who filled the room in front of the stage.

The crowd whooped and screamed.

Dylan swallowed. This had been his life. He couldn't believe he was walking away.

'Right you are,' Linden said with a grin. 'But before we sing this final time, I have news. This is Instantaneous Rock's last gig.'

The room went silent.

'We have loved singing and playing for you, but it's time for new adventures.'

'Boo,' someone called from the audience.

'Ah, now there's no need for that, because we have something special for you. Our fabulous drummer, Dylan McKenzie, has a solo gig here tomorrow night. Dylan is the power behind our band, making us all look good. And he's ready to show you just how talented he is. I will be here cheering him on, and I hope you'll join me.'

There was silence, and then a single cheer. Finally, the

room erupted.

Dylan let out a breath he hadn't realised he was holding. He stood up and held his drumsticks high. The volume increased.

'Let's do it,' Dylan said, grinning widely. 'If this is our last song, let's make it count.' He sat down and started a drum roll.

There was a whoop from somewhere near the front, and then the crowd quietened down.

Dylan fell into a steady heartbeat that reverberated through his body and down through his feet into the floor. He closed his eyes, feeling his way through the song on the vibrations of Linden's voice, the bass and GJ's guitar riffs. He chest tightened as sadness welled through him. This was a lot to leave behind.

His eyes were wet as he opened them and he blinked to clear his vision. Linden was lost in the song, but GJ was watching him, a sad smile on his face. Dylan held his gaze as he played the final chorus of the song.

As the sound faded, Dylan could hear his heart pounding in his chest. He swallowed the lump in his throat, and then stood up and stepped round the drum kit to the front of the stage. The crowd watched in silence as he reached for Linden and GJ's hands, and then raised his arms into the air.

The crowd erupted in screams and cheers.

They stood there, still and silent, feeling the waves of emotion that poured over them from the audience. This hadn't just been theirs. They were a part of this village, a part of everybody's lives and they would never lose the magic they had created.

Linden looked over at Dylan and nodded, and then he

dropped Dylan's hand and pulled him into a rough hug. 'This isn't the end for you. It's only the beginning and we will be there with you every step of the way.'

GJ joined them and hugged them both.

The crowd cheered even louder.

DYLAN DIDN'T HAVE TO BUY A SINGLE DRINK. PEOPLE WERE queueing up to speak to the band and push pints into their hands. He was overwhelmed by the number of people who had told him what the band had meant to them and wished him luck with his new venture. The pub was beginning to clear now. Rain was pounding down on the skylight above his head, pushing the regulars towards home.

'You won't really stop, will you?' Dylan said to Linden, downing the dregs of his pint.

Linden shrugged. 'We don't have a band without you. I meant what I said. You were always the powerhouse. We've gone farther than I ever thought we could, but I think this is the end for us.

'Linden, I'm not sabotaging your chances. These people have followed us for ages. I'm sure they can handle enjoying more than one band.'

'Huh,' He knocked back a shot of amber coloured liquid. 'I appreciate your faith in us, but I know when to stop.'

'I'm still your friend, Linden. If I'm here, I'm happy to help.'

Linden took a deep breath and sighed. 'Thanks, man. Look, I'm sorry if I've upset Tabitha. You can tell her I'll back off.'

Dylan ordered two bottles of beer and pushed one

towards Linden. His friend nodded and took a gulp.

'I'd love you guys to come and visit the new flat. Would you do that? Have we patched things up that much?'

Linden grinned. 'Of course we have. Is now a good time? GJ are you coming to visit Dylan's new pad?'

'You go,' GJ said. 'I've got a headache. I'll drop by tomorrow.'

Dylan pulled on his coat then put a hand on GJ's arm. 'Are you okay?' he said, too quietly for Linden to hear. 'It's not like you to duck out like this. Is your headache really that bad?'

GJ smiled. 'You guys have stuff to sort out and Linden will only open up one on one. Take the moment. Remember what good friends you are. I'll be at your flat tomorrow and we can have a proper knees-up then. In the meantime, I'm going to walk your mum home.'

GJ and Rachel went with them as far as the old flat. Dylan leaned against the outside wall of the building while Linden dropped his bass inside.

He came out clutching a pack of beer. 'Lead the way.'

Dylan couldn't help glancing over to Tabitha's house as they came up to the flats. Her curtains were drawn, but light shone through the cracks. An owl shrieked.

Dylan's flat was dark.

'Do you always keep it this warm?' Linden said, flicking on a light switch. 'I had no idea you felt the cold so much. The old place must have felt freezing.'

'Nah, I've left the heating on by mistake. Would you like a glass for that?' Dylan nodded at the cans of beer in Linden's hand.

'Thanks.' Linden snapped off two of the cans and handed them to Dylan.

Dylan took them and went through to the kitchen, leaving Linden to poke around.

'This is nice,' he said peering into Dylan's bedroom.

'Thanks.' Dylan grinned. He hadn't expected Linden's opinion to matter. He had convinced himself he was immune to worrying about what the guys thought. Tabitha's words flitted through his mind. *They are a part of you.* She had been right. She had known he needed his friends even when he hadn't. 'You know, Tabitha was never the issue. We were.'

'Is this going to get heavy?' Linden raised one eyebrow.

'You know, it is.' Dylan waved him through to the living room and sat down on the sofa, propping his feet up on the footstool. 'I'm fed up of all this drinking buddy crap. Either we're proper friends, or we're just people who say hello when we pass. We've known each other too long for this rubbish.'

Linden sighed. 'Okay, I'll bite. How were we the problem?'

'We've spent so many years trying not to grow up, like Peter bloody Pan. But it doesn't work. That shit gets boring. We can't make time stand still and, quite frankly, I don't want to. I want a career and a relationship. I can't be everyone else's magic ingredient for youth.'

'Here's to you having a future.' Linden nodded and reached out to clink his beer bottle against Dylan's. He got up and walked over to the window. 'That's her house isn't it?'

Dylan sighed. 'Yeah, that's the one, but she's cut me off. I have to look at her house every day knowing I'm not welcome. I guess you got what you wanted.'

Linden frowned, but said nothing.

43

TABITHA SCOWLED AT THE WINDOW IN THE SHOP. FROM where she worked, she had a constant view of Dylan's flat. Right now she could see him wandering around his living room, shirtless, a guitar strung over his chest.

The commission sat on her easel virtually untouched. She was desperate to paint. The lack of an outlet was leaving her edgy and unfulfilled, but the distance from Dylan only made her more obsessed. At night her dreams were on a loop. Dylan and Max fighting. A storm. A tiger climbing up a fallen tree trunk. A tiger creeping up, silently, behind Dylan. She shuddered. She had no idea whether these dreams were prophetic, or the product of an under-used imagination, but she wished they would stop. Dylan turned, walked to the window and stared at her. She felt his gaze as though the road, the walls and the people between them weren't there. Her hand started moving automatically over the paper in front of her. The barriers she had put up disintegrated just a little.

The door banged open, the bells clattering against the

glass in the strong wind. Linden stood in the doorway, his gaze darting around the room. He licked his lips, shoved his shoulders back and ran a hand through his hair.

'Do you ever enter a room quietly?' Tabitha snapped. 'There's glass in that door, and it's original. If you keep slamming it like that it's going to shatter.'

'I'm— Aghhh!' Linden yelled as a barn owl flew over his head and into the room with a screech. Moments later it was followed by another one.

Tabitha stood, transfixed, staring at the two birds that had settled onto her windowsill. 'Shhh, don't frighten them.'

'Frighten *them*? What the hell are they doing in here?'

'Shh, I have no idea. They've never come in before. Maybe they're getting out of the storm. Whatever, just be quiet. Don't scare them away.' Reaching for her sketchbook and a pencil, she started drawing them, taking down the lines she had never seen so closely before.

'It is getting filthy out there,' Linden said, shutting the door carefully behind him. 'Have you seen the storm warnings? They're saying something big is on the way.'

'I have.' Tabitha looked up from her sketch pad and frowned at the window.

'Watch out for falling branches and that kind of thing. You should be careful here on your own. Remember you have Dylan over the road now if you ever have any trouble.'

Tabitha waved a hand dismissively, not looking up from her sketch. 'I don't want to bother Dylan. He moved there to get some space, not to be harassed by a needy neighbour.'

'Is that how you see yourself? A needy neighbour?' Linden tilted his head, smiling, a furrow between his eyebrows. 'I can't say I'm seeing that woman anywhere nearby. I think Dylan would be delighted if you harassed him a bit, actually.'

'Last time we spoke you warned me off.'

'Yeah, well, sometimes I'm really wise, other times I talk a load of rubbish. Your job is to work out which is which.'

Tabitha laughed in spite of herself. 'Anyway, it doesn't matter. Dylan has already told me he wants space.'

Linden frowned. 'I thought he serenaded you with a specially written song? That doesn't sound like a request for space to me.'

'Oh, that didn't mean anything.'

'Seriously? You always struck me as a pretty intelligent woman. Now, I've gotta be honest, I'm starting to wonder. But I can tell you for sure that Dylan does not want space, at least not from you. He'd seriously like some space from me, but he's not going to get that. You, he wants to have around.'

Tabitha stared at Linden. He seemed serious, but how could this be the same guy she had met before? How could he be warning her off one moment, and all but begging her to date his friend the next? Was this the next stage in his attempt to humiliate her and drive her away?

Linden was looking around now, staring intently at her paintings. She was pretty sure he was trying to give her time to think, but she wasn't sure why. If he left, she'd have all the time in the world.

'I'll take one of these,' he said, pulling a greetings card of a barn owl out of the display. He nodded towards the bird. 'This will be a nice reminder to watch my tongue.' Linden put two pounds on the counter and tucked the barn owl card into his inside pocket. 'Right you are.' He nodded again and then turned his back and walked to the door. Just as he stepped through, the owls swooped silently through the shop and out over his head. He yelled and the door banged shut behind him. He turned to look at Tabitha through the window, his face burning.

She walked over to the window and pulled back the net curtains. The owls were settling into their usual nesting spot, fluffing up their feathers and screeching. It was getting dark now and the wind was showing no sign of abating. The image of the men fighting flickered involuntarily through her mind. She shivered.

A leaflet fluttered off the table. Tabitha frowned. She couldn't feel a draft. She picked up the piece of paper and turned it over. It was dark blue and there was a picture of Dylan playing the guitar in the middle. She felt breathless as she gripped the small piece of paper too tightly. It had not been there before, so Linden must have left it. Dylan was playing at the pub tonight, on his own, and Linden had just invited her.

44

DYLAN HAD NEVER BEEN SO NERVOUS. HE WASN'T SURE whether he was more worried about Tabitha turning up or not turning up, about people hating his music, booing him for leaving Instantaneous Rock, or not coming at all. All he knew was that his stomach was a mass of squirming worms and he felt sick. He closed his eyes, focusing on the sound of the guitar as he plucked the strings, turning the pegs until the notes sang. He missed his drumsticks. He loved the guitar, but he loved his drums even more, and right now he felt naked without them hiding him from view.

The door banged open. Linden. Dylan grinned in relief. At least there would be one friendly face in the audience. He hadn't realised how much the argument with Linden had been dragging him down until things were fixed. Linden winked, and then went to the bar. He raised his eyebrows and tapped his watch. Time was ticking by and the audience was becoming restless. He was completely in tune, he had warmed up his voice, but he'd never begun a gig before and had no idea of where to start. He held

Linden's gaze until the other man nodded, walked through the increasingly packed room and vaulted up onto the low stage.

'Welcome Wildley Forest!' Linden shouted over the noise and the room stilled. 'This is a very special gig for me, because for once I get to sit back, have a drink and enjoy the show. Dylan is an incredible musician. He was the power behind Instantaneous Rock and I'm so excited to hear what he has for us. Ladies and gentlemen, I give you Dylan McKenzie.'

Linden vaulted off the stage. The crowd parted as he made his way back to the bar. He picked up his pint and held it up in salute, a grin of anticipation on his face.

This was it. Dylan had to deliver, or he wouldn't get another chance. The pause stretched out. He had always imagined Tabitha in the audience and her absence was like a yawning hole that swallowed up his will to go on. He took a deep breath. Either he was a professional or he wasn't. He closed his eyes, blocking out the room, and played. The rolling chords felt so familiar under his fingers and the sound calmed his nerves. He had this. His connection with the guitar grew. The feel of it under his arm, the solid wood curving perfectly against him. The vibration filled him, and he moved with the notes as they engulfed his body and mind with sound.

Eyes still closed, he felt the shift in energy. He opened his eyes and searched the room. The tiger was standing in the middle of the crowd. She was watching Dylan, her clear blue eyes so familiar he felt his heart expand. A smile spread across his face and he started singing.

The room fell completely silent and his voice filled the space. They had never heard him sing and he felt the jolt of their surprise, and then an easing as they began to ride with him. He felt Tabitha more than he saw her, her tiger form flickering in and out of his vision.

His break came so fast. He put his guitar down and the audience groaned. 'I'll be back in twenty minutes,' he said with a chuckle. 'Recharge your glasses, have a chat and we'll reconvene.'

Rather than going to the bar, he ducked out the back, gulping down air as the adrenaline hit. There was a jug of water and an empty glass on a small round table in the corner. He downed the first glass, and then refilled it and sipped at a second. He was entitled to free beer while he played, but he never drank alcohol until he'd finished. Drinking dulled the senses and persuaded people they were performing better than they were. He didn't want any part of that.

'Dylan?'

The voice behind him sent chills down his spine. He took a deep breath and turned. Tabitha stood just inside the door. Her long hair fell in copper waves around her face and down past her shoulders. Her skin shone with an other-worldly glow. She wore jeans and a long-sleeved, fitted tunic with a beaded pattern that glinted in the artificial light.

Dylan swallowed. The moment seemed unreal. He felt breathless, disconnected somehow from his body and completely aware of it at the same time. He longed to reach out, to touch his fingertips to her fine-boned hands, to stroke her cheek. Her huge eyes were pools of liquid blue that pulled him in. He couldn't look away. He walked towards her, drawn too strongly to resist. 'You came,' he whispered.

She nodded. 'You have Linden to thank. I can't say I like him, but he's a good friend to you.'

Dylan swallowed and nodded. 'I owe him for that. Will you stay for the rest of the gig? I saw you earlier. I saw your tiger. God, I've missed her. I can't tell you how sorry I am for freaking out. I have regretted that moment more often than I can possibly say. Is there any chance you might forgive me?'

'It's not about forgiving you. I can't always control where I go when I travel, and I can't paint if I tether myself. I'm trying to stop myself travelling to you. I don't want to intrude, but I need to be able to draw and paint. So if you don't want my company in that way, we need to stay away from each other for good.'

Dylan closed the distance between them. He took her hands in both of his, felt his heart race as the smooth skin of her delicate fingers touched his own. 'Please, don't keep away. You are always welcome in my space whatever form you are in. Please, visit me tonight after the gig. Come into my home and you'll see that you're welcome. Just promise me that if you're there, you'll be visible, so I know.'

Tabitha nodded. Her chest rose and fell. Her hands gripped his with strength despite being so delicate. Her slight form belied a strength of character that he knew was formidable. This woman was so much more than she seemed.

She reached up on her toes, holding his gaze.

Dylan's heart was hammering in his chest as he lowered his mouth to hers, allowing their lips to meet with a featherlight touch. He pulled back slightly, searching her intense blue gaze for any sign that he may have read things wrong.

Putting her hands around his neck, she pulled him back.

His head swam as she leaned in to him, her breathing grounding him into a sense of wonder. This was actually real.

The door banged. Linden stood there, hands on his hips, a grin fixed on his face. 'Are you coming? Everyone's waiting.'

Dylan swallowed. He took a deep breath, stepped backwards and rolled his shoulders. 'Wait for me after?'

She smiled.

45

DYLAN

DYLAN WAS FLYING. HE FELT AS THOUGH TABITHA WAS feeding him a personal stream of inspiration. From the moment she stepped into the room he had got everything right. The crowd was made for him, shouting his name between songs and whooping and screaming with their applause.

There was one song left to go. Tabitha was sitting at the bar, a pint of Guinness in her hand. Her huge blue eyes were pointed right at him and they held him transfixed. He tuned his guitar again. This was the song. This was the one he had poured his heart into. He swallowed. He *would* hold it together. It was the only way. He stilled his fingers, allowing the sound to die away. Raising his eyebrows, he took an ostentatiously big breath and waited. The room stilled. A smile played around Tabitha's parted lips.

He plucked the guitar string so lightly, the sound wouldn't have carried beyond the first row or two of people, but the anticipation started there and he still felt the buzz when he began to sing. The room was silent and he breathed into the note, making it soft, gentle and seductive. He sang louder, weaving a web with his voice and pulling in his audience. Looking over to Tabitha, he met her gaze. Her eyes were burning, their blue more fire than ice now. There was a mirage of the tiger next to her, completely still, watching Dylan.

> *Stripes in the moonlight*
> *Silent paws on glassy ground*
> *Eyes flash in the darkness*
> *Eyes flash and my heart drowns.*
>
> *You shatter my defences*
> *You fill my heart with fire*
> *With you I am creation*
> *With you I find my wild.*
>
> *But when the shadow fades,*
> *My world is small and dark*
> *I can't find my way forward*
> *I can't light my inner spark.*

The tension in the room rose, lifting him, carrying him through the emotion of the song as he soared over the crowd, pulling them up with him. His heart expanded, the fingers of his energy reaching towards Tabitha.

He felt her respond, her tiger snaking through the crowd towards him. He surrounded the creature with sound, feeling the pull of the thick white fur, the memory of her delicate hands in his. He closed his eyes and saw only her face, her big, blue eyes drawing him in, captivating him and holding him forever.

Wild Shadow you consume me
With your flames that burn so bright.
Come back to me my tiger
Come back to me my light.

Wild Shadow

As the last notes dissipated, Dylan was breathless. Eyes still closed, he sat motionless, fingers millimetres from the strings while the sound faded.

The room exploded in applause: clapping, whooping, screaming. Linden jumped onto the stage, pulling Dylan to his feet and wrapping him in an enormous hug.

'Take a bow, and then come to the bar. The first round's on me. You were incredible.'

Dylan was beaming. He stretched his arms out on either side of him, bending low to accept the applause.

'Thank you so much,' he shouted above the noise. 'If you'd like to download my album, take a leaflet. It has all the information. I am looking for a record deal, so if you know anyone in the music industry, please do let me know and I'll give you a free album to pass on, as well as one for yourself as a thank you. You guys are my first audience and you will always be my favourite.'

He bowed again and the crowd roared. Clipping his guitar into the case at the side of the stage, he vaulted down to the floor. Hands grasped at him as he made his way through the crowd. His name floated continually through the air. He had seen this happen to Linden, but he'd never been on the receiving end of it before.

'Here you are, my man!' Linden clapped him on the back and handed him a pint of lager.

'Dylan, that was unbelievable.' GJ was staring at him, eyes wide.

'Coming through, coming through, make way for the hero's mother!' The crowds parted and Rachel came into view, her arms stretched out to Dylan.

'I *always* knew you were that good,' she whispered into his ear. 'Those boys were fools not to have made more of you sooner.'

'Thanks, Mum.' Dylan smiled and squeezed her tighter.

Tabitha had stepped through the chaos and was standing behind his mum.

He stood up. Baring his soul through his songs had seemed like a good idea when he was alone in his flat. Now that he had to face her, he had gone off the plan.

'Your songs are beautiful,' she said. She stepped closer, so close he could barely breathe. Then she reached up on tiptoe and wrapped her arms around him, putting her cheek to his. His heart exploded in his chest. The rightness blew through him, taking his breath away. He put his arms around her, closing his eyes and blocking out the world.

'Tabitha,' he said, his voice hoarse.

She pulled back.

He opened his eyes and his breath caught when he saw that she was smiling. 'I really am sorry.'

'I know. I heard your songs.'

'Is there any chance we might take up where we left off? I mean … carry on getting to know one another?'

Tabitha stepped backwards.

Rachel was watching Dylan, a huge smile on her face. 'Go on, Tabitha. Give him another chance. He's worth it, I promise you.'

Tabitha looked at Rachel and smiled. When she turned

to Dylan, the light was still there. She reached out, took his hand in her own and squeezed. 'Come to the gallery tomorrow after work. About seven. I'll get in some nibbles.'

Then she was gone.

Dylan swallowed. He took a deep breath, and then looked over at his mum.

She was beaming. 'That really was a great gig, darling. Here's to the future.'

46

MAX THUMPED THE DESK. HE HAD PUT THE REPORT OFF FOR too long. He knew nothing about tiger conservation and it was too late to figure it out now. He had hours before the report was due on Ursula's desk, not the days or weeks he needed to pull it out of thin air. He looked after captive tigers. He did not reintroduce them to the wild.

The Wildley Forest Zoo website was filled with information about conservation, but he hadn't bothered to look. He had ignored the posters plastered to the walls in visitor centres and skipped staff meetings. He had ignored his pigeonhole, which he now knew was filled with information, reminders and official warnings. Basically, he was screwed.

The phone rang. Sophie's name flashed up on the screen. She had always given him immunity, but his phone was now filling up with messages from her demanding information. There were more from Ursula. He was tanking big time and he had no idea how to get this under control.

He looked around his office. He wished it felt more familiar. He had been so proud to get a job with an office and staff. But he'd barely stepped into it since that first day. The drawers and cupboards were empty. The computer was covered with dust. The room was musty and unused.

He hadn't cared when his staff had all resigned within a few weeks of his appointment. He was happier with the cats than with people anyway, so when the positions weren't filled, he didn't complain. There always seemed to be someone around to help, even if they were managed by Ursula.

Max rolled his shoulders, and then rubbed at his neck. There must be a way out of this. He may have fudged his CV, but he was clever enough to have faked it this far. He would find a solution, or he would find someone to help him.

47

DYLAN

We can now confirm that London and the Home
Counties are on course for a direct hit from Storm
Benjamin. The advice is to cancel all unnecessary travel.
Where possible, stay inside and check on any vulnerable
friends, family or neighbours. The storm is forecast to be
at its height for the next twenty-four hours.

THE VOICE ON THE RADIO SOUNDED SERIOUS. DYLAN
sighed. The trees were bending further and further in the
wind. The few visitors who had braved the zoo seemed to
have left, but the place was still open.

'Damn it,' Dylan muttered to himself as he checked his
watch again. It was only five minutes later than last time. 'If
I don't get out of here soon, I'll be stuck.' The tree outside
the Playbarn bent ominously in a huge gust of wind. Dylan
shivered.

He picked up the phone and dialled Sophie.

'Hello?' She sounded distracted, but less fierce than
normal.

'Can we close up here? There isn't a single visitor.'

Silence.

'The trees outside are swaying alarmingly,' he added, hearing the stress creeping into his own voice. 'I'm worried my staff won't get home safely if we leave it any longer.'

He could hear the howling wind from the other end of the phone. She was clearly outside. There was a loud crash, and Sophie screamed.

Dylan jerked backwards from the handset, the noise cutting through his eardrums.

'Do it.' Her voice was shaky. 'I'll shut the whole zoo to all non-essential staff. Get your people out as soon as. Keep an eye on your phone. You'll be notified when we need you.' She hung up.

'Come on, guys,' Dylan shouted across the echoing Playbarn. 'Get out of here. Go home. If anyone has a long way to travel and can't get back safely, tell me now. I won't see anyone in danger or stranded.'

'Thanks, boss. We're all good.' Ed, a guy with an open, friendly face and long, brown dreadlocks nodded at Dylan. 'Stay safe.'

'You too, mate.' Dylan held the door open as they all filed out. The wind caught it and pushed it backwards. He held on, trying to stop the door from slamming against the wall and smashing the glass. When the gust eased, he shoved the door shut and locked it tight. He stood with his back to the solid surface and looked around him. The trees were bending further than he would have thought possible. Dead, muddy leaves flew around as though they had newly fallen.

He heard a growl to his right. The white tiger glared at

him and then growled again. She walked over, rubbing against his legs. He gasped. She felt so real.

She took his coat in her teeth and tugged. He jerked forwards, straight into a gust of wind that pushed him backwards.

Putting his head down into the wind, he pushed forwards towards the exit, foot by hard-won foot. The wind was still getting stronger and was joined by sheeting rain that soaked him in moments. He was freezing, but the going was slow. His hands turned pink, and then took on a strange tinge of blue.

Tabitha growled more urgently this time, tugging at his coat again and propelling him faster towards home.

By the time he reached her house he was shaking with cold.

She nudged him up the path towards her front door, but he shook his head. 'I need to shower and change. I'll freeze if I stay like this. I'll be back in half an hour.'

She growled.

'I promise.'

She rumbled and then dissipated.

He looked up and saw Tabitha's face at the window, pale and wide-eyed. He raised a hand and then turned for home.

The water in the shower felt roasting, but the dial was barely turned to warm. His teeth chattered as he stood under the spray, allowing it to heat his bones and still the incessant clattering of his teeth. He didn't want to get out of the water, but Tabitha was over the road, and soon he might be unable to cross even that small distance. Forcing himself to turn off the spray, he towelled off and dug his warmest clothes out of the wardrobe. Fully dressed, he reached for the hairdryer, and then put it back. His hair would be soaking again in moments when he stepped out the door. Instead he combed it, and then hunted for his raincoat in the pile of boxes still waiting to be unpacked.

A movement on the other side of the road caught his attention. A tall, dark-haired figure stood in front of Tabitha's door. The door opened. He couldn't see Tabitha's face from here, but her shoulders went from relaxed to hunched in a moment.

Max was gesturing, but she wasn't letting him in. He was getting more agitated now, pointing up at the sky and his now-soaked clothes. Then he went inside. Something streaked through the air over Max's head, and then the door closed behind him.

'Damn,' Dylan muttered to himself. What was the man up to now? Every time Dylan got close to Tabitha, Max got in the way. He could tell how much Max put Tabitha on edge and that just exacerbated his own irritation.

Pulling on his raincoat and dragging the hood as far as he could over his head, he picked up the bottle of wine from the kitchen worktop and ran out into the rain. His feet were soaked in moments from the enormous puddles on the road, but he was beyond caring. Max was in there with Tabitha, and he didn't trust him.

He hammered on the door and it swung open.

Max leaned against the door frame, a tight smile on his face. 'And what might you be doing here?'

'I was invited. What's your excuse?'

'Tabitha, is that true?' Max turned but didn't move his bulk out of the narrow doorway.

'Yes. Let him in.'

His brows pulled together, but he stood upright and

stepped back. Dylan ducked as he came through the low door.

He pulled up short and straightened. Two barn owls sat on the windowsill, their sleek white forms silhouetted against the sky while they watched him with inky-black eyes.

Tabitha stood next to him, her long, copper hair framing her delicate face. Her bright blue eyes were so familiar he felt his heart squeeze. She was his tiger and the woman he wanted to spend the rest of his life with. How could it have taken him so long to realise?

He swallowed. Reaching out his hand, he offered her the bottle of wine.

She took it, smiling. 'Would you like some?'

He nodded, his throat too dry for words.

'I'd love some, thanks for asking.' Max cut across the connection, breaking the mood. His lips compressed and his eyes narrowed as he glared at Dylan. 'It looks like we're all going to be stuck here together for a while, unless you're planning to head home, Dylan? After all, I'm sure it's safe to cross the road, even in this weather.'

'I was invited. Were you?' Dylan repeated, allowing irritation to flow into his words.

Max stepped back, his jaw tightening. 'Some of us don't have the luxury of living nearby. Luckily I have good friends willing to take me in during a storm.'

'How poetic.' Dylan said through gritted teeth.

'Boys, boys, please stop the tantrums.' Tabitha turned on a small TV in the corner and set it to a twenty-four-hour news channel. 'Here you are.' She handed them each a large glass of red wine, and then gestured to the table next to the small kitchen. 'Help yourself to nibbles. I only catered for two, but I'm sure I can pull more together if anyone's still hungry.'

'This is perfect, thank you.' Dylan took the wine. Putting a canapé in his mouth whole, he wandered over to the paintings and stopped in front of the picture of the white tiger that had caused so many problems before.

'This is my favourite,' he said, turning to Tabitha and holding her bright-blue gaze. 'I have a soft spot for white tigers.'

A smile played around the edges of her lips. She sipped her wine but said nothing.

'I prefer the yellow kind myself.' Max scowled. 'They seem fiercer, somehow. More primal. White tigers are every bit as dangerous, but for some reason we've romanticised them. They are killers, predators to be feared not adored. Only a fool believes anything else.'

'You're right,' Tabitha said, putting her wine down and walking over to him on feet as silent as the cat she was barely containing. Her voice was soft, but deadly. 'You won't hear the tiger coming and you'll be dead before you know she's there, unless she wants you to live. Never underestimate her.'

Max shuddered. 'I saw one, you know. I saw it outside your house and then again in the cat enclosure playing with my tigers. By the morning it was gone, and nobody else had seen it. Nobody apart from Dylan.'

'Then you're lucky.' Tabitha leaned on the edge of a wooden display table, crossing her delicate arms across her chest. 'How many people can say they've seen a white tiger on the streets near their home?'

'Near *your* home,' Max said, eyes narrowed.

Tabitha laughed. 'Yes, near my home.'

Max stepped closer, tilting his head to one side. 'I just think it's strange, that's all. You turn up with a tiger obsession and suddenly a white tiger is prowling the streets of Wildley Forest Village and playing with the tigers you like to draw. Then it turns out you have a painting of an identical tiger in your showroom, set to sell for a small fortune. I know you draw from life. You're there by my tigers every day doing just that. So which particular tiger modelled for this picture, I wonder? Private collections are a risky business when you're talking big cats.'

Dylan let out a bark of laughter. 'You think Tabitha has a tiger stowed away in here somewhere?'

'Well, not in the showroom, obviously. But I've never been out the back, or upstairs.'

'Good to know,' Dylan said, not caring that the grin spreading across his face was a direct taunt.

'What are you getting at, Max?' Tabitha said, her jaw tight. 'Were you *really* unable to get home, or is there something else you wanted?'

He tilted his chin up. 'I'd like to have a look around. If there is a tiger here, we need to get it secured as soon as possible.'

Tabitha rolled her eyes. 'Have you seen the size of my home? Can you really imagine a tiger in here?'

'Maybe that's why it's getting out. Dylan and I were lucky to escape that last encounter alive. Next time, it will confront someone who *doesn't* know what to do.'

Dylan raised his eyebrows. Max had not been so self-assured when the tiger faced him down, but he was doing an admirable job of pretending otherwise. If Tabitha hadn't actually been there, she might even have believed this story. He suppressed a smile.

'Oh for goodness' sake, have a look then. The back door's over there.' Tabitha inclined her head towards the rear of the shop. 'But this is your one and only chance, so you'd better do a thorough job. Make sure you check the shed and the path around the side of the house. Oh, and the gap behind the rockery. A tiger could definitely lie in wait there. Wildley Forest is relying on you, Max. Don't let them down.'

48

DYLAN

Max slammed into Dylan's shoulder as he walked to the back door.

Dylan grunted, but didn't react.

The door clattered against the wall as a gust of wind shoved it out of Max's hand, knocking it inwards.

'I'd like to have a door at the end of the night please,' Tabitha called after him. 'Particularly if there are tigers on the loose.'

Max's jaw tightened, but he said nothing as he stepped outside and shut the door behind him.

'I'm sorry,' Tabitha said with a sigh. 'I didn't invite him. He just turned up, but I couldn't send him packing in this weather.'

'I know. I saw him arrive and I saw how pleased you didn't look. But I can't believe you're letting him poke around.'

Tabitha sighed. 'I know, but I wanted to speak to you alone, and I couldn't figure out another way to get rid of him. Don't worry, there's nothing tiger-like out there.

There's nothing tiger-like anywhere apart from my paintings.'

'And you.'

She nodded. 'And me. But Max wouldn't understand that.'

'I'm not sure I do either, but I'd love to try if you'll give me the chance?'

Tabitha looked at him for a moment. 'What happens in your mind when you play music?'

Dylan furrowed his eyebrows. She watched him, her huge, blue eyes glowing in the dim light. He was breathless, but forced his voice to sound steady. 'I step out of my normal reality and into something bigger. I connect to the people I play with through the music, but also through the way my body interacts with my instrument. When I'm performing well and my audience are loving it, we are all part of the same, beating organism, flying together.'

Tabitha smiled. 'It's the same thing. When I draw or paint, I feel that too. But I actually take the next step and travel consciously outside of my body.'

'But sometimes you're solid. I've felt the tiger's fur. It's so soft.'

Tabitha shrugged. 'I'm not really sure how I do that. But when I'm travelling, the difference between light and matter isn't an issue. I can be whatever I want to be.'

'So could you travel as a different animal? Like these barn owls, for example?'

One of the owls shrieked and Tabitha laughed. 'I don't know. Maybe I could. I've never tried. I don't set out to be a tiger, that's just how I look when I'm on the move.'

'That's how you knew all that stuff, isn't it? You knew

about my compositions, that I'd made up with my friends, and more.'

Tabitha nodded.

'You supported me. I remember. You sat on my feet when I needed strength. You stopped me from being alone, but do you watch me when the tiger isn't there too? How do I know when I have privacy?'

Tabitha swallowed. 'Most people can't see me when I travel, but you always have. If I'm there, you'll see me. I'm so sorry. I didn't mean to spy, but I'm convinced there's a purpose to all of this. That kind of magic doesn't appear without a really good reason.'

'What are you saying?'

'I don't know. I think … I think I'm trying to convince you that I'm not crazy, that I'm not some kind of weird stalker.'

Dylan walked towards her, slowly. 'I don't think you're crazy. I never have. I'm a bit embarrassed that you've seen my unguarded moments. You saw me composing, arguing with my friends, goodness knows what else. Have you seen me in the shower? In bed?'

'Nothing like that. I swear it. I have only been pulled to you when I was needed or when there was something I needed to know. I saw you arguing with your friends because you needed the support I had to offer. I'm not sure why I saw you composing, but I'm so glad I did. Your music is incredible.'

'When you turned up, things started to flow. I have been thinking of you as my muse. Every time the white tiger arrives, I become the best version of myself, but I thought she was a part of me. Now it turns out she was you all along. Part of me loves the idea, part of me is mortified. I really don't know what to think.' He sat on the armchair in the corner of the room and dropped his head into his hands.

Tabitha knelt on the floor in front of him. She took his hands in her own and a thrill ran through him at the touch of her skin. 'All I did was make you feel you weren't alone. Everything else came from you. I didn't give you creativity or confidence. I just showed you an image of something fierce, as a reminder that you can be fierce too. You stood up to your friends by yourself. You wrote that music by yourself, and recorded it too. I was privileged to be there with you, but that's all I did.'

Dylan turned to face her. She looked as beautiful as ever, her long, copper hair falling in waves around her shoulders, her huge eyes staring at him. For the first time, he saw something that looked like fear in her gaze. He reached up and stroked her cheek. 'Tabitha, I—'

The door rattled and then slammed open, caught by a gust of wind. 'There's nothing bloody well out there, and you knew it.' Max stomped inside.

Tabitha let out her breath in a rush and sat back on her heels. 'Of course I knew it. I told you I wasn't keeping tigers. You can look upstairs too if you like, but there's nothing there either. There are signs of my tiger obsession in every inch of this house. I make my living drawing and painting them. It fills me up to have them around in every way I can, but I'm no fool. I'm not going to keep an enormous predator in my home. I wouldn't want to even if I could. My dream is to take your tigers and release them into the wild so they don't have to live in a cage and be subjected to your abuse, day in day out.'

'You visit the zoo often enough and pay money for that

access. That makes you just as much a part of the tigers' captivity as me.'

Tabitha reached out and traced one finger over the painting of the white tiger. She took a few deep breaths, before she turned to him again.

'I know.' She swallowed. 'I spent a lot of time talking to the staff at the zoo before I joined. I moved here because Wildley Forest Zoo is doing so much conservation and reintroducing so many animals to the wild. I could have moved anywhere in the country to find tigers. I came here, for that reason and that reason only.'

Max's face coloured. He ground his teeth but said nothing and turned to look out the window. The wind was roaring, and a bin skittered down the street as though it were an empty wrapper. Rain lashed at the glass. A car horn blared, and the brakes squealed.

Tabitha sighed. 'Look, since we're all stuck here together, have something to eat. Sit down. Chat with us, but stop picking fights with Dylan, and stop trying it on with me.'

Max ground his teeth again. 'I'm going to get some air.'

'Max, there's a storm outside, for goodness' sake, come and sit down.'

He yanked the front door open, stepped through and slammed it behind him.

She strode after him and peered through the glass pane on the door. Coming back into the room, she shook her head. 'He's sitting on the doorstep. He won't come to any harm there. I have tried so hard to head this off. Some people just don't listen. He hears just enough of what I say to launch into his own story, never enough to understand.'

Dylan's hands were still clenched into fists. He could

hear his pulse throbbing in his ears. 'Has he ever threatened you?'

'No.'

'Has he ever actually tried it on with you?'

'He's made plenty of suggestions, but he's never done anything I couldn't get out of easily.'

Dylan swallowed. 'Okay then.'

'I know he's confrontational. I know you don't like him and he's done everything he can to wind you up. I get all that. But I need you to let it go. I have been dreaming about you and Max fighting for weeks. I've tried to keep you out of my head, but something is coming, and someone out there wants me to know about it. I can only assume that's so I can do something to stop it. Please, don't let him wind you up. Don't give him that power over you. This storm is enough by itself. There's something in it. I'm not sure what's going on, but this energy is volatile. Barriers are breaking down and it's up to us whether we use that for good or for bad.'

A shiver ran down Dylan's spine. 'How do you know this?'

'I can feel it. I can see what could come. It keeps playing out on the back of my eyelids, in my dreams both sleeping and waking. Believe me or don't, but it is more real than anything else and could change the course of everything. Max is a difficult guy. Don't let him spill over into your life any more than he needs to.'

The door opened and Max came back in, a frown furrowing his forehead. 'It's getting worse out there.'

There was a crash outside. One of the barn owls screeched and fluffed out its wings. Tabitha peered through the window. 'The tree has blown down. Thank goodness you came in when you did. And thank goodness the owls were in here too. She crouched down, eye level with the birds and looked straight into their dark gaze.

Dylan watched, his heart beating fast as some kind of silent conversation went on in front of him. Tabitha nodded and then stood up, reached for the TV remote and turned it up.

Travellers are being urged to stay at home tonight as lashing winds reach unprecedented levels. There have already been numerous fatalities from falling trees and branches. Livestock have been seen roaming the increasingly flooded roads, released by fallen fences and broken gates. Unless it's an emergency, stay indoors. Bring your pets in and keep warm.

'What happens to the zoo animals in this kind of situation?' Dylan asked, wandering over to the window. The glass was cold and the wind was blustering through the wooden frames and old-fashioned glass.

'They stay in their sleeping quarters,' Max said. 'There's always staff at the zoo and the rest of us are on-call. They'll be fine.'

'We won't find them wandering the flooded streets of Wildley Forest Village then?'

Max laughed. The sound was grating and added to Dylan's unease.

A sharp ringing cut through the tension. Max pulled his phone out of his pocket. He walked over to the window as he listened, turning his back to the room.

'Look, Dylan ...' Tabitha held his gaze. She reached out one delicate hand.

His heart beat faster. He took it. Her skin was warm and sent tingles through his own hand and up his arm. He swallowed.

'Lock them in their sleeping quarters.' Max's voice jarred Dylan out of his reverie. Max lapsed into silence, listening to the voice on the other end of the phone. 'Well try to get them back in. I'm on my way.' He slid the phone back in his pocket, grabbed his coat from the hook opposite the door and shoved his arms into the sleeves.

'Where are you going?' Tabitha said, frowning. 'It's not safe out there.'

'I've been asked to check on the tigers. One of the trees is leaning towards the perimeter. I need to make sure the cats are secure.

'You can't go out in *that*,' Dylan said.

'I have to. If a tree breaches the wall of the enclosure, who knows what could happen.'

49

DYLAN

DYLAN BLINKED. HE SQUEEZED HIS EYES TIGHTLY SHUT, AND then opened them again. The world felt distorted. The wind howled around the tiny, stone cottage and one of the barn owls on the windowsill shrieked. It fluffed its feathers and then settled back down.

'If a tree lands on the fence, the cats might be able to climb it and leap onto the high bank at the back of the enclosure,' Max said, an edge to his voice. 'I have to make sure that doesn't happen.'

Dylan took a deep breath and let it out slowly. 'We could have tigers on the loose in Wildley Forest Village?'

Max nodded but said nothing.

Tabitha turned. The painting stood right next to her, the tiger mid-leap from the top of the fallen tree onto the steep bank.

Dylan swallowed.

Max frowned and then walked over to the painting, bending down to look closer. 'What made you paint this?'

'I've seen it over and over. I've dreamed it, drawn it and tried to forget it, but it keeps coming back.'

Max's eyebrows shot up. 'You dreamed it? Seriously? That's a bit of a coincidence.'

'What are you suggesting?' Tabitha's voice was flat, controlled.

'You have been talking about freeing the cats.'

Tabitha gaped. 'Not in Wildley Forest Village! I wanted to front a conservation project to release them into the wild, in their proper habitat!'

Max laughed, but the sound was hard edged. 'You wanted to front it, did you? You think a lot of yourself.'

Tabitha flushed.

'Now listen, Max—' Dylan started.

'No, it's okay. Max needs to go. It may surprise you to know that I *don't* want the tigers getting out of their enclosure.'

Max glared at her. 'You're right about one thing: I do need to go.' He walked over to the door, reached for the handle, and then paused. He turned. 'How does the dream end?'

Tabitha swallowed. 'I've never seen it the whole way, but I'm pretty sure that if you two fight, things will end badly.'

'Us?' Max frowned. 'Who do you mean? Me and the tiger?'

'You and Dylan.'

'Well that won't be a problem. I'll be at the zoo. Dylan will be here.'

'Hang on,' Tabitha jumped up and grabbed her coat, pushing her arms through the sleeves. 'I'm coming with you.'

Max let out a bark of laughter, and then frowned. He

looked at Tabitha speculatively. 'Why? I know you love the tigers, but why would you put yourself in their way when you think they're going to escape?'

Tabitha advanced on Max. Already Dylan could see the haze of something different around her. She had an aura of danger. A soft growl rumbled through the air.

Max shivered.

'The cats don't like you, Max. You know they don't. They're much calmer with me.'

Max's eyes darkened and his jaw tightened. Then his eyes narrowed and a smile played at the corners of his mouth. He looked at Dylan and smirked. 'I guess you have more time to move into your new flat then, Dylan. Come on, Tabitha. Let's get those tigers secured before someone is killed.'

'If Tabitha's going, I'm coming too,' Dylan said, his voice quiet, but firm.

Max rolled his eyes. 'You heard her. If we argue, things end badly. The best way to avoid that is to leave you here.'

Dylan clenched his fists, forcing them down by his sides. He stood up, walking slowly to Max. 'You want me to believe you'll look out for Tabitha? That you'll keep her safe? I've seen what you're like around those cats. You get drunk with the power of it and antagonise them. Tabitha will always put them first, even if it means putting herself in danger and you won't do anything to protect her. I am coming. It is the only way to keep Tabitha safe.'

'And you'll do that how? Using all your knowledge of tigers? From what? Working in the Playbarn?'

'At least I'll be paying attention. I am not staying here.'

'You talk as though I'm a child that needs babysitting,'

Tabitha snapped. 'I have ways of protecting myself that neither of you could come close to matching.'

'I don't have time for this.' Max swung the front door open, stepped through and slammed it behind him.

'I know you're right.' Dylan turned to Tabitha and took both of her hands in his. He swallowed. 'I know how powerful you are. But if you travel away from your body, it must be left vulnerable. Who will watch over you while you travel?'

Tabitha held his gaze. Her huge, blue eyes seemed to grow even bigger as though she were absorbing everything in and around him. 'What is it you think you can do? If the tigers get out, you wouldn't stand a chance.'

'And you would?'

'If I change form, I can protect myself and hopefully keep everybody else safe.'

'But you can't really change form, can you? You can leave your body, but an abandoned body is a perfect treat for a tiger. I won't leave you alone. Max isn't going to protect you. He would let you die and then claim sympathy for having lost the woman he loved. That's the kind of man he is.'

'I know.' Tabitha sighed. 'I'm not going to protect Max. I'm going to protect the tigers. If they get out, he will shoot them. I'm the only one who can get them to safety.'

'You really believe they're going to escape, don't you?'

She squeezed her eyes tightly shut for a moment, and when she opened them, they glistened with tears. 'I've seen it.'

Dylan nodded. 'I believe you, and I'm coming with you.'

'I might not be able to keep *you* safe.'

'I'm not asking you to. I'm not asking for permission either. Afterwards, if we both come out of this alive, you can tell me what you think of me. But for now, you can't stop me from going to my own workplace.'

Tabitha took a deep breath. She nodded and a tear slid down her cheek. 'Let's go.' She opened the door and held on tight, fighting the strength of the wind while Dylan went through.

He ducked out of the way as the owls swooped through the door over his head, and then he bent into the next gust. He didn't hear the door slam behind Tabitha, but felt her push past him.

'I have a car on the other side of the road,' Dylan shouted through the roar of the wind.

'A car would be more dangerous in this weather. We need to walk.' Tabitha started up the road without waiting for an answer.

By the time they reached the zoo they were soaked and shivering from the cold. The owls circled above them, riding the currents of the wind. The zoo was shut and the barriers were locked. Tabitha leaned one hand on the car barrier, and then vaulted neatly over the top. Dylan followed, stopping on the other side to brush off his hands. Here, on this side of the fence, reality began to hit.

If the tigers had escaped, they could be anywhere. They would be stressed and on the defensive, spooked by the howling wind, and almost certainly unpredictable. He was the least qualified person to deal with them, and nobody would be watching out for him. If Tabitha hadn't been so determined to come, he would not have stepped outside the house on that night, but here he was, in the middle of the storm, ready to face down full-grown predators.

50

MAX

MAX GRUMBLED ALL THE WAY TO THE TIGER ENCLOSURE. HE had been soaked within moments of stepping outside Tabitha's house, and the wind was buffeting him all over the place. He hated being out of control and the weather was reminding him how badly things could go.

He scanned the shadows. Where was everyone? There were always keepers around, and he had expected more than usual in this storm. But there wasn't a person to be seen.

It was pitch black, but he shone his torch around the top of the tiger enclosure. He couldn't see a thing, so he started walking around the perimeter, looking for any sign of a wonky tree. He heard a growl in the darkness to his left and his heart accelerated, sending adrenaline pumping through his system. Suddenly, the cold and wet didn't seem to matter anymore.

He climbed the bank behind the enclosure, pointing his torch at the trees nearby. A flash of lightning lit up the hill. He froze. A single tree was leaning against the fence. On the top of it, about to jump onto the bank, was a tiger. The cat grunted a warning, and then bunched his powerful body up to leap.

Max was plunged back into darkness. He backed away from the enclosure until his feet hit the path. Coming face to face with the cats outside the cage on a dark and stormy night was a world away from his adventures into the enclosure. Why weren't the tigers locked in their sleeping quarters? His heart raced, his mind flitted over every eventuality, and then one thought penetrated the chaos: run.

He turned, racing back down the hill as thunder rolled across the zoo. He stopped on the other side of the cage. This area was more open and he swung his torch in wide arcs, hoping to scare the cats off. Rummaging in his pocket for a key, he let himself into his room to the side of the enclosure and closed the door. Leaning on the wooden barrier, he breathed heavily and spread his palms flat against the surface, taking comfort from its solidity.

He flicked the light switch to the left of the door, but nothing happened. Damn, the electricity must be down. That didn't bode well for the phone. He ran the beam of his torch over the tigers' sleeping quarters. The door to their outside area was almost closed, but there was easily enough space at the bottom for the cats to get through. Whoever had tried to shut it clearly hadn't been concentrating. He forced himself to step away from the comforting protection of the door, reached for the phone and pressed the button. Silence. He pressed it again. Still, nothing. He reached into his pocket for his mobile and fired it up, but there was no signal.

He was completely alone.

There was a growl outside the door, but it was cut off by

another roll of thunder. Max swallowed. The temptation to hole up in here was almost irresistible, but even he knew he couldn't leave tigers on the loose for the staff and visitors to find in the morning. They were his cats. He was accustomed to being in close proximity with them. He alone went into their enclosure. He alone had proved he could better them and come out of it alive.

He walked over to the wall next to the cage and yanked up the big, red lever that opened and closed the sleeping quarters. Now the cats could get back in easily if they chose. Rubbing his hands clean on his trousers, he went through to the small room at the end and opened the locked cupboard. There was a solid black box tucked in one corner. Max grinned. He pulled the box towards him, clicked open the catches, and ran a finger over the cold, heavy metal of the closest pistol. Standing up straight, he took a deep breath and filled his lungs with musty air. Then he picked up the pistols, tucked them into his belt, and zipped his jacket over the top of them. Shutting the cupboard door, he locked it, and put the key back into his pocket.

Max looked at his hands in the torchlight, turning them over and over. The shaking had stilled. They were completely steady. Adrenaline was pumping around his system and excitement bubbled up in his chest. This was his moment. He had been born for this.

Putting his ear to the door, he listened. The wind was howling, but the growling had stopped. He pulled out one of the pistols, pointed it at the door and eased it open.

A gust of wind shoved the door back and a flash of lightning floodlit the room. He skittered backwards and slammed into the heavy, metal mesh of the tiger cage, gasping as the air was knocked from his body. He heard a grunt outside and stilled, forcing himself not to breathe.

After a few moments, he pulled himself up to standing, grabbed the pistol from where it had fallen and shoved it into his belt.

The door was still swinging uselessly on its hinges. He walked over, leaned against it, and peered outside. There was nothing to see. Letting out the breath he hadn't known he was holding, he stepped out into the storm. Another roll of thunder cut off any last hope of hearing the cats before he saw them, but he knew they were close. He felt it in the prickling adrenaline that flowed through his veins. He rolled his shoulders and cracked the knuckles in his hands. He would show them all.

51

TABITHA CLOSED HER EYES. THE WIND RACED AROUND HER, but she didn't feel cold despite the drenched clothes that clung to her. Warmth came from the middle of her chest, radiating out to the tips of her fingers and toes.

She sent her awareness into the enclosure and felt the disturbance immediately. It was cold and empty, with the broken tree trunk acting as a bridge to the outside world.

They were out there, free at last.

She started walking, moving instinctively towards the cats. Her awareness split. She was barely holding in her white tiger and wondered what Dylan could see. One way or another, she had to get those cats to safety. Max was volatile and Dylan was the most vulnerable of them all. She loved his impulse to protect her, but wished he had a bit more self-preservation. She hoped she was strong enough to protect them both.

Her human body felt strange, distorted, and the storm wasn't helping. She followed the pull of the cats and then

248

froze. A yell rose over a sudden lull in the wind. Max. She pushed her legs faster.

Dylan was behind her. She recognised his proximity in the prickles that ran down her spine and the backs of her legs. She could hear his laboured breathing as though his body was an extension of her own. She had to keep him safe, even when she travelled from her physical form and out into the elements.

She was almost there when she saw a figure dash across the road. Bright lightning zigzagged through the sky, lighting the enclosure and the space in front of it like a stage. The figure disappeared into the bushes next to the fence. She sent out her awareness. The tigers were on the other side of the enclosure. They recognised her energy and she felt the vibration as the larger cat yowled.

'Max,' she called into the darkness.

She waited, but thunder silenced any attempts he might have made to speak.

Slowly, he stepped out of the bushes. 'Tabitha?' He straightened and puffed out his chest. 'You've come to join the fun? You're lucky, the real action hasn't started yet.'

'No, the tigers are on the hill on the other side. But they're coming this way.'

Max walked over to her, standing too close. 'When did you see them there?'

'A few moments ago.' Tabitha stepped back, putting space between them.

Max peered into the darkness. 'They move fast when they want to.'

'Move!' Dylan yelled, running out from the shadows. 'The tigers are coming!'

'Shit,' Max muttered, looking around, nervously. 'Which way?'

Dylan pointed to the bushes. Tabitha reached out her awareness. The tigers were right there, watching them silently. Dylan's hand tightened like a vice around her own. She squeezed back gently, hoping it conveyed reassurance.

'The tigers trust me,' Tabitha said, looking Max in the eye.

'And?' Max said.

'I'll lead them back to their enclosure.'

'You? Are you kidding me?' Max's voice cracked. 'Do you have any idea what you're dealing with?'

She laughed, tipping her head back and baring her face to the wind and the rain, glorying in the wild air on her skin. 'They won't eat me. Open the doors to the safety cage. That's the only way to get them back in.'

He shook his head. 'There's no way they're going to just walk in there.'

'Is there any harm in doing what I ask?' Tabitha said.

He looked at her for a moment, eyes narrowed, and then walked over to the enclosure. He unlocked the outside door to the safety cage, and then crawled inside and opened the inner door. Climbing out, he put the keys in the outer lock and left them hanging.

He walked back over to Tabitha. 'They may not eat you, but they'll certainly kill you.' Opening his coat, he pulled two pistols from his belt.

'What are you doing?' Tabitha said, her voice carrying over the wind even though she didn't shout. 'You are *not* shooting those tigers.'

He raised the guns. 'It's either them, or us.'

Tabitha felt a rush of energy as she reached out her

mind to connect with the tigers. A cat rumbled in greeting and she felt her white tiger begin to disconnect. 'I have run with them and spent lifetimes by their side,' she said, feeling the power of the giant predator course through her veins. 'I am at one with the cats in a way you will never understand. You seek to dominate and control. You keep them captive. I set their souls free even though you constrain their bodies. I see through you, Max. You have never fooled me, and you never will.'

Max stared at her; lips parted. 'For God's sake. What is wrong with you? You sound *pleased* they've escaped.'

'Pleased? Pleased that you're here with your guns ready to shoot them down? I am here to protect *them* from *you* and I will put them back in their cage to do that.'

A growl sounded from the bushes, and then there was only the roar of the wind.

Max swore. He backed away. 'I take no responsibility for either of you.'

A roll of thunder cut through the sheeting rain.

'Please put the guns away, Max. I will keep you both safe and put the cats back in their cage. Just don't use your guns.'

'You're delusional,' Max said from between gritted teeth. He backed away, but kept his gun trained on the bushes.

Dylan put a hand on Tabitha's arm. 'Ignore him. Focus on the cats. Everything else can wait.'

She closed her eyes, drawing reassurance from the warmth of his touch, re-orientating herself. She would not let Max get to her again.

She reached out her consciousness, searching for the tigers. They were so near, near enough to pounce, near enough to surround her and obliterate any one of them, near enough to be shot and killed.

She walked towards an area of thick undergrowth. 'Come with me, my lovelies,' she sang to herself and felt them follow. 'Stay with Max,' she called over her shoulder.

'No.' Dylan's voice behind her sounded panicked but determined.

A tiger growled.

Dylan stepped back, his face pale. 'I am here to protect *you*.'

She swallowed. The howling of the wind gave them a strange privacy. 'And who will protect you? I can't do that while I'm trying to reach the tigers. They'll kill us in a moment. Now, back away.'

Tabitha closed her eyes. She was shaking and not from the cold. She shook her head. 'I can't,' she whispered.

Dylan stepped closer. 'You can't what?'

'I can't put them back into that cage.'

Dylan laid his palm against her cheek and she opened her eyes.

'You have to put them back in that cage to keep them safe. If we can't secure them quickly, Max *will* shoot them.'

Tabitha swallowed.

'Please, Tabitha.' Dylan took her hands in his own, gave them a squeeze, and then backed away as she had asked. 'Only you have the wildness to reach them.'

52

DYLAN

Tabitha smiled, sending chills down his spine. He knew in that moment that he loved her, and that he was stepping into a world so far outside his experience, he had no idea where he would end up.

She wasn't all human. He could see it in the wildness of her eyes, in the flow of her rain-drenched copper hair and in the translucent glow of her skin as she closed her eyes and raised her arms. She began to hum, and the low rumbling in her throat was halfway between a purr and a growl.

He felt a shift in the energy and shivered again. The tigers were so close. Connected to her as he was, open to her energy, he felt their danger like a hum through his bones. He had no idea whether or not he would come through this in one piece, but in this moment he felt more alive than ever before.

All pretence was stripped away. All the silly drama became irrelevant as the air crackled between Tabitha and the two enormous beasts.

There was a grunt in the bushes to Dylan's right. He stepped away and Tabitha moved in closer.

She turned to look at him, her eyes glazed. 'I know what I'm doing. Keep yourself safe.'

Dylan swallowed.

'Please stay back.' Tabitha's lips peeled back from her teeth and she snarled. She split into two as a flash of lightning lit the sky. A huge white tiger hurtled out from her human body, which dropped to the wet ground. The white tiger pulled up, crouching low in front of Tabitha's prone form and growled.

'Crap, what just happened?' Max's voice was high-pitched. 'Did that thing come out of Tabitha?'

Very slowly, a flame-coloured tiger emerged from the undergrowth. Ears pricked up, amber eyes glinting in the light of the full moon, it peeled its lips back from huge curved teeth and roared.

The white tiger walked towards the other cat and reached her muzzle towards the tiger. The cat held rigid for a moment, and then its posture relaxed. Its body became fluid as it moved towards the white tiger, rubbing its head against hers.

Dylan let out his breath in a rush. Now she just had to get it into the enclosure. He looked up at the expanse of metal caging behind them and shuddered. An image of the white tiger's face staring at him from behind bars ghosted through his mind and sent a chill straight to his heart. How could he be a part of putting these incredible cats back into captivity?

His heart grew increasingly heavy as Tabitha led the tiger towards the enclosure.

A shiver shot down his spine and he turned. The

smaller tiger was watching him. There was nowhere to go. The cat was coming straight for him. It wasn't rushing, but it was close enough to be on him in one leap. He crouched down, gathering up Tabitha's limp body in his arms.

'Tabitha,' Dylan shouted over the roll of thunder. The white tiger turned around with a yowl. The larger tiger bounded over to join its mate who reared up, meeting it head on with a playful swipe.

Dylan let out a slow exhale. The tiger had forgotten him for a moment, but both cats were now mere feet away. They were staggeringly beautiful, but a pervasive and instinctive fear beat in Dylan's chest, turning his legs to jelly and sending his mind into a blind panic. Holding Tabitha's unconscious body in his arms, he stepped backwards, but after three paces, one of the tigers turned to watch him. It sat down, tilting its head to one side, and then stood up and started walking silently towards him.

His breathing grew laboured. He had been so sure he could protect Tabitha, but he was freezing cold, exhausted, and right now he had no plan at all.

The white tiger walked over, placing itself between the yellow cats and Dylan. She waited, teeth bared, a rumble coming from her chest.

The male lowered into a crouch, tensing its legs as though to spring.

A shot rang out through the storm.

The cat stopped and turned.

Max.

'Put the guns down,' Dylan said, his voice low and even. 'I'm safe.' He backed away, putting as much space between him and the tigers as he could without drawing attention.

'Are you crazy?' Max didn't shift his aim.

The tiger froze at the familiar voice. It turned to look at its mate, and then back at the white tiger. Without a sound, it sank into an even lower crouch, and stalked Max.

'Shit,' Dylan said, 'help him, please?'

A rumble came from the white tiger's chest.

'You think *that* is going to help us?' Max said, edging closer to Dylan and Tabitha. 'I don't know what it is, but it's not real and if you think it can protect us from flesh and blood predators, you're crazier than I thought. What's wrong with Tabitha?'

'She fine, just unconscious.'

'Did the tiger get her?' Max's finger moved. The pistol clicked, ready to fire as he pointed it at the male's forehead.

'No!' Dylan cried. Adrenaline shot through him. If he let Max shoot one of the tigers, Tabitha would never forgive him.

He put Tabitha down and lunged towards the other man. Max lurched out of the way, swinging the butt of his gun towards Dylan's temple. Dylan ducked and leapt to the side.

The roar was deafening.

A weight slammed into Dylan and Max was launched through the air. He landed with a thud, his eyes wide as he lay on the ground gasping for breath.

The white cat stood over Dylan and Tabitha's body, its heavily muscled frame protecting them, lips curled back into a snarl.

Dylan yelled as the huge male pounced, its claws raking down Max's body. Max screamed, arching off the rain-drenched ground as huge, bloody tears opened up in his clothes.

The white tiger looked down at Dylan, her icy-blue gaze

holding his for a moment before launching at the male tiger, knocking it away from Max. The man groaned at the impact, which sent him rolling into the mud a few feet to his left. The male reared, but the white tiger met it head on. They clashed, a whirlwind of heavy, clawed paws and curved teeth. Blood spattered Dylan's clothes, but he had no idea who it had come from.

'Oh god, Max!' he screamed. He ran over to the fallen man and crouched down. Max was soaked, covered in mud and drenched with blood. 'Are you alive?' he said, hearing the shaking in his voice. 'Max, talk to me.'

Max groaned and curled in on himself.

'Ambulance, get an ambulance,' Dylan muttered to himself as he pulled his phone out of his pocket. Damn, there was no signal. The storm must have knocked it out. He could have done with some backup. Max had said there were always people on duty, but he hadn't seen a single one. He stood up, looking backwards and forwards between Tabitha and Max. How could he protect them both?

He picked Tabitha's body up and started backing away. He had to get her to safety, and then he'd come back for Max. The key to the Playbarn was in his pocket, digging into his thigh. He would take her there. Tabitha's tiger form was unwaveringly solid now, as she fought with the enormous male.

He had to run for it. He staggered a few steps but then turned and froze. The tawny female tiger circled him. Her silence chilled his blood as she closed in on him, and then walked towards Max. Dylan gasped as she went up to the prone man and sniffed him.

The white tiger let out a series of grunts and the female raised her head. The white tiger bounded over, circled Max and then stood over him, nudging the female towards the enclosure. She grunted, but then walked over to the male. The white tiger followed, staying behind them, crowding them towards the open safety cage at the side of the enclosure. There was a moment of deafening silence. Even the wind stilled. The male paused, yowled and then kept going. The female came in behind him as they all moved towards the enclosure that had held them captive for so long. The tigers baulked as they reached the entry to the safety cage, but the white cat rounded them up, coaxed them through the door and followed them inside. They disappeared into the darkness.

Dylan stood, stunned, his plan forgotten. Then he put Tabitha on a nearby bench and ran over to Max.

The other man's face was deathly pale.

'Max, the tigers are in the cage. How do I shut them in?'

Max groaned.

'Please, Max, how do I close the access cage?'

'Key in the door,' Max mumbled.

'And the sleeping quarters? If they go in there can I shut them in?'

'Red lever by the ...' Dylan leaned in, trying to hear the words as they faded away.

'Damn,' he said as Max passed out. Then he got up and ran over to the access cage. The door swung open, but a key was firmly in the lock, with a heavy, loaded key ring hanging from it. The tigers were nowhere to be seen. Dylan yanked the key out and then crawled into the access cage, pulling the inner door firmly behind him. The third key locked it and he leaned against the wire for a moment, trying to catch his breath. Crawling out of the cage, he slammed the outer door. He slid the key into the lock and turned it.

'The tree trunk,' he muttered to himself. 'How am I going to stop them getting out again?'

The grunt of a cat in the darkness sent a wave of fear through his body. His legs almost buckled, but he held on tight to the wire mesh of the safety cage. The white tiger pulled up and held his gaze for a moment, before throwing her head back in a gut-wrenching roar. The other cats joined in, and then followed her as she led them into the sleeping quarters.

Dylan yanked the key from the lock and then ran to the door of Max's room to the side of the enclosure. The door was hanging open on its hinges. Dylan darted through and flipped the light switch. Nothing happened. The room was pitch black.

The grunt of a tiger sent him skittering backwards. He squinted, trying to see through the darkness, but the sound of their feet padding on the straw was his only clue.

'Ow, crap,' he snapped as he stumbled into the corner of a wooden table. Pulling his phone out of his pocket, he turned on the torch. A beam of light shot out straight ahead. Three sets of eyes stared at him.

'Ahhh,' Dylan shouted, leaping back out the door and slamming it behind him. He leaned on the wall, taking in huge, gulping breaths. It was okay. There were bars between him and the tigers. He had to go back in.

He pushed the door open, more slowly this time. A flash of lightning lit up the room for a moment. The large male was pacing up and down on the other side of the bars. The female was lying in a corner, but when she saw Dylan she pushed to her feet and charged at the bars, throwing her heavy body against them with a monumental crash.

The sound blended with the thunder, mere seconds after the lightning. The storm was almost on top of them.

Dylan forced himself to keep breathing as he scanned the walls with the torch, looking for Max's lever. It was there on the right-hand side of the cage, a large, red lever with a rubber handle on the end. The sign next to it said, 'Push up to open, down to close.' The lever sat at the top of the track.

Dylan inched forwards. Every cell in his body screamed at him to run away, but Tabitha was vulnerable lying on a bench in the storm unconscious, and Max was dangerously in need of medical attention. This was the only way. It felt like an hour's journey to the lever, but Dylan knew it must have been seconds. He reached out, jarring as the male grunted, but then he grasped the rubber handle and pulled.

The door lurched, and then stopped, the female jumped back from the opening and growled.

'No,' Dylan whispered under his breath. 'No, you have to shut.'

The female padded over to the door sniffing it. She turned and grunted at her mate and he ambled over to join her.

Dylan tugged hard at the lever. He had to get it down before the cats got out into the enclosure and went back up that tree trunk.

The door jolted down a bit further.

The lightning and thunder were simultaneous this time.

The female made a run for the door.

A white blur flew across the cage, knocking her from her

feet. She scrambled back onto her paws, dropped low to the ground and pulled her lips back in a snarl.

The white tiger positioned herself in front of the door.

Dylan grasped the lever with both hands and threw his weight into it. It creaked as the door juddered, and then slammed closed.

Dylan collapsed to the ground, pulling in deep breaths and waiting for his heartbeat to slow.

There was a growl in the cage. He sat up. The female was stalking the white tiger, her hackles raised, teeth bared.

The white tiger grunted, and then vanished.

The female roared in frustration. She paced, backwards and forwards across the tiny sleeping quarters. The male growled softly. He didn't take his eyes off Dylan.

Dylan pushed himself onto hands and knees and then up to standing. Every muscle in his body ached from the cold and his head was pounding. He tried the light switch again. Nothing happened. The phone lay on the table and he picked it up, but there was no dial tone.

Outside, the wind was slowing. Dylan ran over to Tabitha. She was soaked through, but breathing. He reached down and touched his lips to hers. Her skin was cold, but she moved. He pulled back. Her bright blue eyes were open. 'We did it,' she said.

A flash of lightning lit her face and her lips parted in a smile.

'Yes, we did.' He bent and kissed her again. She put her arms around his waist and pulled him closer. 'You were very brave,' she whispered.

'You were the one in there with them.'

'I always knew I could disappear. You were the one at risk.'

The rumble of thunder was more distant now.

She sat up and slipped her hands into his. 'You don't need to be scared anymore.'

There was a groan.

'Oh God, Max!' Tabitha leapt up and ran over to the huddled shape on the ground. 'Max, are you okay?'

He groaned again.

'Dylan is your phone working?'

'No. I'll run to the Playbarn. You stay with Max.'

Dylan shoved his hand in his pocket and pulled out the key. 'I'll be as fast as I can.'

The ground was slippery, and the rain was pounding down on his back, but the wind was dying down. He ran as fast as he could, unlocked the sliding door and left it propped open as he went into the office. The phone and lights weren't working, but he used the torch to find his radio and turned it on. It crackled but worked.

He ran his finger down the instructions and turned the dial to the frequency designated for emergencies.

The line crackled. 'Is anybody there?' Dylan said into it. His voice was rough from shouting into the storm. 'Please, is anyone there?' His voice cracked on the final word, and he felt a surge of overwhelm as the white noise continued uninterrupted.

'Hello?' The voice on the other end was quiet, but there.

'Hello, can you hear me?' Dylan was shouting into the machine now. 'Please, we need help. We need an ambulance at Wildley Forest Zoo. A man has been mauled by a tiger.'

'Mauled by a tiger? I'm dialling the ambulance now. Who is this? Where are you? And who is hurt? You're speaking to Sophie.'

'Oh thank God. I'm Dylan and Max is badly hurt.'

'Max?' Her voice was high-pitched. 'Is he okay?'

'I don't think so. He's bleeding everywhere, drifting in and out of consciousness. I have no idea how long he'll last.'

'Are the tigers still on the loose?'

'No, we've contained them.'

'I'm on my way,' she said, breathing more heavily as though she were running. 'The ambulance too. Stay with Max.'

53

DYLAN

THE AMBULANCE PULLED UP NEXT TO THE TIGER ENCLOSURE
and the window opened a crack.

'This way!' Dylan jumped up from his place on the
soggy ground with Max and Tabitha, and jogged over to
the vehicle.

The man looked around. 'Is it safe?'

'Yeah,' Dylan said. 'The cats are back in the cage.'

The man nodded, and then turned the engine off and
jumped out of the ambulance, followed by a woman. She
got a bag out the back, and they ran over to Max,
crouching down on either side of him.

Tabitha got up, giving them space to work, and came to
stand with Dylan.

Another woman climbed out the back of the ambulance. 'Were either of you hurt?'

Dylan shook his head. 'I'm bruised, but we're both
okay.'

The woman gestured to the bench. 'What kind of
bruising?'

Dylan shook his head. 'I bashed my leg hard on the corner of a table. Nothing to worry about.'

She turned to Tabitha. 'You look pale. Did you hit your head?'

'No.'

'Cats didn't get you?'

Tabitha held her arms wide. 'Not a scratch.'

'You're lucky. Not like that guy.' She stepped out of the way as one of her colleagues ran to the ambulance for a stretcher.

Frantic footsteps pounded towards them in the dark. Sophie pulled up short, breathing heavily. 'Oh God, Max!' she covered her mouth with both hands as he was carried towards the ambulance. She blinked several times and a single tear fell down her cheek. They loaded him into the back.

'We're off.'

Sophie nodded. 'I'll call his family.' They watched the ambulance dart away, the blue lights flashing through the trees.

Sophie turned to them. 'How the hell did the cats get out in the first place?'

'Come, I'll show you.' Tabitha started walking over to the enclosure.

Sophie didn't move. She swallowed.

'They can't get out,' Dylan said. 'I shut them in myself.'

Sophie nodded, and then followed Tabitha up the hill.

'There was nobody here,' Dylan said, hearing the desperation in his own voice as they walked. 'No people, no electricity, no phone signal.'

Sophie swallowed. 'I was told the tigers were secured in their sleeping quarters. I had staff here, but they were all looking after their own animals and I was trying to get the electricity and phones sorted. Of course, nobody would go outside in the storm.'

The wind had calmed down, and the rain had slowed to a drizzle. 'Look.' Tabitha pointed to the tree.

Sophie gasped. 'Oh God. The press will have a field day.'

Tabitha was shivering, her thin body shaking hard, her teeth chattering. 'I've bought the land, Sophie. And my friend has a place for our cats at his wildlife sanctuary in India. There's plenty of space for them, and it's as close to being in the wild as they could handle. He'll take them as soon as we can get them there. You just need to sign it off.'

Sophie swallowed. 'You're right. They shouldn't be here. Not after tonight. Now get home and warm up. I'll need to talk to you both properly tomorrow.'

'Of course,' Dylan said. 'You know where to find me.' They started back down the hill. 'You did it,' he whispered to Tabitha, sliding his hand into hers. 'You got them to safety.'

Tabitha sighed. 'I hated putting them back in that cage.'

'There was no other way. Max would have shot them.'

Tabitha closed her eyes and leaned into Dylan's side. 'I just want to get them out of here for good.'

Dylan looked at her thoughtfully. 'What was all that about? With Sophie?' he asked.

'I've bought some land in India to rewild. I'll be extending a tiger reserve, and I've also found a place for our tigers in a sanctuary with someone I trust.'

Dylan shook his head, trying to make sense of her words. 'You're extending a tiger reserve? Doesn't that cost a fortune?'

She didn't look at him.

'God knows how much it would cost to extend a tiger reserve. I thought artists were poor?'

'Most are.' She didn't look at him. She kept walking, her eyes on the ground in front of her, but she drifted further away from him, wrapping her arms around her middle. 'I'm one of the lucky few. I have money put aside. And that makes it my responsibility to do something important with the exposure I have.'

He stopped walking. His heart was pounding. Her hair whipped around her head in the wind from the tail end of the storm. She stopped, stood frozen for a moment, and then turned to face him.

'Who are you, Tabitha,' he said, his voice hoarse.

'You know who I am. I'm the girl you kissed, the girl you've been talking to, the girl who changes into a tiger and paints cats. It's just, when I sell my work, I use a different name. It helps me keep boundaries and live a normal life.'

'What's your real name?'

She swallowed. 'Dylan, my *real* name is Tabitha. I haven't lied to you.'

'So what is your *work* name.'

He saw the muscles contract in her throat. His heartbeat rose another notch.

'My given name is Tara McLoughlin. I changed my name to Tabitha a couple of years ago.' Her voice barely carried over the whistling of the wind.

'Tara McLoughlin?' Dylan repeated, his voice a whisper. 'But … you were on the news. You just sold that painting, for a million pounds.'

'That money all went to the tiger reserve.'

Dylan let out a slow exhale. 'You didn't tell me.'

'I didn't think it mattered.' Tabitha shrugged. Her eyes clouded over. She stepped back, crossed her arms over her chest. 'There's a reason I use two different names. People act differently when they know I have money and reputation. I don't like that. I am who I am.'

'I get that,' Dylan nodded. 'But I've held nothing back from you.'

'I have told you more than I've ever told anyone before.' Tabitha's voice was a whisper, but it carried over the dropping wind. 'I have too much experience of people to think I can tell everything to anyone.'

'I'm not people,' Dylan said, stepping closer.

Her arms tightened around her chest, her knuckles turning white where she clenched her hands into fists.

Dylan took one of her hands and prised the fingers open. He began to massage her palm, his fingers soft as they drew circles over the tense muscles. 'You *can* tell me anything. You can trust me.'

A single tear slid down Tabitha's cheek. She pulled her hand from his and knocked the tear away. 'Come on, let's get out of here. We both need to warm up.' She started walking, her pace uncomfortably fast for the length of her stride. Dylan fell in beside her, his longer legs easily compensating. 'You know Max saw the white tiger appear. He knows it's something unusual and he knows it came from you.'

Tabitha sighed. 'I'll deal with Max later. He has more to worry about than my tiger right now.' She staggered, and then leaned on a tree for a moment, before forcing herself to carry on walking.

'Here, lean on me.' Dylan put an arm around her shoulders and pulled her into his side. 'I'll get you home.'

54

MAX

PAIN JARRED THROUGH MAX'S BODY, JOLTING HIM BACK TO consciousness. He screamed as the ambulance went over a speed bump.

'Here, the meds'll kick in soon.' The voice was low and soothing. 'Just keep breathing.'

'Did they get the cats?' Max croaked.

'Yes. They locked them in their sleeping quarters before we arrived.'

'Thank God,' Max whispered. Another jolt sent his mind reeling and his body jettisoned his consciousness. He swam in a pool of awareness, in and out of his body as the ambulance swerved and bumped, all to the soundtrack of blaring sirens. This time, the cats had won. If there was a next time, it would be different.

'I need to get back.' Max tried to push himself up onto his elbows, but he couldn't move.

'There'll be plenty of time later for that,' the man said. 'You're with me for now.'

'I've been scratched before. I can handle it. I know what

I'm doing.' He lifted his head, and then sank under a wave of dizziness, as the pain threatened to pull him under. The ambulance drifted away. He could still hear the man talking, but had no idea what the words meant, they just floated around as his body jolted, immovable where it lay strapped to the stretcher. His teeth were clamped together and he ground them when the ambulance swerved around a corner. It pulled up and stopped.

'Here we are, you'll be in soon. Just try and breathe while we get you out of here. You might want to close your eyes to block out the lights.'

Max kept his eyes wide when the stretcher was lifted from the ambulance onto a trolley. There was chaos as he was wheeled through a brightly lit corridor. People were talking fast over the top of him. There was a moment of silence when the word 'tiger' was absorbed. Max would have laughed if a jolt hadn't sent another knife edge of pain through his body.

'Tetanus ... infection ... internal damage ... stitches ...' It went on and on. Max rolled his eyes, the only movement he was capable of. This was definitely one point to the tigers, but next time it would be all about him. As the image of the large male flashed through his mind, fear spiked through Max's system. He gagged, and then threw up all over the person to his right. Point taken. This was not the moment to think about tigers.

He wondered if Tabitha would visit him in hospital. Maybe seeing him like this would stir her sympathy. Unbidden, the image of the white tiger shivering into existence from her body flooded his mind. He screamed again, not sure this time whether it was from pain or fear.

55

DYLAN

THE WALK TO TABITHA'S HOUSE SEEMED ENDLESS. THE WIND
had largely abated and the rain was a drizzle. Tabitha shivered. She pulled her keys from her bag, but fumbled the
lock, her hands pink with cold. Dylan reached for the keys,
but she shook her head and tried again. This time the lock
clicked and she pushed the door open.

The room was exactly as they had left it, the remnants
of their food spread out among the artwork. There was a
mew and Emily ran up, weaving through Tabitha's ankles
and leaning into her hand when she bent down to stroke
her. Tabitha picked the cat up, holding her close to her
chest.

'Here, sit down.' Dylan pulled the chair out from
behind the easel.

Tabitha shook her head. 'No, I'm too cold. I'm going
upstairs to shower. Go home. Get some dry clothes on, and
then come back.

'I don't want to leave you alone.'

Tabitha put the cat down and walked over to him.

'Dylan, I wasn't the one in danger. You were. I was bigger than either of them. They knew that. You were at risk the whole time; that's why I didn't want you to come.'

Dylan closed his eyes for a moment. He took a deep breath and then looked Tabitha in the eye. 'It didn't feel like that.'

'I know, but it was like that. I will be okay. I'm only going for a shower. You will be fine too, because the tigers are locked away now. So get dry and warm before you get ill.' She picked up the cat and went up the stairs, shutting the door firmly behind her.

Dylan sighed. He went out the front door and pulled it hard to hear the click of the lock. Then he ran down the path and over the road, determined to get back to Tabitha's house as soon as possible. Logically, he knew she was right. He had been in far more danger than her, but the vulnerability he had felt when she lay in his arms, limp, pale and surrounded by vicious predators had been shocking. He never wanted to feel that helpless again. He shoved the door open, bending down to scoop up a packet from the floor. His fingers were numb and he fumbled as he tore it open. It ripped and a memory stick fell onto the floor. He stared at it, heart racing. The name of the studio was printed on the side. It was his music.

Bending down, he picked it up and put it on the sideboard, backing away from it and then turning and bolting for the shower. He couldn't face *that* kind of moment until he'd warmed up.

The shower was scalding hot on his frozen skin, but it warmed his blood. He washed, shampooing his hair, removing every speck of mud from the rain-sodden zoo. By the time he stepped out, pulling the towel around him, he was flushed, his hair sticking up in all directions.

He stared into his wardrobe and scrutinised his clothes as though they were life choices. In the end he chose one of his performance tank tops, hoping the tiger on his bicep would remind Tabitha of their connection. But even he wasn't prepared to go over the road in shorts in this weather, so he pulled out one of many pairs of almost identical jeans.

He looked over the road. The lights were on upstairs, but the gallery was pitch black. Tabitha must still be in the shower. Sitting at his desk, he powered up his laptop and slotted in the memory stick. He held his breath as his own voice filled the room. Emotion rolled over him through the words he had written. The pain of the loneliness was so palpable, it took his breath away. He had spent years hiding behind an image he had outgrown. Tabitha had shown him that. She had faced down his masks and dug underneath to wake up the part of his soul that had been in fitful sleep. She had offered her hand, promised connection, but he hadn't been brave enough to take it, until now.

The light over the road had moved from the bedroom down to the gallery. He copied the song to his phone, pulled on biker boots and his jacket, and then went out into the street, running his fingers through his hair. It was still wet and it would be even wetter by the time he'd crossed the road. The street was still empty. People would stay locked up in their houses for tonight, at least, and he relished the quiet aloneness of it.

He slowed as he approached Tabitha's house, nerves fluttering through his bloodstream. This was the moment.

If he couldn't tell her how he felt now, after being on the edge between life and death with her, he had no chance.

The owls hooted behind him, but they stayed put this time and he took that as an endorsement. They had not trusted Linden or Max, but today Dylan had their confidence.

Reaching up, he rang the bell and then waited, heart thumping in his chest.

The door opened. Tabitha looked rosy now, warm and healthy. Her hair tumbled in damp, copper waves around her shoulders. Her tunic was pulled in over her tight jeans with a wide belt, and flared sleeves hung to a point over the backs of her hands. She looked stunning and otherworldly.

Dylan swallowed. 'Can I come in?'

56

TABITHA LET THE CURTAIN DROP AS DYLAN CAME OUT OF his front door. She fluffed up her hair, and then straightened it out. 'Urgh, what am I doing,' she said, crouching down to stroke Emily. 'I was sodden when he saw me half an hour ago. He's not going to care if my hair is arranged wrong now.'

The knock on the door set her heart racing. 'Come on, Tabitha. It's raining. Let the guy in.' She stood up and then walked over to the front door, feeling the prickling energy that always told her when Dylan was close. She had never been this aware of anyone before.

She swung the door open, forcing herself to breathe steadily.

Dylan smiled. His hair was still damp, but was styled back from his face now. He rubbed the back of his neck and cleared his throat.

'Come in,' she said, her voice rough. She coughed as she closed the door behind him. He bent down to untie his boots, put them in the corner of the hall, and then pulled off his jacket. He was wearing one of his gig tank tops, the ones that showed the tiger on his arm. Her breath caught. She swallowed. 'Can I get you something to drink?' Her voice was steady now, controlled – unlike the pounding of her heart. 'I still have the wine we opened earlier.'

'I'd love some, thank you,' Dylan said, following her into the gallery. He stopped in front of the painting of the tiger standing on the top of the tree trunk, ready to jump onto the grass verge.

Tabitha felt her face flush. This was hard to explain away.

He shook his head. 'You really are incredible. You know that?'

'Incredible? Not terrifying? You don't want to run for the hills and accuse me of witchcraft?'

'You have a thing about that, don't you?'

She shrugged. 'That happens when the accusations come your way often enough.'

'You've been hanging around with the wrong kind of people.' He grinned. 'I wouldn't know a witch from a goddess, but I'd be very happy to meet lots of them to learn the difference.'

Tabitha let out her breath. She laughed. 'You really know how to break the tension.'

'You never need to be tense around me, Tabitha.' His eyes burned a clear turquoise. He stepped closer and she tilted her head, holding his gaze. He reached out one hand and ran it down her arm until their fingertips touched.

She was holding his glass of wine and she raised it, slowly. He took it from her. Tingles ran along her arm where he had touched it. Her body felt alive and she sank into the energy around her. She could sense Emily, the owls outside, the cats sleeping at the zoo. She felt the vibration of a lion roar even though she was too far away to hear it. She moved towards Dylan, her body pulled by the electric charge of her energy. The blue of his eyes deepened as they almost touched. She was breathless. Her heart was racing, and she reached up to trace the tiger on his bicep, feeling the curve of his muscle. His skin was soft and warm. He tensed at her touch, making the cat move. She shivered.

'You walked away last time,' she whispered.

'That was a mistake.' His voice was low and rough. 'I won't walk away from you again. I have never met anyone like you, Tabitha. I doubt I ever will.'

Tabitha chuckled. 'Well, that's true at least, but I'm sure you'd survive.'

Dylan swallowed. 'I wouldn't bet on it. Before you came along, my life was stunted. Since you arrived, everything has changed.' He paused. 'Do you have a speaker?'

Tabitha blinked. 'A speaker? You mean for music?'

He nodded.

'Over there. The Bluetooth details are on the side.'

Dylan tapped on his phone as he walked over. He didn't turn when the music started, but leant both his hands on the table and hung his head, flexing the muscles in his shoulders and back. A single guitar melody drifted from the speakers followed by Dylan's voice, soft and husky.

> *Stripes in the moonlight*
> *Silent paws on glassy ground*
> *Eyes flash in the darkness*
> *Eyes flash and my heart drowns.*

Tabitha's breath caught. The sound was so raw, so real,

that it grabbed at her heart and pulled. This was a side of Dylan so intimate that he kept his face averted, his body still while he waited.

> *You shatter my defences*
> *You fill my heart with fire*
> *With you I am creation*
> *With you I find my wild.*
>
> *But when the shadow fades,*
> *My world is small and dark*
> *I can't find my way forward*
> *I can't light my inner spark*
>
> *Wild Shadow you consume me*
> *With your flames that burn so bright.*
> *Come back to me my tiger*
> *Come back to me my light.*
>
> *Wild Shadow*

The music faded. 'Is that me?' Tabitha asked. 'Am I the Wild Shadow?' She walked slowly towards him, touched his shoulder and felt his muscles tense. She wrapped her fingers around his arm and pulled him towards her, turning him to face her.

He swallowed and nodded, his eyes searching her own for answers.

She cleared her throat, but it constricted again. She didn't know what to say. The words of his song laid his soul bare, but she spoke with brush strokes, with colour, not with sound.

She turned and walked over to her easel. Picking up the sketchbook, she walked back to Dylan, who watched her, his forehead creased.

She handed him the book and nodded.

He turned the first page and gasped. His own face stared out at him. It was impressionistic but caught the light in his eyes and the curve of the cat on his shoulder. The image gazed up at him from under heavy lashes, a small smile playing around the edges of his mouth.

'Keep going,' Tabitha said, her voice hoarse.

Dylan turned the page. There was another one. This time he was playing his guitar, his eyes closed.

On the next page he sat behind his drums. There was picture after picture. His fingers shook. Tabitha's throat was dry, but the sound of his voice coming through the speakers helped her hold her nerve. He had laid his soul bare. It was time for her to do the same.

Dylan's breath caught and he looked up at her. The picture showed a hard look on his face as he glared out of the page, his expression full of anger.

'That was when I told you. That was how you looked at me when you realised I was the tiger.'

Dylan's jaw tensed. His eyes looked glassy, and then his shoulders slumped. 'I'm sorry.'

Tabitha nodded. 'I know. Me too.'

She turned one last page. In that final picture Dylan stared out through a window. The light from the room lit him up against the black night. His eyes were full of longing.

'That is the one that was real,' he said, putting the book down and taking her hands. 'The other was embarrassment. I couldn't remember what you might have seen, whether I'd done anything to humiliate myself, when all I ever wanted was for you to think well of me. Don't believe the mask.'

'I never believe the mask,' Tabitha said, her voice a whisper. I can sense the dissonance between what is said and what is real, but that doesn't mean I know what is causing it, or what the truth is. I have been rejected by so many people for being me.'

Dylan closed his eyes. He took a deep breath then opened them again. 'By showing me who you really are, you forced me to be more honest about myself, to stop hiding behind the facade *I've* used as a shield. I've grown so used to hiding my own differentness, I didn't realise it was my ground for creating. Whatever happens now, I will always be indebted to you for that.' He traced her jaw with one finger. She felt the pull of his energy and leaned into him. He bent his head and she tilted her face towards his, closing her eyes, blocking out the world as their lips touched. She reached up, feeling the roughness of stubble over the softness of his skin. He pulled her closer, wrapping his arms around her and she sank into the beating of her heart. For once, she wasn't a tiger. She wasn't different. She was all Tabitha.

57

THE MARQUEE WAS ENORMOUS AND SURROUNDED BY A RING of wigwams covered in fairy lights. Tabitha had to remind herself that she was on home ground in the zoo. It was so glamourous it felt a world away from the usual mud and animal smells.

Her heart beat fast as she turned to Dylan. He was breath-taking in a sharp DJ and black bowtie. His short blond hair was styled away from his clean-shaven face. The scent of aftershave drifted from him but didn't mask the new familiarity of his body next to hers. She smiled at the memory of the tiger hidden away under his flawless jacket. Her grin grew broader still when one of the flesh-and-blood cats grunted in greeting, sensing her presence in the darkness. She really was on home ground, no matter how unfamiliar it all felt.

'You're here!' Ursula ran over and gave Tabitha a hug. Turning to Dylan, she gave him a peck on the cheek, her face reddening. 'We can really get going now the stars of the show have arrived.' She led them into the main marquee and they were handed fine-stemmed champagne flutes, filled almost to the brim.

The marquee was enormous. There were tall round tables dotted all over the room. Some already held abandoned glasses. Some supported enormous displays of exotic flowers. Tiny paper butterflies clung to the stems and there was a background hum of rainforest sounds. A screen high up on one side of the tent showed a prowling tiger that paced back and forwards, projected by a light beam. Its roars could be heard periodically over the birdsong and the hum of insects, prompting answering grunts from the tigers in the nearby enclosure. A stage at one end had a single chair with a microphone. Behind it were two display stands, one with the new album cover, and one with an image of a tiger. Tabitha's painting stood between them in a glass case. The room was already heaving with people dressed in black tie and evening gowns. Tabitha smoothed down her chiffon dress. She had felt like a medieval princess when she pulled it on, the floaty skirt dropping from the high waist which was lined with tiny crystals. A mesh of spaghetti straps covered her shoulders and back, and a large amethyst pointed down into her cleavage.

'There are some collectors over here who would love to meet you,' Ursula said.

Tabitha nodded, but frowned up at Dylan.

'You go. I need to tune up. I'll be on soon.' Dylan smiled. 'Is there a backstage area?'

Linden strode up in a tuxedo identical to Dylan's own. He took Ursula's hand and kissed it, and then winked at Dylan. 'Come on, man, I'll take you.'

'What are you doing here?' Dylan frowned.

Linden laughed at his friend's surprise. 'I'm your roady,

of course. Who else knows how you like things? Your guitar's at the back. GJ tuned it for you, so you have time to warm up before you hit the stage.'

Dylan nodded, his focus on the coming performance already clouding his eyes.

A woman in a fitted trouser suit walked over to Tabitha. 'Tara?'

Tabitha smiled. 'Yes.'

'Charlotte.' The woman held out her hand. 'It's such an honour to meet you. Your work has always spoken to me. I've always felt as though you understand me in a way nobody else does. Your tigers reach into my gut and put my fiercest desires on display.'

'Do you have many of my paintings?' Tabitha shook her hand, and then stepped back.

'I have a few, but not enough. I love this one here, and I will bid to win. But I'd also like something bigger, immersive in proportions. Could you do this for me? I have a large and beautiful room that needs a worthy painting.'

'I would love to.' Tabitha felt breathless as an image of a painting on the wall of an enormous ballroom sprang into her mind.

The woman smiled. 'Excellent. I want the painting that puts that look on your face.'

'Darling.' Tabitha's mum put a hand on her arm, spun her around and kissed her on each cheek. 'How lovely to see you. What a glorious event. Are you going to introduce me to your friend?'

Her father grabbed her hand and squeezed it.

'Mum, Dad, I'm so glad you made it. This is Charlotte.'

'It's very nice to meet you.' The woman held out her hand.

'Not Charlotte Byron?' Her mum's voice was breathy.

'Do we know each other?' The woman smiled and tilted her head.

Her mum swallowed. 'No, but I read a feature about you the other day.'

'Of yes, of course. Don't mind that.' Charlotte laughed. So you're mother to the fabulous Tara McLoughlin! You must be so proud.'

Tabitha gave an embarrassed laugh.

'Ladies and gentlemen.' Linden's voice rang out across the marquee, coming through speakers dotted around the outside of the tent. 'I am delighted to introduce the artist who was the power behind Instantaneous Rock, my best friend, Dylan McKenzie.'

Tabitha breathed a sigh of relief at the distraction and turned to face the stage.

There were screams from one side of the tent, to the backing of polite applause on the other. The two elements in the room were marked in their difference. Dylan's fans were young, wearing figure-hugging dresses. Tabitha's were older, drenched in wealth and watching Dylan with amused indifference.

'Thank you, thank you.' Dylan perched on the stool in the centre of the stage and adjusted the microphone. His guitar hung on his shoulders on a black, leather strap. 'It's so wonderful to see so many of you here today. Wildley Forest Zoo has redoubled its focus on tiger conservation and all the money we make at this event will go towards saving the tigers. Every penny made from album sales tonight will go to funding the conservation efforts. From tomorrow, I will donate ten percent of every sale. And if you look behind me, this wonderful painting by Tara McLoughlin will be auctioned later in the night.'

Dylan smiled at the applause and then started finger picking rolling chords. The lights dimmed. The tiger on the screen began to prowl around the side of the marquee, no longer restricted to one single screen, but moving across the canvas of the tent itself. Dylan sang with his eyes closed. He was larger than life on that stage, his tuxedo unexpected and mesmerising given his usual tank top and shorts. He opened his eyes and looked directly at Tabitha. The words flowed as the notes soared and the tiger prowled.

Tabitha felt her own consciousness shift, felt herself separate. She remained so aware of her body, saw Dylan on stage through her physical eyes, but the more real part of her shimmered into her feline form.

She knew Dylan saw her and felt his emotions soar as their connection intensified. She walked to the stage and then leapt up, manifesting her image more strongly. There were gasps in the audience. The white tiger flittered in front of them, one minute appearing solid, the next like a holo-gram and then completely vanished. She walked around the stage, echoing the movements of the cat on the screen. She kept her image vague enough to camouflage as another digital projection and the gasps soon turned to oohs and ahhs. As Dylan's song built, she became more and more solid until the climax, when she jumped from the stage, her paws making an audible thud on the floor. Those at the front moved sharply back, and then breathed again when she flickered out of existence. Tabitha walked back to her body, feeling the emotions of the crowd ebb and flow around her. She kept herself invisible now, adding her own energy to the intensity of Dylan's song, knowing they had the audience gripped.

She integrated fully, taking note of her racing heartbeat, of how breathless she felt. Dylan's voice was soaring, the power shimmering from him captivating every single person there. Tabitha was enchanted, proud and vulnerable as he sang their story, her own painting punctuating his words and mirroring her heart to the world.

Then there was silence. It stretched out as the audience took a collective breath, and then the applause started. At first it was just one person clapping slowly, the sound sinking into the many bodies in the room. Then a smattering of applause slowly grew to a roar that overwhelmed Tabitha, pouring over her, threatening to pull her under. Dylan stood at the front of the stage, his face pale and stunned. She wanted to reach out to him, to be his tiger, but the thunder held her grounded, rooted in the very human scene unfolding in front of her.

The applause kept going, rolling higher and then ebbing in continuous waves of sound. Tabitha started walking through the crowds, pushing past people to get to Dylan. She got to the foot of the stage and reached up, putting a hand on his leg. He jerked and seemed to break out of his daze. He looked at Tabitha, crouched down and kissed her. She clutched her arms around his neck and then smiled as he pulled back and lifted her up onto the stage.

'How did you get so strong?'

He winked at her, and then took her hand and spun her around to face the audience. 'I give you Tara McLoughlin, your artist and my inspiration. The tigers need us, all of us. Please join with us to help them before they dwindle into extinction. Bid for the painting, buy an album, donate, volunteer, spread the word. Whatever you are able to do would be perfect. We need to work together. If we do, I absolutely believe we can make a difference.'

Ursula climbed up the steps to the stage and beamed at them both. 'Thank you so much to Dylan and Tara. Now, get your credit cards ready, because it's nearly time for the auction. Please remember that anything you are able to give will help these beautiful cats.'

Dylan jumped down and reached up to take Tabitha's hands, but she winked at him and vaulted to the floor, landing lightly and easily despite her formal shoes. He grasped her hand and led her to the bar. 'Fizz?' he said, grinning. His face was alight with hope and she laughed, buoyed up by the joy in his eyes.

'Actually,' Tabitha said.

'Ahem,' a familiar voice called over the din.

'Mum!' Dylan was by her side in two strides and bent down, pulling her into his arms. 'Did you see what happened?'

'Of course I did!' Rachel beamed. 'I always knew you could do it.'

'You were amazing,' a familiar voice said.

Dylan looked up. GJ stood there, his hands shoved in his pockets, a smile lighting his face. 'I am so proud of you.'

Dylan strode over to him and pulled him into a hug. 'Thank you for all your support. I'm not sure I would have found the strength to take the plunge without your encouragement.

'Time for a toast, I think.' Rachel nodded towards a tray of drinks at the bar. There were two pints of lager, a Guinness and a dainty glass of clear liquid.

Tabitha laughed and claimed the Guinness. 'You read my mind.' She took a sip, closing her eyes to savour it.

Dylan handed his mum the small glass and gave one of the lagers to GJ. He held up his own pint. 'To the tigers.'

'To the tigers.' Ursula snuck up behind them and put her arm around Tabitha's waist. 'I think this is actually going to happen.'

Tabitha grinned. 'It'd better. I've bought the land.'

Ursula laughed. 'That you have. And Sophie has finally agreed to let us take the tigers to the sanctuary.'

'She has?' Tabitha handed her Guinness to Dylan and then threw her arms around the other woman's neck. 'That's the best news I've heard in a long time.'

'Look, there's a photographer over there from the local paper.' Ursula pulled back and pointed to the bar. 'I'm hoping the story might get picked up by the nationals. Would you go and talk to her?'

'I'll leave that to Dylan,' Tabitha inclined her head. 'Go on, handsome. If anyone can win over the press, you can.'

Linden vaulted onto the stage and took his place behind the microphone. 'Ladies and gentlemen, it's time for the auction.'

'I'm going to need another drink to get through this,' Tabitha said, taking a large gulp of Guinness.

'This is your moment, don't wish it away.' Ursula pulled up a stool and sat beside Tabitha. She looked calm, except for the faint tremor of her hands where they clasped her clutch bag in her lap.

'Huh,' Tabitha rolled her eyes. 'My moment is when I'm painting. This …' she gestured around her, 'enables me to spend my day doing what I love. I'm lucky, but I do wish it was possible to be lucky in a more private way.'

Ursula smiled. 'Just think of the tigers.'

Linden cleared his throat. The crowd turned towards the stage. 'Thank you, folks, it's the moment you've been waiting for. We are auctioning an original oil painting by world-renowned artist Tara McLoughlin, showing two tigers, one yellow and one white, standing on either side of something that looks like a mirror. Is that right?'

Tabitha nodded.

'Good. They are looking at each other through the mirror, which is placed amongst thick foliage. The painting is ninety centimetres wide by sixty centimetres high, plus the frame. I trust you have all taken the time to look at the painting in advance? We will now proceed with the auction.'

Tabitha zoned out while the bidding went on. She generally left the selling of her major works to someone else. The shop front enabled her to sell prints and cards, and it gave her a professional base, but this process embarrassed her.

The numbers were climbing. Bidders were dropping out one by one. Ursula's eyes were wider by the minute. Dylan, who had finished with the journalist, was by Tabitha's side and gripping her hand too tight. She pried his fingers open.

'Sorry,' he said, his voice a mere whisper.

There was a crash.

'Hey, what are you doing?' a man yelled.

Another crash.

Tabitha scanned the room, and then froze. Max stood near the doorway, looking around the room. He was dressed in faded black joggers and an oversized T shirt. His beard was unshaven. He took a glass of champagne from a tray, and then wove to the centre of the room.

58

TABITHA

DYLAN MADE TO STEP IN FRONT OF TABITHA, BUT SHE TOOK his hand and pulled him back until they stood side by side.

Max's face hardened as he scanned the crowd and then snaked across the room, weaving from side to side, to stop in front of Sophie. 'How could you do this to me,' he said, loudly enough for his voice to carry.

The chatter in the marquee died down until everyone was staring at Max.

'What are you doing?' Sophie said, trying to hold her smile. 'You're making a scene.'

'And you hate that, don't you?' Max chuckled. 'But look at this place, tigers everywhere. I should be the guest of honour, the tiger keeper who got the cats back into their cage when they escaped. Instead, you're celebrating without me and I'm under investigation.'

'*He* got them back into their cage?' Dylan's voice was high-pitched.

'Shhh,' Tabitha hissed, but it was too late.

Max spun around.

Tabitha was expecting anger, but Max paled and skittered backwards. He held his hands up in front of his face. 'I'm sorry. I didn't mean to intrude. I'm going now.'

Tabitha stepped forwards. 'Are you alright, Max?'

He tried to back away but slammed into the muscled bulk of a security guard. 'Erm, I'm fine thanks. I just … give me a minute.' He turned and walked out of the marquee into the cold air.

Tabitha followed at a distance, giving him time to gather himself.

He pulled his shoulders back. When he turned to face her, they were near the tiger enclosure. She could see the spot where Max had been mauled and the safety cage she had led the cats through. She shivered.

Walking over, she put a hand on Max's arm, but dropped it when he flinched. 'They told me you were recovering well, but that night took a greater toll than physical injuries. Are you getting counselling?'

'Please don't hurt me.' Tears were streaming down Max's face now.

'Why would I hurt you?' Her heart was hammering, and she could feel her tiger-self reacting to the sense of threat. 'Oh God.' She clapped her hands over her mouth as realisation dawned. He had seen her white tiger appear. He knew it was her. 'Max, please …'

He swallowed. 'It's okay,' he muttered. 'I won't tell anyone. Your secret is safe with me. Just don't hurt me, please.'

'I wouldn't,' she whispered. 'I have never hurt anyone. I knocked that tiger away from you and protected you from it. I led the cats to their cage so Dylan could lock them in. You are in no danger from me.'

He shook his head. 'I'd like to believe that, but I'll never trust a big cat.'

She dropped her head into her hands. A tiger grunted and she wandered over to the enclosure, needing a moment to gather her thoughts. It was right there by the bars. It flexed its muscles then reared up onto its hind legs, landing its front paws on the heavy wire fence.

'Shit.' Max yelped. He jumped backwards and threw up into the bushes. Leaning his hands on his thighs, he took a few deep breaths before turning back to Tabitha. She walked back and stopped a few feet away.

His gaze was flickering between her and the cage. 'Did Dylan know? When we saw the white tiger in the street, did he know it was you?'

Tabitha nodded.

Max let out a slow exhale. 'You must have thought I was such a mug.'

'I was just amazed you saw me,' Tabitha said, her voice quiet. 'Most people don't.'

'Please.' Max held his hands up. 'Don't try and pretend it wasn't a betrayal.'

'A betrayal?' Tabitha raised her eyebrows. 'We weren't involved. We didn't swap secrets.'

'But they were *my* tigers and you took them from me.' His fists were clenched at his side.

Tabitha felt a prickle down her spine and looked back into the enclosure. The tiger watched them, eyes burning yellow in the dark.

'Running with the tigers like that; I can't even begin to understand what that might be like.' His voice was hoarse.

'Look at my pictures. They might give you an idea.'

'Max,' a voice called from the darkness. Linden jogged

up, his bowtie loosened and hanging around his neck.

'Max, I thought I saw you,' he said. 'Look, I've been thinking about you ever since we met in Tabitha's showroom. I'm sorry for how I treated you at school. Dylan told me you still think about it and I'm not proud of that.'

'That's not what you said before,' Max said from between gritted teeth.

'Yeah, well. I was being an arse. But it was Dylan I was angry with, not you. I shouldn't have taken it out on anyone else, Tabitha included.' He held his hand out. 'Can we leave it in the past?'

Max stared at Linden for a painfully long moment, but Linden didn't budge. Max swallowed, and then stepped forwards and took his hand. 'Thank you. I appreciate it.'

Linden nodded, and then jogged back to the marquee.

Max sighed. 'I don't understand you, Tabitha, I'm not going to lie. You must have a strange life.'

Tabitha shrugged. 'It's all I know.'

He nodded. 'If I can make peace with Linden, I guess I can do the same with you. You were right. You did save my life that night. I won't tell anyone your secret. I know you think I'm some kind of monster, but I've always loved you, Tabitha. I wouldn't do anything to hurt you.'

On impulse, Tabitha stepped closer and pulled him into a hug. He tensed, and then relaxed.

She stepped back. 'Thank you, Max. I wish you all the best.'

He held her gaze for a moment, nodded, and then shoved his hands into his pockets and walked off.

Tabitha walked over to the bench by the cage and sat down. She closed her eyes. Moments later, the shadow of a white tiger walked through the safety barrier that kept visitors from the enclosure wall. Inside the fence, she solidified and then huffed and grunted in greeting.

The huge yellow cat rubbed its head up against her white muzzle. The chaos of the marquee seemed a world away as she circled the perimeter of the enclosure with the cat. The other tiger joined and they moved together, gaining pace.

'Your painting sold.' Dylan's voice called her back to the present. 'It went for one and a half million pounds. I can't believe it. I think there was some obscure competition going on between a woman and her father. She was jubilant when she won.'

Tabitha let her breath out in a rush. 'We can do a lot with that.'

Dylan sat down and took her hands in his own. They were cold and shaking. 'You're pretty special, you know that? What you've done for those tigers ...'

Tabitha shrugged, but she squeezed his hands. 'There's not much I wouldn't do for those tigers.'

'I was thinking.' Dylan let go and leaned back on the bench. 'Can you imagine the impact you could have settling the tigers into their new sanctuary if you ran with them?'

Tabitha smiled and felt her attention shift. She felt the pull of the tigers that stood just behind the foliage in the enclosure, watching her. 'Don't think I haven't considered it, but it would never work. I'd have to tell people what I do, and that wouldn't go down well.'

'Has it ever occurred to you that people might be intimidated because they don't understand your differentness?' Dylan said. 'Maybe if they knew what you were able to do, and how you were using your abilities, the fear would ebb away.'

'With some people it would. Others would call me evil and hunt me down.'

'What if we didn't tell anyone?' he said. 'It's not about people or publicity, it's about the tigers. After tonight, I think the zoo would give you whatever you asked for. I'm sure we could do this without you becoming a target.'

Tabitha smiled. 'I'm open to ideas.'

'You're shivering.' Dylan took off his jacket and wrapped it around Tabitha's shoulders.

Tabitha grinned. 'You're a smooth talker, you know that?'

Dylan smiled and laced his fingers through hers. 'I have been told that, yes. It's part of my charm, apparently.'

She felt a prickling through her palms where their skin met. She swallowed. He was so close, but just too far away. She leaned forward. Their lips touched and she shivered, allowing him to pull her in closer. She breathed in the scent of him, feeling her heart pound. She was aware of the tiger on the other side of the fence; she could hear the noise from the tent, but everything was drifting further and further away as she lost herself in Dylan.

She pulled back slightly and tilted her head. 'I've never kissed a rock star before.'

Dylan threw his head back and laughed. 'I've never kissed as a rock star before either. Life is about to change for both of us, I think.'

'All because of the tigers.'

'Well, not *just* because of the tigers.' He smiled. 'I'd like to think we had something to do with it too. Funnily enough, I reckon even Max could take some of the credit.'

Dylan's song started playing on the sound system. A few white flakes fell from the sky, and then all of a sudden snow was everywhere, muting the real world and painting the zoo with a magical, glittering brush. Dylan laughed, stood up and spun around. He tipped his head back, allowing the flakes to drop onto his closed eyelids. Then he slowed, stopped and held out a hand. 'May I have this dance?'

Tabitha smiled. 'Here?'

'You'll never have a more magical dance floor, or a more appreciative audience.' He nodded towards the two tigers, who sat close to the barrier, their gaze fixed on Tabitha.

She stood up and went into his arms, pulling him closer and leaning into his warmth. For the first time, she could truly be herself.

The tiger let out a yowl and then ran for the shelter of his sleeping quarters.

Dylan laughed. 'He looks like you, now.'

He did. He was covered with snow and his golden fur was fluffed out, making him look bigger than normal. 'How do you feel about being with a woman who turns into a tiger?' She smiled, but her heart sped up and fear knotted her stomach. He seemed to have come to an easy acceptance of her weirdness, but they had barely talked about it since that night at the zoo.

'I feel the world is more magical than I ever thought possible, and I can't wait to find out what else is real.'

She let out her breath and laced her fingers through his. 'It'll be a wild ride if you stick with me.'

'I can live with that. I'll have nothing to write songs about if life is too simple.'

Tabitha laughed. 'Here's to the next adventure.'

She reached up onto her tiptoes and kissed him.

Somewhere nearby, a tiger roared.

EPILOGUE
TABITHA

THE HEAT HUNG THICK AND HEAVY OVER THE CLEARING AS the sun set behind the trees. The cage was at odds with the lush environment. The ground was made up of hardened mud, but the trees that surrounded them were thick with pale green leaves and the hum of insects. The birdsong had stilled as the growling cats made their presence known.

Keeping herself insubstantial, Tabitha pawed at the ground. Her body was safely in the truck parked at the edge of the clearing. She knew Dylan sat over it, protecting her physical form, wishing he could protect her astral self too. She had been nervous, but now the land buzzed in her veins, filling her with a purpose bigger than she had ever experienced before.

The tigers in the cage growled and she prowled closer, sniffing at them through the bars. They relaxed for a moment, and then tensed as a loud creaking reverberated through the clearing. The bars began to rise.

The male yowled, putting his nose close to the gap, pawing at the ground.

Tabitha roared, trying to encourage him backwards, away from the danger of a faulty door. For a moment, the bars stuck. The cat put his head to the ground, hoping to slide through, but the door was still too low. He snarled, batting at the bars with one enormous paw, and then skittering to the back of the cage as the door moved.

The bars finally locked into place and Tabitha grunted in welcome. There was a moment of stillness, and then the male shot out of the cage and into the trees. The female followed. Tabitha launched herself after them, her muscles bunching and stretching as she ran, elongating her stride to catch up with the panicked animals. When she took her place beside them, they began to settle. Together they ran to the edge of the sanctuary and then began to scout the perimeter as they had done so many times at the zoo. She led them to the watering hole, launching herself into the crystal-clear liquid with a single leap. The cats jumped in after her, and then they waded out the other side, pausing to rehydrate after their long journey in a hot cage.

The female stood in the water, a rumbling growl coming from her chest. The male looked up, but made no sound. Stepping out of the pool, the female walked over to the trees.

She yowled as she discovered the meat that had been left out for them. The male straightened up, and then started walking out of the water to join her. Tabitha watched for a moment, and then focused her attention on her body in the back of the truck and allowed her tiger form to disintegrate.

A finger stroked her face. She felt the whisper of a breeze over her skin, cutting briefly through the muggy air.

'Tabitha? Are you awake?'

She smiled at the sound of Dylan's voice and opened her eyes.

'Did it work? Are they okay?' he whispered, and she nodded. She had done it. The tigers had a new home, she had her sanctuary, and Dylan was by her side. Life was as it should be.

Tabitha pulled herself up to sitting and took a swig from the water bottle next to her.

'Are you okay? Ursula asked from the front. 'You've been up all night. You must be exhausted.'

Tabitha suppressed a smile, and then faked a yawn. 'It was worth it to see the new reserve at work. It really is going to be wonderful.'

'I think this calls for a celebration,' Ursula said, the grin obvious in her voice. Let's head back to base camp. I have some rather warm sparkling wine we can drink.' She started up the truck, driving unperturbed over the unmade road, throwing her passengers around in the back.

'You're okay?' Dylan asked, leaning over to pull Tabitha into a hug.

'I'm okay. I'm better than okay. It worked. The tigers will be so happy here.'

Dylan cupped her cheek in his hand. He leaned forwards and kissed her, his lips soft against her own. 'You've done something more valuable than most people achieve in a lifetime.'

Tabitha smiled. 'I've *begun* something more valuable than most people achieve in a lifetime. There's still a lot of work to do.'

The radio crackled to life and Dylan's voice came

through the speakers, hauntingly beautiful. In the distance a tiger roared.

Tabitha shivered. 'Will you help me?'

Dylan's face broke into a wide smile. 'I thought you'd never ask.'

LETTER FROM THE AUTHOR

Dear Reader

Tabitha has been in my head for a long time. She started as a nature spirit, twirling around branches and following her tiger around the jungle, but she finally agreed to settle into a more grown-up form for the sake of Wild Shadow.

I have spent years dreaming about tigers and lions on the loose (spoiler: I never die,) and so in Wild Shadow I decided to bring my little nature spirit in on the act. She dealt with it admirably, I think, and I thank her for saving my more breakable characters, even Max.

Wildley Forest is a fictional village, but it is inspired by Sandridge, which is just outside St Albans. I imagine the zoo to be where Heartwood Forest sits. There is no zoo there in real life. Instead, it is a beautiful, Woodland Trust nature reserve.

If you have enjoyed Wild Shadow, please do consider leaving a review. Even a few words help make the book more visible to new readers. Reviews are one of the best ways to support authors, and help them write more stories.

If you would like to find out more about me and my books, you can visit me on my website and social media. If you sign up for my mailing list at www.marthadunlop.com, you will receive book news and extra content first. You can also follow me on Amazon.

Best wishes

Martha

ACKNOWLEDGMENTS

First and foremost, thank you to Kathryn Cottam, structure genius, cheer leader and all-round amazing friend. She has had my back through the whole process of creating Wild Shadow, and has always been ready and willing to look through yet another version. Kathryn, thank you so much for everything. You truly are a star.

Thank you to Eleanor Leese, my fabulous copy editor, to Ravven for my beautiful cover and to Kate Tremills for being ready to answer questions and brainstorm at the drop of a hat. You are a wonderful team and I'm so glad to be able to collaborate with you.

Thank you to Chantelle Nassari for being my expert on all things Rachel, for talking things through with me before I got going and reading her afterwards to make sure I had written her as she should be. You are a huge inspiration to me, and I am honoured to have you as a friend.

Thank you to James Godber for being my tiger guru! Thank you for being ready to answer all my questions, however strange, and for helping me make my tigers more realistic, and a lot quieter!

Thank you to Sam Reynolds and John Douglas for helping me with GJ, Kyle Coetzee for vetting Dylan and Linden's fight scene, Clare Abbott for being my resident medical advisor and Dave Pack for being my all-round drumming and recording studio expert.

To Miriam Leary-Joyce, you have been an absolute star, offering me your forensic view. Thank you so much. And thank you to Mum and Janet Hamer for hunting through my words for the errors I could no longer see.

And of course, thank you to all my friends and family for supporting me every step of the way. I love you all.

ABOUT THE AUTHOR

Martha is a dreamer and lover of stories who likes nothing better than spending her days getting to know the characters in her head.

She is a tarot card reader and reiki master, and loves to chat reading, writing and all things mystical on social media, as well as posting pictures of her fellow pack-member, Bertie the Cavalier.

Martha is a fiddle player who fell in love with traditional music, particularly Irish, and is also teaching herself to play the Irish Bouzouki. She played her way through her English degree at York and remembers that time as much for the music as the books.

You can keep up with Martha's news, book releases and extra content at marthadunlop.com. Picture by Gene Genie Photography, www.genegenie.photography

facebook.com/MarthaDunlopStories

twitter.com/home

instagram.com/marthadunlop

Destiny calls. Soulmates draw closer.
One woman stands in the way.

Beth trusts her psychic senses. So when her birthday visit to a daytime TV talk show takes a weird turn, she knows something is wrong. Amelia, the celebrity on stage, is oddly fixated on Beth and the man with the microphone is hauntingly familiar. Things become even stranger when she buys a tarot deck, and they are all pictured in the cards.

Jonan has waited an eternity to be with the woman who haunts his dreams. When he finally sees her at the TV studio, he hopes life with his soulmate is within reach. But as Amelia refuses to let go of their past together, his hopes fade.

Amelia stands between Beth and Jonan. Spinning tales of supernatural threats to her adoring fan base, she builds a personality cult through fear of the paranormal. As her power grows, she does her best to scare Beth away from Jonan and plans to reclaim him for herself.

United by a destiny that spans lifetimes, Beth and Jonan are determined to stop Amelia's fear-mongering. But Amelia has more than one card to play. Even though they are fated to be together, Amelia's destructive nature may once again tear them apart.

STARFOLK FALLING

BOOK 2
OF THE STARFOLK TRILOGY

COMING SOON

Subscribe at www.marthadunlop.com
to hear about new releases first.